# KEN SANCHEZ

# Soul Reckoning

*Shadowguard Files 1.5*

# Contents


 1  Leo                          1
 2  Finn                        11
 3  Leo                         23
 4  Finn                        33
 5  Leo                         47
 6  Finn                        59
 7  Leo                         68
 8  Finn                        80
 9  Leo                         90
10  Finn                        98
11  Leo                        109
12  Finn                       118
13  Leo                        132
14  Finn                       142
15  Leo                        151
16  Finn                       162
17  Leo                        174
18  Finn                       184
19  Leo                        194
20  Finn                       204
21  Leo                        215
22  Finn                       220
23  Leo                        225
24  Finn                       232
*About the Author*            241

1

# Leo

"Leo, I want you in my office immediately." Director Daniel Hernandez ordered over the phone.

Leo Rodriguez, a seasoned medical examiner at the Human Investigation Bureau (HIB), had never heard his director order him like this before. The way the words tumbled out of the director's mouth sent a shiver down Leo's spine, making him wonder if he'd messed up somehow.

In their department, nobody knew the real Leo. He was a necromancer, but these days, he rarely practiced his craft. Being a necromancer came with its perks and problems, but for Leo, it was mostly a nuisance. People, knowing their history, usually feared necromancers and kept them at arm's length. It had taken the old master necromancers ages to integrate with other magic users and supernaturals, but they had eventually succeeded. Still, Leo often felt like they were more tolerated than truly accepted.

Leo had longed for a life without relying on his magic, a chance to prove to his parents that he could make it in the world on his own terms. When he saw a job opening as a medical examiner with the HIB, he seized the opportunity. The HIB conducted tests to determine if a person had supernatural origins. Leo believed everyone deserved acceptance, regardless of their background.

To hide his aura, Leo had resorted to using death magic. This decision came with a price—a shortened lifespan that he felt in his bones every passing day. Yet, it had been worth it. He'd proven himself time and again, but sometimes, it felt like it wasn't enough to earn his parents' recognition.

As he mused about his past, Leo's gaze wandered around his office in the morgue. The pale morning light filtered through the blinds, casting long shadows on the steel tables and cabinets filled with medical instruments. He reached for his coffee, its warmth spreading comfort through his hands as he continued to reflect on his life.

Hiding his true nature weighed heavily on him. Fear gnawed at him daily. The thought of exposure terrified him, not just for himself, but for the fragile acceptance he'd fought so hard to secure for necromancers like him.

Memories of prejudice and isolation flashed through his mind, like a movie reel. He remembered the days when he'd been shunned, called names, and pushed away by other supernaturals. Those scars ran deep, etched into his soul.

Leo's mind wandered to a pivotal moment in his life—a confrontation with a group of supernaturals who had wanted him gone. It had taken all his strength to protect himself without revealing his true abilities. That day, the price of conformity had felt too high, but he had endured.

With a sigh, Leo leaned back in his chair, the creak of leather punctuating his reverie. He knew that despite his efforts, his secret could be exposed at any moment. The tension in his shoulders refused to dissipate, a constant reminder of the sword hanging over his head.

Leo's morning began with the shrill ring of his phone, disrupting the quiet hum of his lab. He frowned as he picked up the call. "What's wrong, director?"

"There's someone here that wanted to see you, and they say it's urgent. You better get over here now," Director Hernandez's tense voice crackled through the phone.

Leo sighed, rubbing his temples. "Sure. I'll be there." He ended the call with an exasperated shake of his head. "That man needs to communicate better," he muttered to himself.

Without missing a beat, Leo straightened his cluttered desk, tossing aside lab notes and empty coffee cups. He shed his lab coat, opting for a casual jacket. The HIB building, standing tall and intimidating next door to the morgue, awaited him.

He stepped inside, greeted by the bustling sounds of a department in full swing. The scent of the corridors invaded his nostrils as he walked through the familiar but imposing skyscraper. Leo couldn't help but admire the architecture; it felt as if the building held secrets within its steel and concrete walls.

Approaching the department, he encountered Kate Leslie, a five-foot-tall African-American woman who commanded respect without saying a word. Kate's strength and Leo's unexpected friendship had bonded them. A warm smile broke across his face as he saw her.

"Rodriguez! What brings you by?" Kate enveloped him in a hug, which he reciprocated.

"Hey, Kate. I'm good, thanks for asking," Leo replied, grinning.

"Oh, just answer the question, Ghosty," Kate teased, rolling her eyes.

Only Kate could call him that. She was one of the few who knew Leo's true identity.

"The director wanted me in," Leo finally revealed.

Kate's expression shifted to concern. "What about? Hopefully, he hasn't found out what you did for the Hansen Wolves."

Leo's mind drifted back to that difficult task—tracking the stolen souls of the wolves. It had taken a toll on him, one he kept buried deep within himself. "I don't know. He just said that someone was in there wanting to see me."

"Well, you better get going before he blows a casket on you," Kate advised with a chuckle. She patted him on the back before striding away.

As Leo approached Director Hernandez's office, curiosity gnawed at him. What could be so urgent? He had worked in this department for years, his relationship with the director had evolved from cordial to something more complex. There had been clashes and reconciliations, but today's call had an ominous edge to it.

Leo knocked and entered without waiting for a response. Director Hernandez sat behind his cluttered desk, fingers drumming anxiously. "You wanted to see me, Director?"

The director nodded, his face etched with worry. "Leo, sit down." Hernandez gestured to a chair.

Leo complied, his heart pounding in his chest. "What's this about, Director?"

"Like I said on the phone, someone wanted to see you," the director explained before pressing a button on his desk phone. "Maya, please send the gentleman into my office. Leo is now here."

In a heartbeat, Maya, the receptionist, ushered in an unexpected face, one Leo never thought he'd see again anytime soon. Justin Rodriguez, his oldest brother, walked into the room, wearing a simple black shirt and jeans.

"Justin? What are you doing here?" Leo exclaimed, his surprise giving way to a hint of irritation.

The director, sensing the tension, decided to make a hasty exit. "I'll leave you two alone to talk," he said as he stood and left the room.

Justin, his features tense, was the elder of the four siblings. He was tall and lean, with a mop of unruly brown hair that had always been his signature look. Despite their parents' denials, it was no secret that

Justin had always been the favorite child. But there was more to Justin than met the eye; he was a master necromancer, skilled in the arcane arts, but he lacked the unique ability that Leo possessed—a talent for tracking missing souls. Leo had kept this hidden from his family, wary of how they might exploit his gift.

As Justin entered, Leo's resentment, which he had carried for years, smoldered beneath his calm exterior. Jealousy had become a curse worse than necromancy itself.

"I am here to take you home, little brother," Justin declared, his voice carrying a hint of desperation.

Leo scowled, his patience thinning. "Why? I'm not going anywhere with you until you tell me what's going on, Justin!"

Justin hesitated, frustration etched on his face. "I can't tell you right now. Not until you come home with me."

Leo's anger flared. "Damn it, Justin. Weren't you the one who told me to get lost because I wanted nothing to do with any of you back home?"

Justin sighed, running a hand through his hair. "Leo, I had no choice, okay?"

Leo's eyes narrowed. "What do you mean you had no choice?"

Justin gritted his teeth, his voice strained. "I can't say."

"Then what can you say?" Leo demanded, his patience wearing thin.

"Look, we need you back home, alright? There's an emergency," Justin finally admitted.

Leo leaned in, his face inches from Justin's. "You're a master necromancer, Justin. Whatever it is you want me for, you can handle it yourself."

Justin's shoulders slumped, and he rubbed the back of his neck in frustration. "Leo, I know it's hard to believe, but I can't do this alone. You're the only one who can help."

Leo's anger clashed with his sense of duty. He weighed his options, realizing that he might be the only hope for his family. But the years of bitterness and resentment were not easily brushed aside.

"You expect me to just drop everything and come running back home because you say so?" Leo muttered, his voice filled with bitterness.

Justin nodded earnestly. "Yes, Leo. It's that important."

Leo's fists clenched as he struggled with his conflicting emotions. "Damn it, Justin," he muttered under his breath, his voice barely a whisper. "Fine, I'll think about it."

Justin nodded, relief flooding his features. "Thank you, Leo. You won't regret this."

Leo grabbed his jacket and headed for the door, his heart heavy with uncertainty. He glanced back at his brother one last time. "You owe me, Justin. Big time."

As he left the director's office, Leo couldn't help but wonder about the nature of the emergency that had brought his estranged family back into his life.

Leo sat at his cluttered desk, his mind still reeling from the unsettling encounter with his estranged brother earlier that day. He wanted nothing more than to push the memory aside, to focus on his work in the morgue, but it lingered like a shadow.

He proceeded to head into the examination area and started working. He leaned over the dead body that had arrived the night before. The lifeless eyes stared blankly at him, but what disturbed him most was the absence of pupils. His heart quickened, but years of dealing with the macabre had taught him to maintain composure.

Something didn't add up with this body, so Leo decided to dig deeper. Glancing around to ensure no one was watching, he tapped into the sliver of necromantic magic he rarely used these days. He knew this case demanded it.

His hand hovered over the corpse, and a soft purple glow emerged. Unlike most necromancers who required incantations, Leo's magic flowed effortlessly. The glow transformed into swirling smoke that enveloped the body. He cast a simple spell to detect demonic possession.

As his magic probed, the room's lights flickered, and Leo's skin prickled with unease. The smoke began to transform, his magic taking a shape he couldn't comprehend. Panic surged through him as he tried to wrest control of his wayward magic, but it resisted.

The smoky form solidified into a menacing face with dark red hues. "Show yourself, demon!" Leo growled, but the only response was a chilling laugh before the entity vanished.

Leo regained control over his magic, his heart racing. What did this mean?

"Leo, are you okay in here? I heard shouting," Jason, his assistant, called from the doorway.

Leo, still panting, collected himself before responding. "Y-yeah, I'm okay. Did you need something?"

"Just wondering if you're ready to head home. You've been here a while."

Leo checked his watch, realizing he'd lost track of time. "Yeah, you can head home too now."

"Thanks, boss. Are you sure you'll be okay in here?"

"I will be, now go home and get some rest, Jason," Leo said, his thoughts a tumultuous whirlpool.

Before leaving, Jason gave him a concerned nod and exited the room, leaving Leo alone with his thoughts.

Leo sighed and looked back at the dead body on his table. Its missing pupils and the demonic presence left a trail of unanswered questions. He couldn't let this go. He needed to find out more about the body and its connection to the demon he'd encountered.

The morgue's sterile environment contrasted sharply with Leo's inner turmoil. He needed answers, and he needed them fast. He glanced at the body again, searching for any clues.

The body was in a state of advanced decay, an unpleasant odor filling the room. Unusual symbols were etched onto its skin, and Leo realized they held a hidden significance. This wasn't just any corpse; it was connected to something sinister.

Deep in thought, Leo muttered to himself, "What were you involved in, and why did a demon take an interest in you?"

Leo sensed that there was more to his encounter with the demon than met the eye. It had felt like a warning, a message from the other side.

For now, Leo shook it off and headed home and regroup. Leo trudged up the dimly lit staircase of his small Manhattan apartment building, his steps heavy with exhaustion. It had been a long day and he couldn't wait to finally unwind.

His apartment, although modest, felt like a sanctuary to him. The cozy living room, with its mismatched furniture and soft, earthy tones, was a reflection of Leo's simple tastes. A few potted plants added a touch of greenery, and a large window offered a view of the bustling street below.

Leo's train of thought was interrupted when he reached his door. There, sitting on the welcome mat, was his brother Justin. Leo blinked, momentarily stunned.

"Justin? What are you doing here? How did you even know where I lived?" Leo asked, his voice laced with surprise as he approached his brother.

Justin pushed himself up from the floor, his weary eyes meeting Leo's. "Does it matter? Look, can you let me in? I really had nowhere else to go."

Leo frowned, puzzled. "Didn't you get a hotel for yourself?"

Justin sighed, running a hand through his disheveled hair. "This visit wasn't really planned. Like I said, it was an emergency."

Leo, unable to ignore the desperation in Justin's eyes, nodded reluctantly. He unlocked his door and gestured for his brother to enter. "Fine, come in."

As they stepped into the apartment, Leo couldn't help but feel a sense of awkwardness. He had been estranged from his family for years, and this unexpected visit from Justin was unsettling.

They both removed their jackets and Leo gestured toward the living room. "So, are you finally going to tell me what this emergency is?"

Justin took a moment to survey the apartment's decor before settling onto the worn-out couch. "Can we sit down somewhere first? Honestly, you have a nice thing going on here, Leo."

Leo didn't know what to make of the compliment but led Justin to the living room, taking a seat across from him. "Speak."

Justin exhaled deeply. "It's Rory. Something happened to him."

The mention of their younger brother hit Leo like a bolt of lightning. He and Rory had been close, but they had lost touch after he left home. "What happened?"

"He came home one night looking like hell, and since then, he's been acting differently. We all thought he was just acting out because of not having any magic, but yesterday, he collapsed. I tried to reach him through our blood ties, but nothing. Our parents left this morning to visit another coven in Seattle, and they said nothing about Rory."

Leo absorbed this information, his mind racing. Rory's lack of magical abilities had always been a sensitive topic, but Leo had always reassured him of his love, magic or not. "How is he doing now?"

Justin's eyes were filled with worry. "I called home earlier, and Harry said he's still asleep. We need you back, Leo. We've tried using all our magic, but nothing worked. We thought you might be able to reach out to him."

Leo pushed aside their differences, focusing on his responsibility as an older brother. "Alright, I'll do it for Rory. But the moment you turn this against me, I'm gone. Got it?"

Justin nodded, his gratitude evident. "Got it."

Leo stood up, grabbing a couple of blankets for Justin, then headed to his room for a quick shower. As the warm water cascaded over him, he couldn't help but let his mind wander back to the past, back to the days when he and Rory were inseparable.

Leo had always been protective of Rory, and they had promised to stand by each other no matter what. But when Leo discovered that he had magical abilities that surpassed the rest of their family, things had changed.

Guilt had gnawed at him, pushing him to leave the magical world behind. He had wanted to escape the expectations and the pressure, but in doing so, he had left Rory behind as well.

Now, as he stepped out of the shower and dried himself off, Leo knew he couldn't escape his past any longer.

2

# Finn

"There you go, all done." Dr. Finn Sloane flashed a reassuring smile as he finished tending to Eryx Ross' training-induced bruises. The medical bay of the Shadowguards was a place of both physical and emotional healing for those who guarded the shadows.

Finn's role in the Shadowguards was multi-faceted. He served as a healer and, occasionally, a therapist, preferred over the intimidating shrink. His healing magic found full utilization within the secretive organization. When Alex Knight had approached him with the job offer, Finn had leaped at the opportunity.

One of Finn's unique talents was the ability to sense souls. It was this gift that had initially told him that Alex was more than just a mere human, something otherworldly. Initially intimidated, Finn had soon discovered that Alex was a gentle giant, misunderstood by many.

Today, his attention was focused on Eryx, the newest addition to the team. Eryx had set aside his career as a musician to wield newfound godly powers. Eryx only found out recently that he was a vessel for the god Apollo.

"Thanks, doc," Eryx said, rubbing the back of his neck and chuckling.

"Alex is gonna blow a fuse when he finds out I'm in here again."

Finn grinned playfully. "Well, you better get your story straight because he's on his way over."

Eryx's eyes widened. "Wait, what?"

Before Finn could respond, the entrance swished open, revealing a furious-looking Alex. Without hesitation, Alex went straight to Eryx, cupping his cheek in concern. Jealousy tugged at Finn's heart, but he was genuinely happy for Alex and the person he'd been waiting for.

"What happened?" Alex's voice dripped with worry.

Eryx sighed. "I was sparring with Olivia, and she threw me for a loop."

Alex's brows furrowed. "What did I tell you? Don't spar without me. You're still new to this."

Eryx sighed again, looking sheepish. "I just wanted to try out my new bow. It worked perfectly the first time I held it, but it turns out it was all Apollo."

Alex kissed Eryx's forehead before turning to Finn, his eyes pleading. "Doc, is he going to be okay?"

Finn nodded reassuringly. "He'll be fine. His healing has already begun, but he should take it easy for a few days while he fully recovers."

Eryx chimed in, gratitude in his voice. "Thanks again, Doc."

"You're welcome. Now, get out of my office before you two start mauling each other." Finn said and the the couple just cackled before getting up and leaving.

Finn tidied up, his thoughts wandering back to his own past. His decision to join the Shadowguards had been rooted in a desire for purpose and a way to make a difference. The organization offered a unique outlet for his magical talents, and he'd embraced it.

Finn's day had unfolded with a rare sense of ease. The headquarters of the Shadowguards, normally bustling with activity, had been unusually quiet. He welcomed the respite, a chance to breathe in the midst of their hectic lives.

As he prepared to leave, Marcus, a fellow Shadowguard and a speedster, appeared in the doorway. Finn turned to him with a raised eyebrow. "Marcus, is there anything wrong?"

Marcus flashed a wide grin, his energy seemingly boundless. "Ugh no. The team was wondering if you'd like to come with us to Luna this evening."

Finn's interest piqued. Luna, a popular bar in the heart of Manhattan, was renowned for its inclusive atmosphere and its famed Karaoke nights. "Sure, I'll meet you guys there. Is there any particular reason for the sudden urge to go out?"

Marcus shook his head, his enthusiasm contagious. "No reason. Alex just thought it would be nice to have some fun and relax tonight."

Finn nodded, considering the invitation. "Alright, what do you need me to bring?"

"Just bring yourself. Oh, and Alex mentioned that if you want to invite someone, feel free to do so. I'm bringing my dad along," Marcus said, his excitement palpable.

Finn couldn't help but smile at the mention of Marcus's father, Hermes. The bond between them was a testament to the power of family. "Sweet, I'll invite Leo. Thanks, Marcus."

With a quick hug, Marcus sped away, leaving Finn shaking his head in amusement. He decided to head back home to get ready for the evening. The Shadowguards provided houses for their members, a luxury Finn had never imagined having. It was far better than any apartment he could have afforded.

As he entered his home, a furry creature greeted him with a melodramatic meow. Finn scooped up his Siamese cat, Pickles, cradling him affectionately. "Hungry, little one?"

"Meow," Pickles replied, his blue eyes fixed on Finn.

Finn chuckled at his dramatic feline friend and carried him to the kitchen. He fetched a can of cat food from the cupboard and began to pour it into Pickles's bowl, the sound of kibble hitting porcelain filling the room.

The atmosphere in the house was serene, a stark contrast to the usual chaos of his life as a Shadowguard. He relished the moments of quiet, knowing that tonight at Luna would be a different story.

As he set the bowl down for Pickles, Finn's thoughts wandered. He appreciated these simple moments, the ones that reminded him of the ordinary joys of life. A quiet day, a beloved pet, and the promise of a fun evening with friends—it was the kind of balance he strived for.

As Finn headed to his room to get ready, he couldn't help but feel a sense of anticipation. Luna had a unique charm, known for its dimly lit interior adorned with colorful lights, creating an inviting ambiance. It was a place where they could be themselves, a haven for those who needed a break from the demands of their supernatural lives.

The thought of reuniting with Leo brought a smile to Finn's face. Leo had become a constant in his life, a person who he now considered as a friend. It also didn't help that the man was hot but he was not going to tell Leo that. Finn couldn't wait to catch up with him and enjoy the night.

Finn leaned back in his comfy armchair, his eyes fixed on the ceiling as he contemplated his next move. He was in his cozy living room, the soft afternoon sunlight streaming in through the window, casting warm patterns on the floor. With a sigh, he decided to seize the day, or rather, the evening.

He reached into his pocket and pulled out his phone, his thumb dancing across the screen to dial Leo's number. After three rings, Leo's voice came through the line, and for some reason, that alone brought a smile to Finn's face.

"Hello?" Leo's voice held a hint of something troubling, though he tried to hide it.

Finn wasn't one to ignore things easily. "Hey, what's wrong?" he asked, genuine concern coloring his words.

"Oh, hi, Finn. Nothing's wrong, just work stuff, you know," Leo replied, attempting to brush it off.

Finn wasn't buying it, but he decided to let it slide for now. "Tell you what. The team invited me to go to Luna tonight. I was wondering if you wanted to come with me and be my plus one?"

Leo's tone shifted to playful teasing. "Oh? Are you asking me out, Doctor?"

A chuckle escaped Finn's lips. "If I was going to ask you on a date, it would be in person. So, are you going with me or not?"

Leo's laughter filled the line. "Yeah, yeah. I'll be there."

"Okay. Good. See you soon." Finn hung up, the faintest blush creeping onto his cheeks as he ended the call.

He held his phone in his hand, feeling a mixture of excitement and anticipation, much like a teenager watching a romantic movie. The idea of spending the evening with Leo was more thrilling than he cared to admit, even to himself.

As he stared at his phone, Finn couldn't help but wonder what was really bothering Leo. He knew his friend well enough to sense when something was amiss, and the work excuse didn't quite cut it. There was more to it, and Finn was determined to get to the bottom of it.

With a sigh, he decided to put his investigative skills to good use. He began to compose a text message to Leo, his fingers tapping on the screen with practiced ease.

**Finn**: Leo, seriously, what's bothering you? You can talk to me, you know.

The message sent, and Finn stared at his phone, waiting for Leo's response. The seconds seemed to stretch into eternity before the familiar notification sound broke the silence.

**Leo**: Finn, it's complicated. I'll explain later, I promise.

Finn frowned, his concern deepening. He wasn't one to pry, but he couldn't stand the thought of Leo going through something difficult alone. They had been through thick and thin together, and Finn considered Leo more than just a friend; he was family.

**Finn**: Alright, I won't push. Just remember, I'm here if you need anything.

**Leo**: Thanks, Finn. You're a true friend.

A warm feeling settled in Finn's chest as he read Leo's reply. Their friendship was a treasure, and he would do anything to protect it.

With a sense of determination, Finn decided to focus on the evening ahead. Luna was one of those places where magic seemed to happen naturally, and he looked forward to experiencing it with Leo by his side. It had been too long since they had a night out together, just the two of them.

Finn glanced at his watch, realizing he had some spare time to burn. He decided to pay a visit to his parents, whose house wasn't too far away. After giving his pet cat, Pickles, one last affectionate pat, he headed out. The Sloane family home was situated close to Canal Street, and Finn chose to hop on the train to reach there. It was a modest two-story house that he had managed to purchase thanks to Shadowguards and the generosity of his friend, Alex. Finn owed his parents a great deal for providing him with the education and unwavering support that had paved the way for his current success.

From the train station, he strolled for a couple of minutes until he reached the familiar front door. He rang the doorbell, and within a heartbeat, the door swung open, revealing his mother, Jane Sloane. Jane was a petite, plump woman with a warm smile, though she currently looked a tad exhausted and was wearing an apron.

"Hi, Mom," Finn greeted, a grin spreading across his face.

"Finn! My boy!" Jane's smile was infectious as she enveloped him in a warm hug. "Come on in."

Finn stepped inside and shrugged off his coat, hanging it on a nearby rack. "Where's Dad?"

"He's at work and won't be back till later," Jane informed him.

Finn's father, Joseph Sloane, served as a captain in the New York Fire Department (NYFD).

"One of these days, I'll time it right and catch him at home," Finn chuckled.

"You know your dad. He'll work till he drops," Jane said with an affectionate shake of her head. "So, what brings you here all of a sudden? Usually, you're knee-deep in work at this hour."

Finn explained, "Well, there wasn't much work to be done today, so I decided to head home early. And I've got some time before I need to be at Luna."

Jane's eyes sparkled with delight. "Well, come to the kitchen. I've baked some cookies you can munch on, and we can catch up."

Finn's mouth watered at the mention of his mother's cookies, a special treat he hadn't enjoyed in quite some time. He followed her into the cozy kitchen, where the scent of freshly baked cookies hung in the air.

As they settled at the kitchen table, Finn couldn't help but glance around. The house was a haven of warmth and familiarity. The walls adorned with family photos, the faint creak of wooden floors, and the comforting hum of his mother bustling about the kitchen brought back cherished memories.

Finn reached for a cookie and took a bite, savoring the sweet, familiar taste. "These are amazing, Mom."

His mother beamed, her cheeks tinged with a touch of pink. "You always loved these. So, how's work treating you, dear?"

Finn leaned back in his chair, a hint of nostalgia in his eyes. "Work's good, but you know how it is. Busy as ever. Sometimes, I miss the simplicity of home."

His mother nodded in understanding. "We miss having you around more often, Finn. It gets lonely in this old house."

Finn felt a twinge of guilt. He knew he should visit more frequently, but the demands of his job often left him with little time for anything else. "I promise, I'll try to make it a point to visit more."

They continued chatting, reminiscing about old family vacations and neighborhood adventures. Each story was a piece of their shared history, and the hours passed like minutes.

Eventually, Finn's phone buzzed with a reminder. He reluctantly stood up and gave his mother a hug. "I hate to leave, Mom, but I've got to."

Jane hugged him tightly, her eyes glistening. "Promise me you'll come back soon."

Finn kissed his mother on the cheek. "I promise, Mom. And next time, I'll aim for Dad's day off."

Jane chuckled, her smile radiant. "That would be wonderful. Take care, my boy."

As Finn walked away from his childhood home, he couldn't help but feel a mixture of emotions. Visiting his parents had rekindled cherished memories and reminded him of the importance of family. He made a mental note to balance his life better, ensuring that he could spend more moments like these with the people who had always supported and loved him.

Finn had barely enough time to rush home, take a quick shower, and throw on an outfit he deemed acceptable for a night at Luna. He glanced at himself in the mirror, adjusting his collar as he aimed for a balance between casual and put-together. Luna, nestled in the heart of Manhattan's bustling city strip, was calling, and he couldn't keep Leo waiting.

Opting for an Uber ride to preserve his attire, Finn arrived at the club, immediately greeted by a burly bouncer who happened to be a wolf shifter. "ID," the bouncer demanded, his gaze scrutinizing Finn.

Finn obliged, handing over his regular ID rather than his department ID to avoid unnecessary complications. The bouncer nodded, returning the ID, and stepped aside, allowing Finn entry into Luna.

The moment Finn stepped inside, the atmosphere enveloped him in its unique charm. Soft, ambient lighting bathed the club in a gentle glow, and the soothing melody of live jazz music hung in the air, enhancing the overall allure of the place.

Making his way to the team's reserved table, Finn was met with a friendly wave from Alex. He settled into his chair, positioning himself close to the aisle, anticipation building as he waited for Leo's arrival.

Eryx, seated next to him, couldn't resist the opportunity to tease. "Hey, Doc, you're looking rather snazzy tonight. Who's the lucky guest?"

Finn's cheeks warmed, grateful for the dim lighting that concealed his blush. "I invited Leo, though I'm not sure what time he'll show up."

Alex, sitting across from him, chimed in. "You two seem to have hit it off quite well."

Finn shrugged, trying to sound nonchalant. "Yeah, he's alright, I suppose."

As the night continued, the club's atmosphere transformed, weaving an enchanting spell on its patrons. The low hum of conversations blended seamlessly with the soothing jazz, creating an intimate ambiance. Candlelit tables cast flickering shadows, and the scent of well-crafted cocktails wafted through the air.

Finn's anticipation grew with each passing moment, and he couldn't help but steal glances at the entrance, wondering when Leo would make his appearance. The team's banter and laughter served as a soothing distraction, but his thoughts kept drifting back to their recent encounters.

Eryx leaned in, his voice laced with mischief. "You've been awfully quiet, Doc. Something on your mind?"

Finn hesitated for a moment before responding, his voice low. "Just hoping Leo shows up soon."

Alex, ever perceptive, arched an eyebrow. "You're looking forward to his visit, aren't you?"

Finn didn't bother to deny it. Instead, he offered a sheepish smile. "Yeah, I guess I am."

As the evening wore on, the team's camaraderie grew stronger, and the atmosphere became charged with excitement. Finn found himself enjoying the company and laughter, his worries momentarily forgotten.

Suddenly, the entrance door swung open, drawing everyone's attention. In walked Leo, his presence commanding attention. He looked effortlessly stylish in a well-fitted suit, and his eyes scanned the room until they met Finn's. A warm smile spread across Leo's face as he made his way over.

Finn's heart skipped a beat as Leo took the empty seat beside him. Their proximity sent a pleasant shiver down his spine. "Hey," Leo greeted, his voice carrying a hint of excitement.

"Hey," Finn replied, trying to sound composed despite the fluttering in his chest.

As the night unfolded, the club seemed to fade into the background, leaving only Finn and Leo engrossed in their conversation. They talked about everything and nothing, sharing stories and laughter as if they had known each other for years.

"Want to head to the bar?" Leo's voice broke through the chatter at the table, and Finn glanced around. His friends seemed deeply immersed in their conversations.

Finn grinned. "Sure thing." He placed his hand in Leo's, and they made their way to the bar.

At the bar, Leo ordered two light drinks from the bartender, who was quick to oblige. As the glasses clinked in front of them, Finn didn't waste any time getting to the point. "So, are you finally going to tell me what's going on with you?"

Leo sighed, his usually vibrant eyes dimming. "My brother showed up yesterday, out of the blue, and he wants me to go back to Salem."

Finn raised an eyebrow. "Salem? What's the deal?"

"It's about my youngest brother, Rory. I don't have all the details yet, but I'll find out soon." Leo's voice was tinged with sadness.

"You're leaving?" Finn couldn't hide his concern.

Leo nodded, taking a sip of his drink. "Yeah, not for long, though. I managed to get some time off work, and I'll be heading back tomorrow morning."

Finn rested a hand on Leo's shoulder, offering support. "You know I've got your back, right? Just a call away, man."

Leo managed a small smile. "Thanks, Finn. I really appreciate it."

Their conversation was interrupted by the soulful tones of Eryx, who had taken the stage at the Karaoke machine. His voice was a silky blend of emotion and melody, capturing the attention of everyone in the bar.

Finn swayed to the music, his eyes twinkling with admiration. "Eryx sure knows how to work that mic. He's incredible."

Leo chuckled, his worries momentarily forgotten as they enjoyed the music. The bar's atmosphere seemed to transform with Eryx's performance. The dimly lit room became a stage, and the crowd's cheers provided the perfect backdrop.

Finn nodded, understanding the weight of family obligations. "Just promise me you'll be careful, okay? And keep me posted on what's going on."

Leo's eyes met Finn's, gratitude and determination shining through. "I promise."

As the last notes of Eryx's song faded, the crowd erupted in applause.

Eryx returned to his friends, flushed with exhilaration. Finn couldn't help but applaud as well. "That was amazing, Eryx!"

Eryx grinned, accepting the praise. "Thanks, Finn. You're up next!"

Finn chuckled, shaking his head. "Not tonight, my friend. I'm just here to enjoy the show."

The night continued with laughter, more drinks, and shared memories. Finn and Leo leaned on each other, navigating the complexities of life and friendship. The bar's ambiance grew warmer, the music and laughter weaving a sense of belonging.

Finally, as the clock struck midnight, Finn and Leo exchanged smiles. It was time to head home.

# 3

# Leo

They arrived in Salem just before lunch. Leo squinted at the morning sun as he rubbed his eyes, secretly wishing he could've slept a bit longer. Justin had shaken him awake with all the subtlety of an earthquake. Patience was running thin, and Leo was doing his best not to let it snap and ignite his brother into a human torch.

Groaning, Leo reluctantly clambered out of bed and gathered a few more necessities for the trip. He hadn't expected Justin to nab the family car, but he couldn't complain; it sure beat taking the train to Salem.

The car ride was a quiet one, and Leo welcomed the silence. But it was also the right time to say something, to address the chasm between them. Justin, however, beat him to it.

"I'm sorry," Justin muttered, his knuckles white as he clung to the steering wheel like it was a lifeline.

Leo turned to him, eyebrows furrowing. "For what?"

Justin's voice was heavy. "For not being able to stand up and say something before it was too late."

Leo's gaze was a simmering cauldron of emotions. "Not gonna lie,

Justin. What you did hurt. I thought you would be different than them, but I was wrong. You are my older brother. You're supposed to have my back."

Justin's grip on the wheel tightened. "I had no choice, Leo. Our parents threatened to take Rory away if I didn't do what I did."

Rory's name hung heavy in the air, and it stoked the embers of Leo's anger. "They did what? Why?"

"I don't know what their motives were, but like you, I didn't want Rory to be taken away from us. I love all of you, but you were leaving, and your mind was already set upon it, so I did it."

Leo was stunned. Justin rarely showed this much vulnerability before. He couldn't help but wonder what had been going through his brother's mind when faced with such a choice.

"And Harry?" Leo's voice was low and dangerous. "What did he know about all of this?"

Justin shook his head. "He doesn't know anything. Harry was the only one innocent in all of this."

"Mother and Father really crossed the line this time around." Finn's voice was steady, but his insides churned with anger.

Leo heard Justin sigh deeply. "They weren't always this bad, you know. I promise I'll tell you more of what I know soon."

Leo nodded slowly, his eyes fixed on the road ahead. "Thank you. For telling me all of this."

"It's the least I can do, Leo. You're family." Justin's voice held a rare vulnerability that threatened to break Leo's composure. He blinked away the tears that threatened to spill.

The car sped along, the tires humming on the asphalt. The landscape outside the window changed gradually, from cityscape to rolling hills and dense forests. The trees whispered secrets, their leaves rustling in the breeze. Leo stared out, lost in thought.

As the miles passed, Justin's earlier confession gnawed at Leo's conscience. He knew he needed to make a decision about his anger. Did he let it smolder, keeping a grudge that would only harm the family more? Or did he find it in himself to forgive his brother, at least in part, for the desperate choice he'd been forced to make?

The tension between the two brothers hung heavy. Leo clenched his jaw, his own anger simmering beneath the surface. He couldn't forgive his parents for what they'd done, but he had to admit that Justin had been put between a rock and a hard place.

"Justin," Leo said, breaking the silence, "we're in this together now. We need to figure out what our parents are up to and how to protect Rory."

Justin nodded, his eyes fixed on the road. "I'm with you on that, Leo."

Leo couldn't help but wonder what other secrets his brother held, and what they might discover in Salem. It was a journey filled with uncertainty, but they were family, and they were determined to face whatever came their way, side by side.

Leo and Justin arrived at the Rodriguez Estate later in the afternoon and Leo finally felt like he could breathe again, even if it was just for a moment. He knew he needed to mend things with Justin, but his top priority was helping Rory.

The Rodriguez Estate, handed down by generations, stood imposingly before them. Leo never cared much about its history; to him, it was just a house.

As they stepped out of the car, Harry greeted them with a hesitant smile. "Hey, Leo, been a while," Harry said, rushing over to help with their luggage.

Once the bags hit the ground, Leo pulled Harry into a tight hug. "Harry, I've missed you," Leo said, and Harry awkwardly returned the embrace.

"I've missed you too, brother," Harry admitted, a sigh of relief escaping him.

"Come on, you two. Let's continue this inside. It's cold out here," Justin chimed in, breaking the moment, and they all chuckled.

Inside, the house showcased a unique blend of old-world charm and modern luxury. Ornate decor, high ceilings, plush furniture, and advanced technology coexisted harmoniously. Leo used to adore this place until he felt smothered by its opulence.

They dropped their bags in the living room and took a seat. Justin turned to Harry. "How's he doing?"

Harry rubbed his neck nervously. "He's still out. I tried my magic, but it didn't work."

Leo knew Harry was a dreamwalker, a necromancer who delved into the dreams of the living and the dead. Justin, on the other hand, practiced blood magic, harnessing blood to fuel his spells. It granted them power but had its costs.

"He's not dreaming?" Leo asked.

"No, there's nothing in his subconscious. I'm worried something might be blocking us from seeing what's happening inside him," Harry admitted.

Leo furrowed his brow. People dreamed all the time; the absence of dreams could mean countless things.

Leo leaned forward, his heart heavy with concern. "Is there anything we can do?"

Harry sighed, a sense of helplessness in his eyes. "I don't know, Leo. It's a mystery. And mysteries in our world tend to be dangerous."

Their conversation hung in the air, filled with uncertainty. Leo couldn't help but feel that their return to the estate had unleashed a series of unforeseen events.

The atmosphere inside the house was both inviting and daunting. The grandeur offered comfort, but it also reminded Leo of the secrets and mysteries that lurked within these walls.

As night fell, Leo, Justin, and Harry gathered in Rory's room. The dim light cast eerie shadows, intensifying their unease.

Leo turned to Justin, his voice filled with determination. "We need to find out what's happening to Rory, no matter the cost."

Justin nodded, his eyes reflecting Leo's resolve. "Agreed. We'll use every resource we have."

With their goals set, they delved deeper into the mystery of Rory's condition.

Leo grabbed his bags, his heart thudding with a mix of emotions. Returning to his childhood home after so many years had him feeling like a kid sneaking into a haunted house. The scent of fresh laundry filled the hallway as he pushed the door to his old room open, revealing a space preserved in time. Everything neat, everything perfect. A smile tugged at his lips; Rory's handiwork, he guessed.

His bags thumped onto the floor as he stepped back into the hallway, eager to see his youngest brother for himself. Justin, his other brother, was already heading the same way. Nods passed between them in silent camaraderie. They reached Rory's room, and Justin swung the door open.

Stepping into the room, Leo's skin tingled with unease. Something felt off, like a shadow lurking in the corners. He knew he needed to tighten his magical shields, just as he'd done back in the day when their games of hide and seek had real stakes.

"Tighten your shields," he urged Justin, his voice low and serious.

Justin frowned, eyes narrowing. "Why?"

Leo's gaze scanned the room, searching for clues he couldn't quite put into words. "Something's not right in here. Whatever had happened to Rory, it's feeding off the energy in this room."

Justin and Harry exchanged a worried glance before both followed Leo's lead, strengthening their magical defenses.

Rory had always been on the lean side, but the sight that greeted Leo now was unsettling. His brother appeared painfully thin, like a shadow of his former self. Leo couldn't help but think that whatever lurked within Rory was responsible for this drastic change.

He approached the bed, his footsteps muffled by the plush carpet. The air in the room felt heavy, Leo's eyes never left Rory's face as he assessed the situation.

Harry stood by the doorway, his brows furrowed in worry. He broke the silence, his voice hushed. "Leo, what's happening to him?"

"I don't know, but I need to see for myself." His voice was tinged with concern, his jaw set with determination.

Leo raised his hand, palm facing up, and conjured a small, shimmering purple ball of energy. He tossed it into the air, and it hung there, casting a soft, protective aura over the room. "That was a defensive ward," he explained to Harry. "Just in case something happens, it won't spread out of this room."

His concern for his brother fueled his determination to stop whatever force was responsible for this, at least temporarily. He took a deep breath, his eyes narrowing as he concentrated.

Extending his hands, Leo began to weave intricate gestures in the air, his fingertips leaving trails of purple sparks that glimmered like spectral fireflies. The room seemed to respond to his command, the very air thickening with magic. A sense of otherworldly power emanated from Leo as he tapped into his necromantic abilities.

With a swift and fluid motion, he brought his hands together, palms facing outward. A pulse of dark energy rippled from his fingertips, spreading outwards like a shockwave. It was as if the very fabric of the room shivered in response to his command.

As the energy drain's influence began to recede, Leo visualized the room's atmosphere changing. The oppressive feeling of being drained slowly lifted, replaced by a sense of vitality and renewal. The air itself seemed to shimmer with a faint, soothing light, casting a gentle, purifying glow over the room.

The room's temperature seemed to stabilize, and the air regained its freshness. Leo's magic had created a protective barrier, a sanctuary where the energy drain could no longer penetrate.

The purple ward he had conjured earlier began to intensify in brilliance. It transformed into a swirling, intricate pattern of arcane symbols, spinning like a celestial dance. This magical barrier pulsed with an aura of defiance, pushing back against the malevolent force responsible for draining the energy.

Leo's eyes blazed with an inner fire as he continued to channel his necromantic power. He willed the ward to hold fast, to shield Rory and the room from harm. The room itself seemed to sigh in relief as Leo's magic took hold, restoring balance and protection.

"I've never seen anything like that before. Did you just take away what was draining the room? It feels like I can breathe now." Justin said.

Leo nodded, relief washing over him. "Yes, though it is not forever. I've placed some sort of stop-gap to temporarily stop whatever it is from draining the energy in this room."

Harry leaned in, his brow furrowing. "How long will it last?"

Leo met his gaze, a weight in his eyes. "It will last for a couple of days. Now I need you two to watch my back and get ready."

Justin scratched his head, puzzled. "Why?"

Leo's voice was resolute. "I am going to try and seek out his soul."

"What? Are you saying that you can track souls?" Justin asked, his eyes wide.

Leo clenched his jaw, determination flickering in his gaze. "I don't have time to explain right now, but yes, I can track souls. Keep an eye out."

With a deep breath, he closed his eyes and focused his energy, channeling his innate connection to the mystical forces that governed the realm of spirits.

As Leo delved deeper into the spirit realm, the boundaries of the physical world dissolved around him. He found himself standing on the ethereal shores of a shimmering, iridescent river that flowed with the memories and emotions of countless souls. The air carried a scent of forgotten dreams, and a mournful melody whispered through the realm.

Around him, crystalline trees reached for the stars, their branches touching the infinite expanse above. Ghostly beings with shimmering wings whispered secrets to the universe.

Leo knew that this place held peril. Malevolent shadows lurked, waiting to ensnare the unwary. But for Rory, he'd brave any abyss.

Following an invisible thread of connection, Leo navigated the spirit realm's labyrinth. Soon, he reached a colossal tower, radiating a dark, foreboding energy—Rory's prison.

He ascended the tower, each step laden with echoes of forgotten moments. At the top, a haunting blue light bathed a chamber, and there, Rory's soul awaited.

Rory's soul, though ethereal, bore his essence. But his eyes held an eerie emptiness.

"Rory," Leo whispered, reaching out to touch his brother's incorporeal form.

Rory's voice, feeble yet wise, echoed through the chamber. "Leo, you must leave this place. It's not safe. I am not alone, and I've harnessed a power I never knew I possessed."

Confusion etched Leo's face. "What do you mean? You don't have magic, Rory."

With unexpected energy, Rory pushed Leo out with radiant light, back into the mortal realm. Leo's heart pounded as he returned, his mind filled with questions about Rory's newfound abilities.

Back in the room, Justin and Harry stared, concern etched on their faces. Leo knew their quest had taken a twist.

Justin scratched his head. "What happened in there?"

Leo shook his head, troubled. "Rory warned me to leave and pushed me out."

Harry frowned. "We can't just leave him there. We need to figure this out."

As the room's atmosphere grew tense, Leo spoke up. "We'll need more answers. I saw something in that realm—a power Rory never had."

Justin crossed his arms, deep in thought. "You think someone's behind this?"

Leo nodded. "I do. And I'm gonna find out who and why."

Justin and Harry exchanged glances, then nodded. They knew they couldn't turn away from the mystery that had enveloped them.

"What now?" Harry asked, his fingers tapping nervously against his thigh.

Leo looked at them both, a determined glint in his eyes. "Do you still have access to the library?" he asked Justin.

Justin nodded, his sandy hair falling into his bespectacled face. "Yeah, I still have the key to it."

"Good," Leo replied. He rubbed his chin, deep in thought. "I remember Mother telling us that there's a book about a person's soul being trapped in the spirit realm. I want you guys to find it."

Harry scratched his head. "How about you? What are you going to do?"

Leo's gaze shifted to the old wooden floor. "I'm going to have to call in a friend of mine who can possibly help us in the matter." With that, Leo nodded to his brothers and left Rory's room.

He retreated to his own room, sinking onto his bed, thoughts racing like a river in flood. He couldn't shake the feeling of power that Rory had possessed. It was an unsettling thought—Rory being possibly more potent than even their parents. Leo wondered if his parents knew about Rory's strength and if they had any role in what had happened to him.

But now was not the time to delve into those mysteries. Leo shook off the unsettling thoughts and retrieved his phone from his pocket. He dialed a familiar number, the one that always brought a smile to his face.

"Hello?" Finn answered at the very first ring.

"Hey, Doc," Leo said, his voice tense. "I need your help. How fast can you get to Salem?"

4

# Finn

Finn's head was pounding like a construction site at rush hour, and he was pretty damn sure it was the booze's fault. He groaned, squinting at the alarm clock as it screamed like a banshee from his nightstand, making his suffering even worse. Just when he thought things couldn't get any worse, his cat, Pickles, decided it was time to show affection by pouncing onto his bed and giving him a good ol' tongue bath.

"Ugh, cat, not now," he grumbled, pushing Pickles away as politely as a hungover guy could manage.

Dragging himself out of bed, Finn stumbled to the kitchen, feeling like a zombie in a B-movie. He managed to pour some cereal into a bowl for himself and dumped cat food into Pickles' dish, who was now giving him the judgmental stare reserved for lazy pet owners.

"Alright, alright," he muttered, his voice cracking like he'd been stranded in a desert for a week.

As he half-heartedly shoveled cereal into his mouth, Finn's thoughts drifted to Leo. He wondered how his buddy was faring on that trip to Salem. Finn decided it was no use stressing over it. Leo was a big boy, and if things went sideways, he'd call. Or text. Probably with lots of expletives, but it would get the message across.

Clinging to his cereal bowl for dear life, he finished his meager breakfast and made a valiant effort to look human again. A quick shower and some clothes thrown on in a haphazard fashion later, he was almost ready for the day.

As he left his apartment, he muttered to Pickles, "You guard the place, alright? And don't throw any wild parties while I'm gone."

Pickles merely yawned, unimpressed by Finn's attempt at humor. Finn sighed, locking the door behind him. Another day, another dollar, and maybe, just maybe, the throbbing in his head would subside by lunchtime.

Finn dragged himself into the bustling headquarters of the Shadowguards just before the place transformed into a chaotic hive of activity. As he made his way to his cluttered office, he exchanged greetings with various agents, offering smiles and nods to those he was particularly friendly with. However, it was no secret that camaraderie flowed through the veins of the Shadowguards like a potent elixir.

The rule, laid down by Alex was clear. Respect was to be maintained at all costs.

Finally reaching his cluttered sanctuary, Finn was met with a warm smile from his eternally youthful-looking assistant, Lucy. She appeared to be in her mid-thirties, but Finn knew that she was far older than she let on – a succubus in disguise. Outsiders might have been wary of her, given the infamous reputation of her kind for sapping sexual energy and manipulating unsuspecting victims. But Finn knew better. Lucy was the living proof that not all denizens from the depths of the hells were as terrible as their reputation.

Lucy's crimson lips curled into a friendly grin. "Hey boss, you look like shit," she quipped, her words laced with playful concern.

Finn ran a hand through his tousled hair, attempting to salvage some semblance of his appearance. "You could say that. I absolutely feel like shit too."

Raising a perfectly arched eyebrow, Lucy leaned in closer. "Fun night?" she inquired, her eyes dancing with curiosity.

Finn sighed, realizing there was no point in hiding it. "Yeah, Alex's team invited me over to Luna."

Lucy's grin widened. "Well, come here. I have some potions that you can use for your hangover."

Finn accepted the small vial that Lucy handed him. The potion had a pungent odor that made his nose wrinkle in disgust. Nevertheless, he downed it in one gulp, hoping that it would perform some kind of miracle.

After a couple of agonizingly long minutes, Finn began to feel the effects. The pounding in his head subsided, and the queasiness in his stomach eased. He marveled at the wonders of supernatural hangover remedies and couldn't help but smile in gratitude.

"Thanks, Lucy," he mumbled, his voice returning to a more normal volume. "Do I have any appointments this morning?"

Lucy's crimson eyes sparkled as she consulted her digital calendar. "You've got a couple of wolf shifter agents scheduled, boss."

Finn nodded, mentally preparing himself for the day ahead. "Send them in as soon as they arrive."

As he settled into his creaky office chair, the first patient of the day limped in. It was clear that this particular wolf shifter had seen better days. His fur was disheveled, and he had a rather comical expression of discomfort on his face.

Finn gestured for the agent to take a seat. "Morning," he greeted, offering a wry smile. "Rough night?"

The wolf shifter groaned in response. "Recon mission," he grumbled, his voice laced with exhaustion. "Chased a rogue vampire all night."

Finn chuckled sympathetically, shaking his head. "Well, take a load off, my friend. Let's see what we can do for you."

And so, the day began in Finn's office, filled with a mix of supernatural maladies, amusing stories, and the occasional colorful language that only the Shadowguards could bring. Despite the chaos, Finn couldn't help but find solace in the fact that he was making a difference in a world where the bizarre and the mundane often collided in the most strangest ways.

It had been a typically hectic morning for Finn. Appointments had piled up faster than he could clear them, and just as he thought he was about to break for lunch, fate had other plans. Lucy, his ever-efficient assistant, waltzed into his office with a look of urgency.

"Lucy, did I have another appointment?" Finn inquired, eyebrows furrowing.

Lucy shook her head, her bobbed hair bouncing. "No, the big guy wants you in their briefing room now."

Finn let out a sigh, mentally rearranging his lunch plans. "Okay, let me just put some things away, and I'll be on my way over."

Lucy nodded and exited the room, leaving Finn to wonder why Alex, the big boss, wanted to see him. He couldn't help but shake off an uneasy feeling as he gathered his things. Whatever it was, Finn was determined to face it head-on.

He arrived at the briefing room, finding everyone already seated, and Alex, their enigmatic leader, at the head of the table. As Finn entered, he received warm smiles from the team, which did wonders for his confidence.

"Hey, Doc! There's a chair here," Eryx, the rookie, chimed in, patting the seat beside him. Finn obliged and took the offered seat.

Alex cleared his throat, commanding everyone's attention. "Alright, thank you for coming, Doctor," he began, and Finn nodded in acknowledgment. "Now, you must be wondering why I've called you in here, but worry not, there's a good reason for it."

Finn leaned forward, curiosity piqued. "What's going on?"

Alex paused for dramatic effect, and Finn's heart raced with anticipation. "The team has decided unanimously that they want you to fully join the team as our medic on the field."

Finn's jaw dropped. "What? I don't mean to sound ungrateful, but why now? And who's going to replace me in the medical bay?"

"As you can probably tell, the team currently lacks a healer," Alex explained. "Though Eryx's abilities can heal, he's still new to it and doesn't have control over his magic. By joining the team officially, you can help Eryx train a part of his magic while assisting the team on missions. As for your current role, you'll still be working there, as you're the person most people trust and confide in. With this in mind, I took it upon myself to get you another hand when it comes to treating agents."

Finn blinked, trying to process all the information being thrown at him. "What do you mean?"

"Marcus, will you please call our new doctor in, please?" Alex said to Marcus, who promptly walked towards the door and escorted a striking African-American woman into the room. He stood beside Alex as the woman stepped forward.

Alex gestured to the woman.. "Why don't you introduce yourself to everyone?"

The woman smiled warmly. "Hey, everyone, I am Doctor Gina Lacroix. I am a part of the Lacroix pack, and yes, I am a shifter with the ability to transfer healing magic to people. It's lovely to meet all of you."

Finn's head was spinning with all these sudden changes and introductions. He glanced around the room at the expectant faces of his teammates.

"Finn," Alex spoke up again, drawing his attention, "Gina will be your right hand, and I want you to give her the best training possible about what we do here in the Shadowguards. So, the question remains: Do you want to be a part of our team or stay in the medical bay?"

It was a lot to take in, but Finn didn't need much time to think about it. The opportunity to be in the field while still contributing to the medical bay was too good to pass up. He nodded decisively. "Of course. I'll do it."

Cheers erupted in the room, and his teammates congratulated him. Finn's heart swelled with a mixture of excitement and nervousness. He noticed Alex's approving nod and couldn't help but smile.

"Marcus, can you please escort Doctor Lacroix to the medical bay and introduce her to Lucy?" Alex instructed.

Finn had intended to do it himself, but just then, the alert went off.

Finn's eyes widened as he watched the team in action for the first time. They moved with an efficiency and professionalism that left him utterly amazed. His heart raced, knowing that he had just become a part of this extraordinary group.

As the team huddled around the blinking alert on the mission control screen, Finn's anxiety grew like a storm cloud. He fidgeted with the collar of his shirt feeling like a rookie on his first day of school. It was then that Eryx sauntered over to him.

"Hey there, newbie," Eryx said, clapping Finn on the back hard enough to almost knock the wind out of him. "Don't sweat it. We were all greenhorns once. You'll get the hang of it."

"Newbie? Aren't you also a newbie?" Finn raised a brow at his friend and managed a weak smile and nodded his thanks. He appreciated Eryx's attempt at reassurance, even though the butterflies in his stomach continued their relentless fluttering.

"Well, that's true but this time, I won't be called a rookie anymore." Eryx replied.

"Eryx you will always be *the* rookie." Alex said from around the corner.

Eryx slapped Alex's shoulder as he came closer to them making everyone chuckle.

Just when Finn thought he couldn't take the suspense any longer, Gabe spoke up. "I've got it! The alert's origin is right here in Brooklyn."

Alex took charge. "Gear up, everyone. We're heading to Brooklyn."

Finn followed the team to the locker room, where Lucas handed him his own uniform. It was sleek, dark, and adorned with an assortment of symbols. Finn hurriedly stripped off his civilian clothes and wrestled himself into the ensemble. He couldn't help but feel like he was cosplaying as a character from a cheesy sci-fi movie.

Lucas grinned as he handed Finn a pair of goggles. "Looking good, rookie. These will help you see things you've never seen before."

Finn put on the goggles, feeling like a cross between a wannabe superhero and a confused tourist. He adjusted them until they were on top on his helmet.

Alex gathered the team, all now clad in their matching ensembles, and gave a quick rundown of the mission. "Alright, team, you know the drill. We're dealing with a witch coven in Brooklyn. Let's keep it by the book, people. No heroics."

As they piled into a blacked-out van, Finn found himself sandwiched between Eryx and Gabe, who seemed to be arguing about the best pizza joint in Brooklyn. Eryx was adamant that it was "Sal's Slice of Heaven," while Gabe insisted on "Tony's Tasty Pies."

"Enough, you two," Alex grumbled from the front seat, clearly amused but acted like he was irritated. "We've got a job to do."

The ride to Brooklyn was surprisingly uneventful, though Finn couldn't help but feel like he was the odd man out in a group.

They pulled up to a nondescript building that looked like it belonged in a neighborhood where nothing ever happened. The team piled out of the van, weapons in hand, and Finn felt a surge of adrenaline.

They were greeted by a woman who looked like she had better days, and Finn guessed that this was the coven's head witch. The lady had wrinkles that told stories of many moonlit spells gone awry, and her hair, a wild tangle of gray, seemed to have a mind of its own.

The head witch introduced herself as Annie and took a brief look at everyone on the team. Her gaze shifted to Finn, and he couldn't help but feel like he was under some kind of magical microscope. Annie's brow furrowed, and she muttered something under her breath, her eyes narrowing.

Finn didn't know what this meant, so he shrugged it off, exchanging a confused glance with Alex. Alex, always the one to cut straight to the chase, asked Annie what the situation was.

Annie sighed heavily, her shoulders slumping. "Well, you see, one of our coven members went a bit... loopy the other night. And this morning, we received reports that she was wreaking havoc in another witch coven by attacking them."

Alex raised an eyebrow. "Attacking? That doesn't sound good. Did you manage to apprehend her?"

Annie nodded grimly. "Yes, we did. She's in the warded room of our coven now. But here's the weird part..."

Finn leaned in, curious. "What's weird?"

Annie hesitated for a moment, as if choosing her words carefully. "The room is empty."

The team exchanged glances, a collective frown settling on their faces. Empty rooms were generally not the best sign, especially in cases involving rogue witches.

Alex, their fearless leader, took charge. "Alright, let's get to the bottom of this. Marcus, you scout the area. The rest of us, we're going to need to see that empty room."

As they followed Annie through the dimly lit corridors of the coven, Finn couldn't shake the feeling that they were walking into something much stranger than they had initially expected. The air was thick with an odd mix of herbs and incense, and the walls were adorned with bizarre paintings of cats with three tails and cauldrons bubbling over with rainbow-colored brews.

Alex, always the pragmatic one, turned to Annie. "So, can you tell us more about this missing coven member? What's her name?"

Annie frowned, her face wrinkling further. "Her name's Agnes. She's been with us for years, always quiet and unassuming, until the other night, that is."

Finn couldn't help but blurt out, "What happened the other night?"

Annie stopped in her tracks, causing the team to halt as well. She turned to face them, her eyes holding a hint of fear. "I'm not entirely sure. But she came back from a midnight gathering with the strangest look in her eyes. It was like she'd seen something beyond the veil, something…unnatural."

The team exchanged uneasy glances. Unnatural was never a good sign in the world of witches.

They finally reached the door of the warded room, and Annie produced a small, ornate key from the folds of her robe. With a shaky hand, she unlocked the door and pushed it open.

To their surprise, the room was indeed empty. It was a small, windowless chamber, filled with dusty spell books, vials of mysterious liquids, and a broomstick that seemed to have a mind of its own, wobbling in the corner.

Alex scratched his head, his voice tinged with confusion. "This is…odd. Where's Agnes?"

Finn peered around the room, his gaze falling on a particularly large cauldron. "Maybe she turned herself into a newt and hopped away?"

Alex shot him a withering look. "Finn, this is serious."

Finn shrugged, not at all offended by the look. "Hey, in the world of witches, you never know. Turning yourself into a newt is practically a rite of passage."

Annie sighed, her shoulders slumping further. "Look, I don't know what's going on here, but we need to find Agnes. If she's out there causing trouble, we're all in danger."

As the team left the room, Marcus returned with a bemused expression on his face. "I scouted the area, and there's no sign of her. It's like she vanished into thin air."

Alex rubbed his temples, clearly feeling the weight of the situation. "Alright, team, let's regroup and figure out our next move. We need to find Agnes and find out what happened to her, no matter how strange things get. Do you have any of her things that you can let me borrow for a bit?"

Annie nodded briskly, her determination clear. "Yes, I do. Let me get it real quick."

Finn exchanged a puzzled glance with Alex before nodding in agreement. "What are you planning to do?"

"I am going to see if I could track her using my magic," Alex explained, his voice carrying a sense of urgency. "Finn, I want you to check each of the coven members in here while we track the missing witch."

Annie returned, cradling a delicate ring in her hand. Finn could sense the weight of its importance in the room. "Here," Annie said, handing the ring to Alex. "This was her ring, handed down by her mother. It was precious to her, so please be careful with it."

Alex nodded solemnly, acknowledging the gravity of the situation.

"Annie, can you please gather everyone in your coven in the living room so I can check them?" Finn said.

"Sure, come with me," Annie said, leading Finn toward the living room. She glanced back at Alex, her concern evident.

"Are you going to be okay in here, Alex?" Finn asked.

"Don't worry about me. Go ahead," Alex replied, his gaze fixed on the ring.

In the midst of the tension, it was clear that Alex was the team leader, calling the shots.

Annie led Finn into the living room, instructing him to wait as she called her coven members. He didn't have to wait long before a group of witches assembled before him, their expressions a mix of worry and curiosity. Annie positioned herself beside Finn, ready to support him.

Finn began to work his Healing magic, focusing on each witch's soul. His brows furrowed as he delved deep, searching for any signs of damage or distress. Fortunately, he found that none of them required immediate assistance. He let out a relieved breath and nodded to Annie, signaling that they were clear.

Annie motioned for Finn to follow her to the cozy kitchen, where she busied herself preparing tea. She handed Finn a cup and poured one for herself. The room was filled with the soothing aroma of the brew.

As they settled at the kitchen table, Alex entered, his expression serious yet tinged with a hint of excitement. "We got a hit," he declared, "but we'll need Marcus to catch Agnes."

Finn, eager to help, inquired, "Do you need me for that?"

Alex nodded, his gaze shifting between Finn and Annie. "Yes, but not right now. You should stay with the coven."

Annie chose this moment to bring up something unexpected. She leaned in closer to Finn and spoke with a mix of curiosity and revelation. "Finn, did you know that you're a warlock?"

Finn nearly choked on his tea, his eyes widening in surprise. "A warlock? But I thought male warlocks were killed off centuries ago."

Annie confirmed his suspicion with a nod. "You're right, but my senses don't lie. You're a rare kind of warlock, Finn—a soul healer."

Finn opened his mouth to ask more questions about his newfound identity when the room suddenly filled with the clamor of the arriving team. Their entrance was nothing short of chaotic, with them was an unconscious woman the he figured to be Agnes.

"We need to bring her to a warded room," he said, his voice cutting through the silence like a knife. The team members nodded in agreement, understanding the urgency of the situation.

Once inside the warded room, Finn couldn't help but feel a shiver run down his spine. Annie wasted no time and pressed her hands firmly against the walls, reinforcing the protective wards that surrounded them. It was as if they were preparing for a storm, and Finn had a sinking feeling that it might be worse than any storm they'd faced before.

"Finn, can you take a look at her, please?" Alex's voice broke Finn's thoughts, snapping him back to the task at hand. Finn nodded and stepped closer to Agnes, who lay sleeping on a nearby bed.

Finn focused his attention on Agnes, closing his eyes in concentration. He called upon his magic, feeling a gentle hum resonating within him. When he opened his eyes, a soft, white light radiated from his open palm. Gently, he placed his hand on Agnes' wrist, allowing his magic to do its work. His unique gift allowed him to delve deep into the mysteries of a person's soul.

As Finn's magic worked its ethereal wonders, Agnes's body began to jerk and twitch. Her eyes flew open, and Finn could sense the rest of the team behind him, ready to spring into action if needed. But Finn was unyielding, his gaze locked onto Agnes's eyes.

However, what he saw there shook him to his core. Her pupils were gone, as if something else were controlling her actions. A possession, Finn realized with a sinking feeling. Panic welled up within him, but he couldn't afford to lose his composure. He conjured a ball of wispy white magic in his hands and commanded it to expel whatever dark entity had taken hold of Agnes.

But it wasn't working. The entity resisted his efforts, its grip on Agnes unyielding. Then, to everyone's astonishment, Agnes began to speak. Her mouth moved, but Finn could bet his last coin that it wasn't her voice. It sounded dark, almost masculine. She spoke of revenge, of payment for some unknown transgression. Her gaze shifted, fixing on Alex, and she smiled with a wickedness that sent a chill down Finn's spine.

"Alex," she hissed, her voice dripping with malice, "your end will soon come."

Finn was about to redouble his efforts to expel the malevolent entity when, in a flurry of darkness, it fled into the aether. The sudden departure left the room in stunned silence, each team member trying to make sense of the bizarre turn of events.

But Finn couldn't afford to dwell on it for long. He turned his attention back to Agnes, still lying on the bed, now free from the entity's grasp. With a weary sigh, he used the healing globe in his hand to encase Agnes in a gentle cocoon of healing magic. It was the least he could do to help her.

Once he was done, Finn turned to Annie, who had been watching the entire ordeal with a mix of concern and fascination. "She'll recover," he said with a hint of exhaustion in his voice. "We just need to give the magic some time to work."

Alex, ever the pragmatic leader, stepped forward and addressed Annie. "We'll be leaving now," he said, his tone firm. He nodded in Finn's direction, acknowledging the work he had done. "Keep an eye on her and let us know if there's any change."

With that, the team filed out of the warded room.

Finn got home later than he expected but the events of earlier still lingered on his mind. He was about to sleep when his phone started ringing. He saw that it was Leo and answered it quickly.

"Hello?" Finn said.

"Hey, Doc," Leo said, his voice tense. "I need your help. How fast can you get to Salem?"

"Why what's wrong?" Finn was now worried.

"My brother can potentially use your help. Something isn't right and we need your expertise."

That didn't sound ominous at all. "Okay. let me just tell Alex what's going on then I can head out there."

"Thank you Doc, I appreciate it." Leo said before ending the call.

Whatever it was, Finn needed to help his friend. He knew that he just started his new role in the Shadowguards but he was pretty sure that Alex would understand and probably even offer his help.

# 5

## Leo

Leo eagerly waited in the car at the airport parking lot, trying not to look too much like a stalker waiting for his prey. He couldn't help but feel excited to scc Finn again, even though their friendship was still in its early stages. There was just something about Finn that made Leo feel at home and safe, and it didn't hurt that Finn was incredibly attractive, with his dark brown hair and mesmerizing blue eyes.

Finn had taken the early flight, and he had told Leo he should be arriving any second now. Leo was practically on the edge of his seat, scanning the crowd for any sign of his friend. Then, like a beacon in a sea of people, he spotted Finn's familiar head. Well, maybe Finn just had a way of standing out, or perhaps Leo was just a tad biased. Yeah, that was probably it.

As Finn got closer, he spotted Leo and waved. Leo waved back, feeling a rush of warmth at the sight of his friend. When Finn finally reached him, Leo couldn't help himself and enveloped Finn in a tight hug.

"Hey, thanks for coming out here," Leo said, his voice filled with genuine gratitude.

"It's nothing, Leo. What are friends for and all that?" Finn replied with a warm smile as they broke apart.

Leo took Finn's bags, eyeing them skeptically. "Are these all you have?"

Finn nodded. "Yeah, I don't mind carrying them."

Leo grinned mischievously. "Nah, it's fine. I'm stronger than I look."

Finn chuckled, and the sound was like sweet music to Leo's ears. "Alright then, lead the way to your chariot."

With that, Leo led Finn to the car and opened the door for him. As they settled into the car, Leo couldn't contain his curiosity any longer.

"So, did Alex know about your travels?" Leo asked as he started the engine.

Finn sighed, leaning back in his seat. "Yeah, I told him last night after our call."

Leo shot Finn a sideways glance. "And what did he say?"

Finn shrugged. "He was surprisingly chill about it. Said he'd hold down the fort while I'm away."

Leo raised an eyebrow. "Well, that's unusual for Mr. Control Freak."

Finn laughed. "I guess he's learning to let go a bit."

As they merged onto the highway, Leo couldn't help but think about the real reason he had picked Finn up from the airport. He had to tell Finn about the whole Rory situation, and he wasn't looking forward to it.

Leo cleared his throat, glancing over at Finn. "So, Finn, about Rory…"

Finn turned to him, his expression filled with concern. "Yeah, what happened?"

Leo took a deep breath. "His soul got trapped in the Spirit realm."

Finn's eyes widened in surprise. "Whoa, how did that happen?"

Leo hesitated for a moment before deciding to spill the beans. "Well, you see, my ability to track souls allows me to enter the spirit realm and that's where I found Rory's soul. Something wasn't right when I found him"

Finn looked puzzled. "And? What's the catch?"

Leo sighed. "The catch is that it eats away at my own soul, and the longer I stay in there, the more it can potentially shorten my lifespan. Also, from what we thought, Rory was human. But I felt his power when he threw me out of the realm."

Finn blinked. "Wait, you're telling me you risked your life to save Rory's soul?"

Leo shrugged, trying to play it cool. "Well, yeah. He's my brother, and family comes first, right?"

Finn shook his head, a small smile tugging at the corners of his lips. "You're insane, Leo."

Leo grinned. "Yeah, I guess I am."

They fell into a comfortable silence as Leo continued to drive. The tension from the heavy conversation began to dissipate, replaced by a sense of camaraderie and an unspoken understanding between the two friends.

Before they knew it, they had arrived at Leo's family estate. The imposing mansion stood before them, a stark contrast to the casual conversation they had just shared.

Leo parked the car and turned to Finn. "Well, welcome to the madhouse."

Finn chuckled. "Thanks for the warm welcome."

As they stepped out of the car and made their way towards the front door, Leo couldn't help but feel grateful for Finn's presence. No matter how crazy things got in the world of necromancers and soul-tracking, having a friend like Finn by his side made it all a little less daunting.

They entered the house, and Leo couldn't help but notice Finn's jaw dropping to the floor. Leo teased him, "You better close that before one of the ghosts flies in it."

Finn responded with a playful slap to Leo's shoulder. "You dick. You never told me you're this rich."

Leo chuckled. "So is that your way of saying you're into rich old men?"

"Stop it. You know what I mean," Finn retorted.

Leo took the lead. "Come on, let's get you settled in your room before I introduce you to my brothers." He grabbed Finn's bags and headed towards the guest room.

Curiosity got the best of Finn. "So, are your parents around?"

Leo shook his head. "No, Justin told me they're currently in Seattle, and we don't know when they'll be back."

They arrived at the guest room, and Leo swung open the door, revealing the spacious interior. Finn's jaw, once again, threatened to detach from his face.

"This room's bigger than my apartment in Manhattan," Finn remarked, his eyes still scanning the room in disbelief.

Leo shrugged nonchalantly. "It's just a room."

Finn turned to Leo with a grin. "Just a room? Man, you've got to teach me your definition of 'just.'"

Finn asked if he could freshen up before meeting Leo's brothers. Leo leaned against the doorframe, waiting patiently. "Sure thing, take your time."

After a while, Finn emerged from the guest room, looking more refreshed and ready. Leo extended his hand, and Finn took it willingly. Leo led the way to the kitchen, where they found Justin and Harry engrossed in their own worlds, sipping tea and reading books.

Leo cleared his throat to get their attention. "Guys, this is Finn." He paused dramatically. "He's a doctor and a healer."

Finn smiled, feeling a mix of amusement and nervousness at Leo's theatrical introduction. "Nice to meet you," he said with a polite nod.

Justin looked up from his book, his eyes scanning Finn with a hint of curiosity. "A doctor, huh? Leo, you finally brought home someone useful."

Leo chuckled, and Finn did the same. "And this is Harry," Leo continued, "our resident dreamwalker."

Harry gave a little wave, his expression friendly. "Pleasure to meet you, Finn. Leo's been telling us all about you."

Finn raised an eyebrow at Leo, who smirked in response. "Has he now?"

Leo moved on to the final introduction, gesturing toward Harry. "And this grumpy-looking guy is Justin. He's a blood witch necromancer."

Justin shot Leo a mock glare before nodding at Finn. "Welcome to the madness, Finn."

Finn chuckled, finding the mix of personalities in the room both amusing and endearing. "Thanks for having me. Leo's been talking about you guys too."

Justin grinned. "Only good things, I hope."

Finn laughed. "Mostly."

As they settled in the cozy kitchen, Leo couldn't help but feel that, despite the playful banter, this was the beginning of something truly special—a new chapter in his life filled with humor, camaraderie, and a hint of the supernatural.

Leo rubbed his temples, feeling the weight of the situation pressing down on him. The kitchen was cluttered with stacks of dusty old books, their spines cracked and pages yellowed with age. Justin and Harry, with furrowed brows, flipped through pages, scanning text after text for any sign of information about souls trapped in the spirit realm.

Leo's frustration simmered just below the surface. "Have you guys found anything?" he asked, desperation creeping into his voice.

Justin, his eyes weary from hours of searching, looked up. "Not yet. We don't even know if these are the right books that you told us to get."

Leo nodded, trying to keep his impatience in check. "Me and Finn will have a look later on. Just keep on looking."

Finn, ever the curious one, looked at Leo. "What are you guys looking for?"

Leo sighed, realizing that it was time to share their mission with Finn. "We are looking for information about the souls being trapped in the spirit realm," Harry chimed in.

Finn raised an eyebrow, his interest piqued. "If you don't find anything, I can try and contact Alex and see if he can shed light on the situation."

"Alex?" Justin asked, a note of confusion in his voice.

Finn nodded. "He's my boss. If Leo hasn't mentioned it already, I work for the Shadowguards, and my boss probably knows something."

Leo couldn't help but notice the hesitance in Finn's voice, a hint of something left unsaid. He made a mental note to inquire about it later. "Any help is good at this point. Let us know if you need anything."

With their brief exchange concluded, Finn turned his attention to a different matter. "Is it okay if I take a look at Rory?"

Leo nodded, relieved for a momentary distraction from the pressing issue. "Sure, this way." They moved towards Rory's room, Leo still feeling the residual energy from the protective ward he had set up the day before. It was less oppressive now, and he hoped it was a sign that things were improving.

Leo watched as Finn glanced around the room, his expression shifting from curiosity to mild discomfort. Finn didn't say anything, but Leo knew he could sense it too—the lingering presence in the room, an eerie sensation that crawled beneath the skin like a shiver.

"Can I get closer to Rory?" Finn finally asked, his voice cautious. Leo nodded, offering a small, understanding smile.

Together, they approached Rory's bedside. Leo kept a slight distance, giving Finn space to work his magic. With deliberate care, Finn reached out and gently clasped Rory's hand. As their skin made contact, a faint, otherworldly white glow began to emanate from Rory's fingers, casting a gentle, ethereal light across the room.

Leo watched in fascination as Finn's eyes closed, his brow furrowing in concentration. The room seemed to come alive with a subtle, yet palpable energy, and Leo could feel the magic coursing through the air. It was stronger than he had ever given the doctor credit for, and it left him both awestruck and perplexed.

After what felt like an eternity, Finn slowly opened his eyes, meeting Leo's gaze. Leo's curiosity got the better of him, and he couldn't help but inquire about Finn's findings.

"So, what did you discover?" Leo asked, his tone a mix of anticipation and concern.

Finn released Rory's hand and let out a sigh, his expression serious yet tinged with a hint of the absurdity of the situation. "Rory's soul is not your run-of-the-mill human soul. You were right, there's something extraordinary about him."

Leo raised an eyebrow, leaning in closer to Finn. "Extraordinary? How so?"

Finn hesitated for a moment before he answered, his voice laced with an odd blend of amusement and gravity. "Well, I could sense it—his soul is restless, like a squirrel trapped in a tiny box."

Leo couldn't help but chuckle at the absurd image Finn painted. "A restless squirrel, huh?"

Finn grinned, the tension in the room momentarily eased by their shared amusement. "Exactly! But here's the kicker. I sense that something else is meddling with his soul. It's like he's being puppeteered by an unseen force."

Leo's laughter faded, replaced by a deeper concern. "Puppeteered? By what?"

Finn shrugged, his demeanor becoming more serious once more. "I can't quite put my finger on it. It's as elusive as a mischievous ghost playing hide-and-seek."

Leo sighed, his mind racing with possibilities. "This just keeps getting weirder. We need to figure out what's controlling Rory and how to free him."

Finn nodded in agreement. "I'm with you on that, Leo. We'll get to the bottom of this."

Leo and Finn stepped out of Rory's room, the heavy atmosphere gradually lifting as they left the emotionally charged scene behind. Outside, the hallway was quiet, illuminated by soft, muted lights. Leo halted, turning to face Finn with a genuine expression of gratitude.

"Thank you for coming down," Leo said, his voice sincere. "I really appreciate it."

Finn, ever the supportive friend, smiled warmly and reached for Leo's hands, his touch reassuring. "Like I said before," Finn began, "I know that we haven't known each other long, but you've become a part of my life that I consider family."

Leo felt a rush of warmth in his chest at Finn's words. It wasn't just the emotion but the undeniable truth in them that touched him deeply. He couldn't help himself; he pulled Finn into a heartfelt hug. It was meant to be a quick, friendly embrace, but as their bodies pressed together, it somehow stretched into something more.

The seconds ticked on, the hug lasting longer than either of them had anticipated. Leo's senses heightened, and he couldn't ignore the intoxicating scent of Finn's cologne. He wanted to bask in it, to inhale deeply and lose himself in that enticing fragrance. Unbeknownst to him, Leo's body began to betray him in ways he never expected.

His heart raced, and his mind, once focused on gratitude and friendship, veered into a more primal direction. Leo's body responded to the close proximity, and he could feel an undeniable stirring in his nether regions. Panic flashed across his face for a fleeting moment.

Just when Leo thought he couldn't take it any longer, he reluctantly broke the hug. His cheeks burned with embarrassment, and he tried to clear his head, fearing that Finn might have noticed his unexpected physical reaction.

As Leo pulled away, he noticed something on Finn's face—a sly, knowing smirk that made him instantly self-conscious. Leo couldn't help but glance downward, his eyes widening in surprise as he realized that he wasn't the only one who hadn't been entirely unaffected by their lingering embrace.

Finn's expression was a mix of amusement and something deeper, something that mirrored the unspoken tension in the hallway. Their eyes locked for a moment, and it was as though an unspoken agreement passed between them, acknowledging the uncharted territory their friendship had just stumbled into.

"Uh, well," Leo stammered, trying to regain his composure and steer the conversation away from the awkward silence that had fallen between them. "I guess we both need some air, huh?"

Finn chuckled softly, his eyes still holding Leo's gaze. "Yeah, fresh air sounds good right about now."

As they made their way, the tension between them remained, simmering just beneath the surface. Their friendship had taken an unexpected turn, and neither of them could predict where it might lead. All they knew was that they had crossed a threshold, and things between them would never be quite the same again.

"Is it okay if I go back to my room and give someone a call?" Finn asked.

"Sure, do you want me to take you back?"

"No, I think I can manage. I'll call you when I get lost," he quipped, a hint of humor in his voice.

Leo chuckled at Finn's response, his eyes filled with a playful glint. "Okay. Just yell if you need me," he said.

With that, Finn turned around and began his journey back to his room, leaving Leo to his own devices. Leo watched him go with a warm smile, appreciating the camaraderie he was developing with his newfound family. Then, Leo turned and headed back to the kitchen where he'd left Justin and Harry engrossed in their books.

Upon returning to the kitchen, Leo discovered his brothers still deep in the pages of their respective books. Leo couldn't help but marvel at the sight before him; it was a rare occasion for them to engage in such shared activities as siblings.

Leo quietly made his way to the kitchen counter and decided to brew some tea for himself and his brothers. They were so engrossed in their reading that they didn't notice his return. Leo, ever the prankster, decided to liven things up a bit. He conjured a small, purple fireball on his index finger and playfully flicked it at Justin.

"Ow," Justin exclaimed, momentarily torn from his book. He turned around to see Leo smirking mischievously. "You little shit," Justin teased, a smile breaking through his initial annoyance.

Leo couldn't help but laugh at his brother's reaction as he joined them at the table while the tea steeped. "Are you guys okay in here?"

Harry, the one who often remained quiet, finally spoke up, "Yeah, though my eyes are starting to become crossed from all the reading."

The comment elicited a shared chuckle, lightening the atmosphere in the room.

Justin, however, had a more serious question in mind. He put down his book and turned to Leo. "So, are we going to talk about how you can track souls and you never told us about it?"

Leo sighed, realizing that he could no longer keep his true nature a secret. "I've known about it since before I left. But it didn't really mean much to me at the time. It was only years later, when I met a master necromancer, that I started to understand my abilities to track souls."

Justin, still processing this revelation, asked the question that had been bothering him. "Why didn't you tell us about this before?"

Leo hesitated before answering honestly, "I was scared. I thought that soul trackers didn't exist anymore and that I was the only one left." Leo then turned his attention to Justin, his eyes filled with a mixture of emotions. "And besides, Justin, during that time, you had already sided with our parents."

The room fell into a charged silence as the weight of Leo's words sank in. It was a reminder of the strained family dynamics that had haunted them for years.

Unexpectedly, Leo noticed tears welling up in Justin's eyes. "I'm sorry for the way I acted back then," Justin admitted, his voice trembling. "I'm here now, and hopefully, you can forgive me."

Leo, moved by his brother's genuine apology, reached out and took Justin's hands, giving them a reassuring tug. "I forgive you, Justin. You told me you had no choice. Speaking of which, you mentioned that our parents weren't always like they were. What did you mean by that?"

Leo could sense that Harry was listening intently to their conversation, and he could also detect a heavy burden of guilt in his younger brother.

Justin brushed away his tears and began to recount a long-buried memory. "You see, they were incredibly kind people. The best parents a person could ever have. But one day, I think you were around three, Leo, they were called to help someone from a nearby pride. I don't remember most of the details, but they came back different."

Leo absorbed this information, his mind racing to process the implications of what Justin had just revealed. Whatever had transpired that day had fundamentally changed their parents, and Leo was determined to uncover the truth.

"Justin, I want you to remember the name of the pride they went to," Leo said with a sense of urgency in his voice.

Justin nodded solemnly, and Leo released his hands before rising from the table, determined to pursue this newfound lead.

58

# 6

# Finn

Finn jolted awake, disoriented by the sudden explosion. Panic surged through him as he hastily threw on some clothes. With each hurried button and tie, his heart pounded louder.

He stumbled out of his room and into the dimly lit hallway, the ancient wooden floorboards creaking beneath his hurried footsteps. The house felt empty, an eerie silence looming like a heavy fog.

"Leo?" he called out, his voice cracking with worry, but his plea was met only with the echoing emptiness of the hall.

Finn clenched his fists, his knuckles whitening as he pushed forward. The echoing clashes of magical combat grew louder with every step he took. It was a chaotic symphony, a bizarre crescendo that fueled his anxiety. He had to find his brothers and figure out what in the magical realms was going on.

He paused for a moment, closing his eyes to focus on the magical energy coursing through his veins. He felt it, a warm and comforting presence in his palm, like a loyal friend ready to guide him. With a determined exhale, he extended his hand, palm up, and let his magic flow.

From his open palm, wispy white smoke swirled and coiled like ethereal serpents. It moved with purpose, spiraling through the air, and then, like a scent carried by the wind, it led him forward. Finn followed the trail, his heart pounding even harder as he realized it was taking him to the back garden.

As he reached the garden's entrance, a surreal scene unfolded before his eyes. Leo stood tall and defiant, his palms radiating a vivid shade of purple. The necromantic magic crackled around him like an electrified aura, ethereal hands and skeletal figures materializing and swiping at unseen foes.

Beside Leo, Justin was embroiled in a bizarre battle of his own. His eyes were wide with a mix of terror and determination as he sliced his forearm with a swift, practiced motion. Blood oozed from the wound, but instead of dripping to the ground, it hung in the air, forming intricate patterns. Justin's blood magic danced like crimson ribbons, entwining and attacking with a fluid grace.

But it was Harry, who caught Finn's attention next. Harry's brows were furrowed in intense concentration as he conjured dark, watery magic that seemed to flow from his fingertips like liquid silk. Streams of this strange blue magic swirled and coalesced into ferocious waves, crashing against some unseen adversary.

Finn sprinted through the chaos, his heart pounding in his chest. He called out to Leo, his voice edged with concern and confusion, "Leo, what's going on?"

The three brothers were in the midst of a frantic battle, flinging arcs of crackling magic in every direction. The air was alive with energy, but Finn couldn't discern the source of their struggle. It was a swirling maelstrom of power, an eerie dance of shadows and flashes.

Leo, his brow furrowed with intensity, responded without taking his eyes off the mystical fray, "Bloody poltergeists are everywhere." As Leo cast another brilliant ball of magic, he finally turned his gaze toward Finn. Worry etched his features. "Can you fight?" he asked urgently.

Finn clenched his fists, determination surging through him. "Yes," he replied, "but I can't see what I'm fighting."

In that moment, a grotesque construct, seemingly woven from blood itself, surged in front of them. Finn's eyes widened in alarm. He glanced at Justin, who was on his knees, looking pale and weak. If this relentless onslaught continued, Justin would soon run out of blood, and that could prove perilous.

Desperation gnawed at Finn's insides, but Leo's next words offered a glimmer of hope. "Take my hand," Leo instructed, his voice tense with urgency. Finn reached out, his fingers trembling, and clasped Leo's outstretched hand. "I'm going to lend some of my power to you so you can see the fuckers," Leo declared.

Without hesitation, Leo transferred a surge of his necromantic magic into Finn. It felt like a rush of icy fire coursing through his veins, and his very soul seemed to vibrate with newfound energy. Finn couldn't comprehend the sensation, but there was no time to dwell on it.

As the magic took hold, Finn's vision shifted and expanded. It was as if he'd been granted a new set of eyes, and he saw the world in a dazzling spectrum of colors and auras. The shadows coalesced, and the poltergeists began to materialize before him.

They were grotesque and menacing, their ethereal forms wreathed in flickering, malevolent energy. Angry crimson eyes glared at Finn, and misshapen limbs reached out with spectral claws. Finn's heart raced, but he refused to be paralyzed by fear.

Leo's voice cut through the chaos. "Can you see them now?"

Finn nodded, his eyes fixed on the spectral assailants. "Yeah, I've got them."

Without wasting a breath, Finn reached deep within himself, tapping into the wellspring of his own latent magic. He summoned it forth, forming a crackling ball of energy in his hands. It pulsed with an eerie, ghostly light, casting eerie shadows on his determined face.

With a swift motion, he hurled the magical sphere into the midst of the poltergeists. It detonated in a burst of supernatural brilliance, sending shockwaves of power rippling through the ethereal creatures. Several of them were banished back into the spirit realm, but Finn knew they wouldn't stay down for long.

Beside him, Justin and Harry continued their relentless magical assault, each of them fighting to keep the otherworldly horde at bay. But Finn could see the toll it was taking on them, especially Justin. The blood constructs he'd created were draining him quickly, and the man was visibly weakening.

Finn gritted his teeth. He couldn't let Justin exhaust himself to the point of danger. His eyes darted to Harry, who was on the verge of being overwhelmed by a fresh wave of poltergeists. Without a second thought, Finn focused his magic, shaping it into whip-like tentacles that shot out towards the encroaching spirits.

The tentacles lashed through the air, striking the poltergeists with ethereal force. They hissed and recoiled, giving Harry the opportunity he needed to regain his footing and launch another barrage of magic.

Harry shot Finn a grateful nod, and for a moment, their eyes met in silent camaraderie. They were in this together, bound by the chaos and the urgency of their situation.

As the battle raged on, Finn couldn't help but wonder why these restless spirits were attacking them. He remembered Annie's words about his unique abilities as a Soul Healer, and suddenly, it clicked. Ghosts were departed souls, and he had the power to heal them.

Turning to Leo amidst the ongoing skirmish, Finn shouted over the cacophony of magic and mayhem, "Leo, fall back with your brothers! Trust me!"

Leo, casting a wary glance at Finn, shouted back, "What are you doing, Finn?"

Finn's eyes burned with determination. "Just trust me!"

Leo nodded and signaled to his brothers to retreat. They began a strategic withdrawal, keeping the poltergeists at bay as they moved backward.

With a deep breath, Finn steeled himself. He closed his eyes and focused on the turmoil around him. The chaotic energy of the poltergeists, the pulsing rhythm of their anguish, it all flowed through him like a torrent.

In that moment, Finn embraced his role as a Soul Healer. He reached out with his magic, extending it toward the poltergeists.

The effect was nothing short of astonishing. His magic intermingled with the restless spirits, and he felt their confusion, their anger, their longing. With a gentle flick of his fingers, he began to soothe their tormented souls.

The poltergeists started to slow down, their violent thrashing turning into a bizarre dance of confusion. Some of them even began to weep spectral tears. Finn could sense their fear and despair, and he used his magic to guide them, to help them find the path to the afterlife.

One by one, the poltergeists dissipated, their spectral forms melting away like mist in the morning sun. It was a surreal and oddly beautiful sight, like watching a chaotic ballet of the supernatural.

As the last of the poltergeists vanished, Finn opened his eyes, his chest heaving from the exertion. Leo and his brothers stood in awe, their expressions a mix of astonishment and gratitude.

Leo stepped forward, his voice filled with wonder. "You did it, Finn."

Finn managed a weak smile, feeling the residual echoes of the poltergeists' emotions still lingering within him. "Yeah, I guess I did."

The brothers regrouped, their battle-worn but triumphant. The threat of the poltergeists had been quelled, and Finn had discovered a new facet of his extraordinary abilities.

The living room was awash with a sense of urgency as Leo and Harry gently helped Justin settle onto one of the longer couches. Finn, the group's resident magic user, watched the scene unfold, his eyes focused on Justin's condition. He knew that time was of the essence.

Justin lay there, his face pale and his breathing shallow. Blood stained his clothes, a vivid reminder of the ordeal he had just endured. Finn approached with a solemn expression, his hands glowing with a soft, soothing light.

Leo's voice trembled with concern as he asked, "Finn, can you help him? Is he going to be okay?"

Finn nodded, his gaze never leaving Justin. "I'll do what I can," he replied, his voice steady but filled with determination. He extended his hands over Justin's prone form, and the soft glow from his palms intensified, casting a warm and comforting light across the room.

As Finn's healing magic flowed into Justin, the room seemed to hold its breath. The air crackled with energy, and the very atmosphere seemed to vibrate with the power of the magic at work. It was as though the world itself recognized the gravity of the situation.

Justin's eyelids fluttered as Finn's magic took hold, and a sigh of relief escaped Harry's lips. "He's waking up," Harry announced, his eyes fixed on his friend.

Finn's brow furrowed with concentration as he continued to channel his healing magic. He could feel the ebb and flow of Justin's life force, like a river seeking its natural course. With each passing moment, Justin's color returned, and his breathing grew stronger.

Justin's eyes finally opened, and he blinked up at the concerned faces of his friends. "What... happened?" he rasped, his voice weak but filled with confusion.

Leo leaned in, his voice gentle as he explained, "You got hurt. But Finn's healing you. You're going to be okay."

Finn's magic danced across Justin's wounds, knitting flesh and tissue back together with an almost ethereal grace. It was a sight to behold, the magic's luminescent tendrils weaving intricate patterns of restoration across Justin's body. The room was suffused with a warm, golden light, and the air smelled faintly of herbs and springtime.

Justin winced as the last of his injuries healed, a bead of sweat forming on his forehead. "That… that was intense," he murmured, his voice stronger now.

Finn withdrew his hands, and the glow faded, leaving Justin looking tired but remarkably better. "You lost a lot of blood," Finn said with a hint of concern. "You need to rest."

Harry nodded, his worry still etched on his face. "Finn's right. You should take it easy for a while."

Justin managed a weak smile, his gratitude evident. "Thanks, guys. I don't know what I would've done without you."

Finn's shoulders relaxed as he stepped back, his healing magic spent but successful. "Just doing what we do best," he said, trying to downplay the gravity of the situation.

The night air outside the balcony was cool and refreshing. A gentle breeze rustled through the leaves of nearby trees, carrying with it the soothing scent of flowers and earth. The sky above was adorned with a myriad of stars, their distant twinkling adding a touch of magic to the atmosphere. Leo and Finn stepped out onto the balcony, the wooden floor cool beneath their feet.

Finn couldn't help but admire the serene beauty of the night as he leaned against the railing. He turned to Leo with a furrowed brow, his curiosity piqued. "Leo, what exactly happened back there? Why did that poltergeist attack you?"

Leo's gaze drifted to the starry sky as he contemplated his response. "I'm not entirely sure," he began, his voice tinged with uncertainty. "I had gone out for a walk earlier, and my magic started acting up. That's when the first poltergeist attacked. Harry and Justin joined me shortly after."

Finn nodded, absorbing the information. "Do you have any idea why they targeted you?" he asked, his concern evident.

Leo let out a sigh, his eyes returning to Finn's. "Honestly, I don't know for sure," he admitted. "But if I had to guess, it might be related to Rory's condition."

Finn's eyes widened with realization. "If that's the case," he said slowly, "then we might be close to figuring out what happened to Rory."

Leo's expression grew somber. "I hope so," he replied quietly, his gaze fixed on the balcony's railing. "Speaking of which, how did you manage to take on that poltergeist? It was incredible."

Finn offered a small, rueful smile. "Well," He paused, as if choosing his words carefully. "You see, we wore on the case the day you called regarding a missing witch. The head witch, Annie, she mentioned something about me being a soul healer and a warlock."

Leo's eyes widened in surprise. "A soul healer and a warlock?" he repeated, still trying to grasp the enormity of it all. Finn nodded. "That's probably why your powers were stronger than mine," he explained. "Your magic, it felt different—more potent, more focused."

As Leo spoke, the air around them seemed to shimmer with an ethereal glow. It was as though the very essence of magic was dancing in the night, a silent testament to the power they both possessed.

Finn couldn't help but feel a mixture of awe and trepidation. He had always known he was different, but this revelation opened up a world of possibilities and dangers he had never imagined.

"I still don't know Leo. She also told me that I am the only male warlock alive. This new found magic is too overwhelming for. I am not sure what to do with it." Finn said.

Leo placed a reassuring hand on Finn's shoulder, his eyes filled with understanding. "We'll figure this out together, Finn," he said, his voice unwavering. "And we'll do whatever it takes to save Rory."

Finn met Leo's gaze, determination burning in his eyes. "We will," he affirmed, a newfound sense of purpose surging within him.

67

# 7

## Leo

Leo woke up feeling like utter crap. His entire body throbbed in places he didn't even know could ache. He yawned and stretched, trying to coax his stiff limbs back to life. It felt like he'd been hit by a truck, backed over, and then hit again for good measure.

After what seemed like an eternity of groaning and contorting in bed, he finally managed to roll out. Leo stood there for a moment, swaying slightly as if he were testing the stability of the floor. With a grimace, he shuffled towards the bathroom for what promised to be a much-needed shower.

The hot water did wonders for his aching muscles. As the steam enveloped him, he tried to massage away the pain, cursing whatever cruel twist of fate had befallen him. His moans and grunts could have been mistaken for the lamentations of a wounded animal.

Freshly showered and slightly less miserable, Leo managed to wrestle himself into some clothes. He had a vague notion of needing sustenance, though the thought of preparing anything more complicated than cereal felt like a herculean task in his current state.

As he staggered towards the kitchen, a most wondrous scent wafted through the air. It was a symphony of bacon, eggs, and something that could only be described as fried heaven. Leo's stomach rumbled in response, and he felt an unexpected surge of energy propelling him forward.

In the kitchen, he found Finn, his two brothers, Justin and Harry, seated around the table, feasting like kings. Leo hadn't known Finn could cook anything more complicated than instant noodles, so the sight before him was nothing short of a miracle.

Finn, with a spatula in hand, looked up from the sizzling pan with a grin that could put the sun to shame. "Well, well, look who finally decided to join the land of the living," he said, his voice dripping with amusement.

Leo blinked, but he managed a crooked smile. "Did I miss the memo about 'Finn's Fabulous Breakfast Extravaganza'?"

Justin nearly choked on his orange juice. He wiped his mouth and let out a hearty laugh. "You could say that. Finn here decided to bless us with his culinary prowess this fine morning."

Harry, the younger brother, chimed in, "It's like we've entered a new dimension of deliciousness."

Leo slid into a chair, eyeing the spread before him. It was a breakfast lover's dream—eggs cooked to perfection, crispy bacon, golden pancakes, and a medley of fresh fruits. He couldn't help but laugh. "Finn, I'm impressed. When did you become a five-star chef?"

Finn flipped another pancake onto a plate with flair. "Oh, you know, I've been secretly honing my skills. Thought it was time to unveil my culinary genius to the world."

Leo grabbed a pancake and loaded it with syrup. He took a massive bite, savoring the explosion of flavors. "This is amazing! You've been holding out on us, man."

Finn chuckled, leaning against the counter. "Consider it a one-time treat. I can't promise gourmet breakfast every day."

Justin raised an eyebrow. "I don't know, Finn. You might have just secured yourself a permanent spot as our designated breakfast chef."

Harry nodded in agreement. "Yeah, this is life-changing."

Leo had to admit, he'd never seen Finn look so pleased with himself. "Well, I, for one, am all for this new breakfast tradition."

As they devoured the feast, conversation flowed easily. The pain and exhaustion that had plagued Leo earlier seemed to melt away in the company of good food and great company. Finn regaled them with stories of his early morning culinary adventure, complete with a few dramatic flourishes and exaggerated gestures.

Justin and Harry joined in with their own anecdotes, and soon, the kitchen was filled with laughter and the clinking of cutlery. It was a simple moment of camaraderie, a reminder of the joys that could be found in the most unexpected places.

Leo leaned back in his chair, a contented smile on his face. "Who would've thought that the day I woke up feeling like death would turn out to be one of the best mornings ever?"

Finn grinned, a mischievous glint in his eye. "Well, Leo, they do say that breakfast is the most important meal of the day. I just made sure it lived up to the hype."

Leo turned to Justin. "How are you feeling? Should you be walking around already?" Leo asked, concern etching his features.

Justin set down his fork and locked eyes with Leo. A sly grin spread across his face. "Honestly, I've never felt better. Whatever Finn used on me did the trick."

Finn, who had been quietly sipping his morning tea, chimed in with a hint of pride in his voice. "I'm glad my magic helped. Though you still shouldn't push yourself today. I can sense that your body is still healing, so only light work today, okay?"

Leo couldn't help but smile as he observed Finn. The man had quickly become a part of their household, and Leo's heart raced every time he saw Finn's happy, smiling face. Leo's self-control was slipping, and he wondered how much longer he could be patient.

"Yes, sir," Justin replied with a mock salute. "Only light work today. Got it." Justin turned his attention back to Leo, excitement in his eyes. "Oh, by the way, I got word from one of the necromancers who was on the scene with our parents, and she agreed to meet with me today."

Leo perked up at the news. "I didn't expect you to get information so quickly. Who's this person?"

Justin leaned in, lowering his voice as if sharing a secret. "I'm trying to make it up to you, and this was the least I could do to make that happen. Her name is Alicia Peterson, and I'll be meeting her in the City today."

Leo nodded, considering the situation. "Take Harry with you. You're still not fully healed yet, and you might need backup. Harry, are you okay with that?"

Harry, who had been quietly sipping his coffee, looked up and nodded. "Yeah, sure. I want to know what happened too."

Leo turned his attention to Finn, his voice tinged with anticipation. "Finn, would you like to join me in the library today?"

Finn raised an eyebrow, his playful side coming to the fore. "A library? You have a library in here? What's next, a bowling alley? But yeah, sure."

After breakfast, the group scattered to their respective tasks for the day. Leo, eager to spend some alone time with Finn, gently grabbed his hand and led him up the grand staircase to the library on the second floor of the house. As they pushed open the heavy wooden doors, Leo couldn't help but grin at the sight of Finn's wide-eyed amazement.

"Wow, Leo, this place is… it's huge!" Finn exclaimed, his eyes darting around the cavernous room filled with towering bookshelves.

Leo chuckled. "You haven't seen anything yet." He guided Finn deeper into the library, the soft glow of enchanted sconces illuminating their path. The shelves seemed to stretch on forever, lined with books of all shapes and sizes. Dust motes danced in the air, caught in the ethereal light.

"Trust me, you won't get bored here," Leo said, his voice filled with amusement.

Finn's eyes landed on a massive tome, and he couldn't resist picking it up. "What's this?" he asked, his fingers tracing the ornate cover.

Leo glanced at the book and grinned. "Ah, 'The Complete Guide to Magical Creatures.' It's a classic. Want to see something fun?"

Finn nodded eagerly, and Leo opened the book. As they flipped through the pages, the illustrations came to life. A phoenix burst into flames and then rose from the ashes, a griffin stretched its wings and let out a majestic roar, and a mischievous-looking imp winked at them before disappearing back into the pages.

"Whoa, this is incredible!" Finn exclaimed, his eyes glued to the magical display.

Leo laughed. "I told you this place was special. Now, let me show you something even more amazing." He led Finn to a section of the library filled with books on various magical disciplines.

Finn raised an eyebrow. "What are we looking for?"

Leo's eyes twinkled mischievously. "A book on elemental magic." He scanned the shelves until he found what he was looking for and pulled out a tome titled "Mastery of the Elements."

As Leo opened the book, a holographic image of a swirling vortex of water emerged from the pages. The water danced and shimmered, and Finn could feel a cool mist on his face as if he were standing by a waterfall.

"Is this… real?" Finn asked, his voice filled with wonder.

Leo nodded. "It's a projection of the elemental magic described in the book. This library is enchanted to bring the words to life."

Finn reached out, tentatively extending a hand toward the holographic water. His fingers passed through it, and he laughed as the sensation of water droplets trickling down his skin filled his senses. "This is incredible! What else can this place do?"

Leo led Finn to a different section, this one filled with books on history and ancient civilizations. He pulled out a dusty tome titled "Chronicles of the Lost Kingdom" and opened it. Suddenly, they were standing in the midst of a bustling ancient marketplace, surrounded by people in colorful garments and exotic animals.

Finn's eyes widened. "Are we… are we really here?"

Leo chuckled. "No, it's an illusion, but a convincing one, isn't it?"

Finn nodded, his gaze fixed on the vibrant scene around them. "I could spend hours in here."

Leo smiled, his heart swelling with affection. "That's the idea. This library has been in my family for generations. It's a place of knowledge and wonder, and now, it's yours too."

As they continued to explore the library, Leo couldn't help but admire Finn's sense of curiosity and excitement. He was content to revel in the magic of the moment and the growing bond between them.

"So what are we in here for?" Finn turned to him and asked.

"We need to find a book," Leo replied, clearing his throat and trying to ignore the proximity that seemed to intensify with each passing second. "One that holds information about trapped souls in the spirit realm. My parents always talked about it, said it should be here somewhere."

Finn nodded, his own eyes scanning the labyrinth of shelves that surrounded them. "Got it. I'll check this section," he said, bending down to inspect the lower shelves.

Leo, still aware of Finn's nearness, tried to focus on the task at hand. "Alright, I'll take the upper section then." He climbed a ladder and began pulling out dusty tomes, scanning their titles and flipping through pages in search of anything that might hold the key to their quest.

As they searched, time seemed to blur. Hours passed, and they exchanged occasional frustrated glances, stacks of books growing around them. The library was silent except for the occasional creak of the wooden shelves and the rustling of pages.

Finally, Leo gathered a handful of books and made his way down to the bottom section of the library, where Finn was engrossed in his own search. He took a seat in one of the creaky chairs, his stack of books teetering precariously.

Leo leaned over and whispered to Finn, "Find anything yet?"

Finn looked up, his face weary but determined. "Not a thing. This place is a treasure trove of dust, but no soul-trapped books."

Leo sighed and ran a hand through his hair. "Maybe we should take a break. Clear our heads."

Finn's eyes lit up at the suggestion. "Yeah, a break sounds good. My back's killing me from all this bending over."

They both rose from their chairs, stretching their cramped limbs. Leo stifled a yawn and glanced around, his gaze landing on an ornate, cobweb-covered mirror mounted on the wall.

"Hey, Finn," Leo said, a mischievous glint in his eye. "Want to see something cool?"

Finn raised an eyebrow, intrigued. "Sure, what is it?"

Leo reached out and tapped the dusty surface of the mirror with his finger. "Watch this."

With a flourish of his hand, Leo traced a pattern in the air, his fingers leaving behind a trail of sparkling blue light. The pattern danced and swirled, casting an ethereal glow around them.

Finn's eyes widened, and he watched in amazement as Leo's magic worked its wonders. "That's... wow," he said, his voice filled with wonder.

Leo grinned, feeling a rush of pride. "It's a little trick I picked up. Now, watch this." With a flick of his wrist, he sent the sparkling light into the mirror, and suddenly, it came to life. The mirror rippled like water, and the surface transformed into a shimmering portal.

Finn's jaw dropped. "Is that... a portal?"

Leo nodded, his eyes sparkling with excitement. "Yup! It leads to another part of the library. Let's see if we can find what we're looking for there."

They stepped through the portal, emerging into a different section of the vast library. This area was bathed in an eerie, bluish light, and the shelves were filled with books that seemed to glow with an otherworldly energy.

Finn and Leo exchanged excited glances, their fatigue momentarily forgotten. "Now, this looks promising," Finn said.

Leo and Finn cautiously navigated the mysterious realm that Leo's father had forbidden them from ever entering. Leo's heart raced as he led the way, following memories of his father's actions to open the portal. The atmosphere around them grew increasingly charged with an otherworldly energy, and a sense of foreboding hung in the air.

Leo looked back to check if Finn was still following, but as he turned, he was met with an unsettling sight: nothingness, a void where Finn had just been. Panic surged within him.

"Finn?" he called out desperately, but only eerie silence answered his plea.

Gathering his courage, Leo pressed forward. The strange, powerful sensation intensified with each step. He reached deep within himself, ready to wield his magic if needed. There was no turning back now.

As he continued, a distant light beckoned him. Leo couldn't resist its pull. Approaching cautiously, he felt the anticipation of an impending discovery. The light drew him in until it consumed his surroundings.

When the light finally faded, Leo found himself standing before a magnificent sight. A solitary pedestal stood in the center of a vast chamber, and above it hovered a shimmering book. Leo's intuition told him that this was the very book they had sought.

With cautious excitement, Leo took a step closer. However, as he advanced, an invisible force halted his progress, and his feet became rooted to the ground. Panic began to set in. He struggled against the unseen restraints, his heart racing.

Suddenly, something materialized before him. It was a woman, ethereal and regal, adorned in a breathtaking ensemble of greens and purples. Leo felt an inexplicable calm wash over him as he gazed upon her.

"Who are you?" Leo stammered, unable to tear his eyes away from her presence.

The woman smiled, her voice a soothing melody. "I am Hecate, dear child. A goddess."

Leo's astonishment grew. "A goddess? What are you doing in this place?"

Hecate's laughter resonated like wind chimes. "Your parents imprisoned me within this book, and I have awaited someone worthy to set me free."

Leo's brow furrowed with confusion. "Worthy? Why me?"

Hecate's eyes gleamed with an otherworldly wisdom. "I can sense the immense power within you, Leo. You are the one destined to release me."

Leo's thoughts raced, his mind torn between the urgency of his quest and the incredible situation before him. "I need the book to save my brother, Rory," he admitted.

Hecate nodded knowingly. "To retrieve the book, you must first release me."

Leo took a deep breath, his decision clear. "How can I free you?"

Hecate's response came with a mischievous glint in her eyes. "You must share your magic with me, young sorcerer."

Leo blinked, not entirely comprehending. "Share my magic? How?"

Hecate's lips curled into a playful smile. "Oh, it's quite simple, really.

Just imagine your magic as a radiant, glowing orb within you."

Leo closed his eyes, envisioning his magical energy as a brilliant sphere deep within his chest. It pulsed with life and power.

"Now," Hecate continued, "extend your hands toward me, and imagine tendrils of your magic reaching out to me."

With hesitant but determined hands, Leo followed her instructions. He felt a tingling sensation as if an invisible thread connected him to Hecate.

Hecate encouraged him. "Now, imagine your magic swirling and dancing as it flows toward me, like a stream of brilliant light."

Leo obeyed, visualizing his magic as a luminescent river surging from his chest into Hecate's outstretched hands. The room began to glow with a soft, ethereal light, and the air seemed charged with magical energy.

Hecate's eyes sparkled with delight as the magic flowed into her. "Yes, just like that, Leo. Your power is remarkable."

As the transfer continued, Leo felt both exhilarated and vulnerable. He could sense his magic leaving him, but he also realized the importance of this exchange.

Hecate absorbed the magic with grace and appreciation, her form growing more solid and radiant with each passing moment. She radiated a warm, comforting energy that enveloped Leo.

Finally, when the last thread of Leo's magic had been shared, Hecate smiled with gratitude. "Thank you, Leo. You've set me free."

The restraints that had held Leo in place dissolved, and he stumbled forward. Breathing heavily, he gazed at Hecate, now fully manifested before him.

Hecate gestured toward the floating book. "The book you seek is yours, dear child. Take it and use it to save your brother."

Leo approached the book, his hands trembling with anticipation. He reached out and gently grasped it, feeling a surge of power and purpose flow through him.

"Good luck, Leo," Hecate whispered, her voice fading as she dissipated into the ether.

Leo clutched the book tightly, a newfound determination burning within him. With Hecate's magic now infused within him, he was ready to face the challenges ahead and do whatever it took to rescue his brother.

Leo felt himself being drawn away from the chamber, his surroundings blurring into a swirling maelstrom of colors. It was like being caught in a tornado of magic. His heart pounded in his chest as he clutched the ancient tome tightly in his hand. The sensation was disorienting, and he couldn't help but wonder if he would ever see the library's secret room again.

As the colors faded, Leo's eyes slowly opened, and he found himself standing once more in the dimly lit secret room of the library. It was a stark contrast to the otherworldly chamber he had just left. He took a deep breath, trying to steady his racing heart.

"Leo? Are you okay?" Finn's voice cut through the haze of disorientation, and Leo turned to see his friend rushing toward him.

"Y-Yeah," Leo stammered, still trying to shake off the remnants of the magical journey. Hecate's touch still lingered on his hand, sending shivers down his spine. He would have never thought that he'd come face to face with an actual goddess.

Finn's brow furrowed with concern. "What happened? And is that the book that we are looking for?"

Leo nodded, his fingers gripping the ancient tome tighter. "Yes, it is. Though it's a long story." He glanced around the room, the memories of the otherworldly chamber still fresh in his mind. "Come on, let's get out of this place."

Finn nodded in agreement. "Let's go. It's giving me the creeps already." He reached out to help Leo to his feet, and together they made their way toward the exit.

The room seemed to close in on them as they walked, the shelves of ancient books looming like silent sentinels. Dust motes danced in the dim light, giving the space an eerie, timeless quality. Leo couldn't help but glance over his shoulder, half-expecting the room to have vanished, just like the other chamber.

As they stepped out of the secret room and into the library proper, Leo's senses were assaulted by the familiar scent of old books and the soft, ambient hum of whispered knowledge. It was a stark contrast to the otherworldly realm they had just left behind.

Finn glanced at him, a mix of curiosity and concern in his eyes. "So, what happened in there, Leo? You look like you've seen a ghost."

Leo ran a hand through his tousled hair, trying to find the right words to describe the indescribable. "I… I met Hecate. The goddess herself. She helped me find the book."

Finn's eyes widened in disbelief. "You met a goddess?"

Leo nodded, his voice still tinged with awe. "Yeah. It was… surreal. She had this aura of power, and her touch… it was like nothing I've ever felt before."

They walked through the maze of bookshelves, the weight of the ancient tome a constant reminder of the extraordinary events that had just transpired. Leo's mind was a whirlwind of thoughts and questions.

Finn couldn't contain his curiosity any longer. "What did she want, Leo? Why did she help us find the book?"

Leo hesitated for a moment, struggling to find the right words. "She said that the book holds the key to helping Rory." He paused, looking at Finn with a mixture of determination and uncertainty. "We need to decipher it, Finn. Whatever is in that book, it's powerful, and it's our responsibility to unlock its secrets."

# 8

# Finn

Finn's curiosity gnawed at him like a persistent itch. He needed answers, and he needed them now. The goddess Hecate had revealed herself to Leo, and they found themselves in possession of a mysterious, ancient book imbued with a power that sent shivers down their spines.

Finn and Leo exchanged uneasy glances before placing the enigmatic tome on the coffee table with great care. Its pages seemed to whisper secrets of long-forgotten realms, and its presence weighed heavily in the room, like a tangible aura of ancient magic.

With hesitant hands, they gingerly turned the pages, revealing inscriptions in a language that neither of them could decipher. Finn's frustration mounted as he ran his fingers over the cryptic symbols.

"Do you know what language this is?" Finn's voice trembled with uncertainty, mirroring his anxiety.

Leo squinted at the text, his brow furrowing in frustration. "No. But it looks old and feels even older," he admitted, his voice laced with defeat. "At this point, we won't be able to help Rory."

Finn's determination flared like a beacon in the gloom. "Maybe there's a way," he replied, his eyes narrowing in thought.

Leo regarded Finn with a mixture of hope and skepticism. "What way? We can't even read this damned book."

Finn took a deep breath, steeling himself for what he was about to suggest. "We can contact Alex," he said, his voice firm.

Leo's eyes widened with surprise. "Alex? How would he know about the language in this book?"

Finn leaned closer, his voice lowered to a conspiratorial whisper. "If anyone can help us decipher this, it's him."

Leo nodded slowly, the weight of the situation sinking in. He understood the gravity of the situation and knew that desperate times called for desperate measures. "Alright, let's do it. Call Alex."

Finn wasted no time. He retrieved his phone and began to snap pictures of the cryptic pages, capturing the symbols and text in vivid detail. The camera's flash illuminated the dark room in brief, eerie bursts, enhancing the otherworldly atmosphere.

As Finn compiled a gallery of images, he hesitated for a moment before pressing the call button. Each ring of the phone seemed to reverberate with anticipation. Finally, Alex's voice echoed through the speaker, rich and commanding.

"Finn? What's going on?" Alex's tone held a hint of curiosity.

Finn wasted no time with pleasantries. "Alex, we need your help. We've got a book here, an ancient one, and it's written in a language we can't understand. We think it might be the key to helping Leo's brother, but we're stuck."

There was a brief pause on the other end, the weight of Alex's consideration almost palpable. "I see. Describe the book to me," he instructed.

Finn relayed the eerie ambiance, the feeling of ancient magic, and the cryptic text that defied comprehension. As he spoke, Leo watched with a mixture of apprehension and hope, aware that this conversation might hold the key to saving Rory.

Alex's voice remained steady and authoritative. "I'll meet you both as soon as possible. Until then, keep the book safe. I will do my best to decipher its contents."

Finn hung up, a mixture of relief and uncertainty washing over him.

In the meantime, Finn and Leo continued to photograph the pages, capturing every intricate detail. The camera's flash continued to dance through the room, casting eerie shadows on the walls. Each image added to the growing collection of cryptic symbols and text, a visual representation of the enigma they were determined to unravel.

The minutes stretched into hours as they meticulously documented the book's contents. Finn couldn't help but feel a sense of awe and trepidation. The magic imbued in the pages seemed to intensify with every photograph, as if the book itself yearned to be understood.

"Alright, let's call it a day," Finn said, his voice laced with exhaustion. He ran a hand through his disheveled hair, sweat clinging to his brow. "Can you ward the book?" Finn asked and Leo nodded.

Leo's fingers danced gracefully over the book's surface, tracing intricate symbols with precision. A soft, ethereal glow enveloped the tome as he chanted incantations under his breath. The air seemed to hum with power as Leo's magic worked its protective charm.

Finn couldn't help but feel the subtle shift in Leo's power. It was different, more potent than before. The room crackled with energy, and Finn's eyes widened in realization. Something had changed, whatever happened in that chamber with Hecate made Leo's magic increase in power.

Once Leo completed the warding, he turned to Finn, his expression grave. "We need to keep the book safe," he said, his voice carrying the weight of responsibility. He surveyed the room, considering their options. "The library," he decided, "it's the best place."

Finn's mind raced as he contemplated returning to the secret chamber where they had found the book. The memories of that place sent shivers down his spine, and he hesitated.

"I can't go back there," Finn admitted, his voice quivering with unease. He knew that whatever lay within the chamber had left an indelible mark on him.

Leo placed a reassuring hand on Finn's shoulder. "You don't have to," he said gently. "Go and check on Rory. I'll take care of this."

Finn nodded in gratitude, his trust in Leo unwavering. Together, they stood and made their way out of the dimly lit room, leaving the ward-protected book behind.

Finn's footsteps echoed down the corridor as he ventured toward Rory's room. The air felt heavy with anticipation, and his heart raced with worry. He pushed open the door and was met with a scene of chaos.

Rory's room was in disarray. Books and belongings were scattered haphazardly across the floor, and the bed was empty, its sheets tangled and askew. Panic clawed at Finn's chest as he scanned the room for any sign of his friend.

"Rory?" he called out, his voice trembling. There was no response, only an eerie silence that hung in the air like a shroud.

His eyes fell upon the open window, curtains billowing gently in the night breeze. Finn cursed under his breath, realizing that Rory had vanished through that very window.

Finn dashed out of the room, his heart pounding in his chest like a drum. He wasn't sure what had happened, but the look on Leo's face told him it was serious. Leo's concern was etched across his features, his brow furrowed with worry.

"What's wrong? Did anything happen?" Leo's voice quivered with anxiety as he confronted Finn in the hallway.

Finn's words tumbled out in a hurry, "Rory's gone."

Leo's eyes widened, mirroring the fear that gripped Finn's heart. Without another word, they both hurried toward Rory's room, their footsteps echoing in the dimly lit corridor.

"Where is he?" Leo's voice trembled as he hurried to the window, his eyes scanning the outside world.

"Do you know a place where he could have possibly gone?" Finn asked, trying to regain some composure despite the rising fear.

Leo turned to Finn, his gaze intense and filled with purpose. Without a word, he closed the distance between them, his lips meeting Finn's in a brief, passionate kiss. It was a moment of reassurance, a shared connection amidst the chaos.

Finn's lips tingled from the touch, a flicker of warmth amidst the fear that threatened to consume him. Leo pulled away, his eyes locking onto Finn's.

"I do," Leo said, determination in his voice. "Come on, we can't afford to waste any time."

Finn nodded, his heart pounding as they hurried out of the room and down the stairs. Outside the house, the world was shrouded in darkness, and the night seemed to hold its breath, waiting for their next move.

Finn could hear Leo's hushed conversation as he spoke urgently into his phone, his words filled with urgency.

"How long can you get here?" Leo's voice was urgent. "Okay... Just get here as soon as you can."

Finn approached Leo, curiosity getting the better of him. "Who was that?"

Leo's gaze met Finn's, and he spoke with a sense of urgency. "It was Justin. They're on their way back. But we can't stand here and wait for them."

Dread settled like a heavy weight in Finn's chest. "Where are we going?"

Leo's eyes met Finn's, and in that moment, Finn saw determination and hope. "There's a clearing in the forest where we used to go when we needed to clear our heads. I'm hoping that we can find him there."

Finn nodded, a mixture of fear and determination coursing through his veins. With Leo leading the way, they ventured into the forest, the trees towering above them like ancient guardians.

The forest path was bathed in silver moonlight, casting eerie, elongated shadows on the ground. Leaves rustled in the breeze, and the air was filled with the scent of damp earth and pine. It was a place they had frequented in their past, a sanctuary away from the world's troubles.

As they walked deeper into the woods, Finn's senses sharpened. He could hear the faint whisper of the wind in the leaves, the distant call of a night bird, and the soft crunch of their footsteps on the forest floor. It was as if the forest itself held its breath, aware of their quest.

Leo's presence beside him was a comforting anchor in the darkness. He kept his gaze forward, his eyes scanning for any sign of Rory. Finn couldn't help but steal glances at him, his heart aching with worry and affection.

Finn couldn't shake the feeling that they were being watched, and he hesitated for a moment.

"Leo," Finn said, his voice barely a whisper, "I feel like we're not alone here. It's like something's following us."

Leo turned to look at Finn, his expression grim. "This forest is ancient, Finn. It's said to be home to countless spirits. What you're feeling might just be their presence. We need to keep moving, though. Rory's in trouble."

Finn nodded, though he couldn't shake the unease that had settled in his gut. They continued deeper into the forest, Leo leading the way with a sense of purpose that Finn admired. He trusted Leo's instincts, even in the face of the unknown.

As they walked, the forest seemed to close in around them, the trees growing taller and thicker, their branches reaching out like gnarled fingers. Finn's imagination played tricks on him, and he couldn't help but glance over his shoulder every so often.

Leo noticed Finn's unease and put a reassuring hand on his shoulder. "We're almost there, Finn. Just a little further."

They walked for what felt like hours until they finally reached the clearing Leo had mentioned. The moonlight bathed the open space in an eerie glow, and in the center stood Rory. Relief washed over Finn, but something about Rory's posture and the strange smile on his face sent a shiver down his spine.

Leo called out to Rory, his voice tinged with concern. "Rory! Thank the gods we found you!"

Rory turned to face them, and Finn's heart sank. There was something off about him, something that sent a chill through Finn's veins. Rory's mouth opened, and when he spoke, his voice was distorted, as if it came from somewhere far away.

"Leo stop. Something is not right." Finn shouted and Leo stopped.

"I've found the magic I've always wanted," Rory said, his words sending a shiver down Finn's spine. "And now, it's time to end the people who made me suffer."

Leo took a step forward, his worry deepening. "Rory, you're not yourself. We can help you."

But Finn sensed the danger, his instincts screaming at him to be ready. He placed himself between Leo and Rory, his magic crackling in his fingertips.

Rory's smile widened, and it was a chilling sight. He spoke again, his voice low and menacing. "I can sense it, Leo. Hecate's magic coursing through your veins. It's a shame I have to kill you."

With those words, something dark and malevolent surged from Rory's form, and Finn knew they were in danger. He raised a protective barrier of magic around them just in time to shield them from the oncoming attack.

The forest seemed to come alive with the battle of magic that followed.  Sparks of light and dark energy clashed in the moonlit clearing, casting eerie and hypnotic patterns in the air.  The night seemed to hold its breath as the three friends fought a battle of magic, each spell and counter-spell a dance of power and desperation.

Leo's voice rang out with determination. "Rory, snap out of it! You don't want to do this!"

But Rory's eyes were filled with madness, and his attacks grew more ferocious. Finn and Leo knew they had to end this before it escalated further. They combined their powers, weaving a spell of purification and healing, and sent it crashing towards Rory.

The magic struck Rory, and for a moment, his features softened. It seemed like their spell had broken through the darkness that had taken hold of him. But just as quickly, the malevolent force within him fought back, and Rory let out a guttural scream.

The battle raged on, each side pushing their magical abilities to the limit. Finn and Leo were determined to save him, but they knew that they were teetering on the brink of a dangerous precipice.

Finn and Leo struggled in the midst of Rory's relentless onslaught, their spells faltering against his demonic might. Frustration etched across their faces as they realized their efforts were in vain.

"You stay here. I am going to go try and hit him from the back," Finn determinedly stated, his gaze locked onto Rory. Leo nodded, sharing the urgency in his friend's eyes.

Finn darted behind Rory, a palpable sense of impending doom looming as the dark magic emanating from Rory's sinister conjurations sent shivers down his spine. This had to end. Finn gathered every ounce of magical energy he possessed, summoning the strongest spell he could muster. With a swift and decisive motion, he unleashed it upon Rory's unsuspecting form.

The spell exploded on impact, a blinding burst of arcane energy tearing through the air.  But as the dissipating smoke cleared, an eerie revelation unfolded—Rory remained unscathed, his twisted smile unbroken.

"You think your puny spells can stop a demon like me? Don't make me laugh, human," Rory taunted, his voice dripping with malevolence.

"Finn!" Leo's desperate cry cut through the tension.

Finn watched in horror as Rory vanished from his sight, only to reappear directly in front of him. The demon's malevolent intentions were evident as he readied a devastating strike. Yet, just as the abyss threatened to swallow Finn, a sudden shift in the atmosphere electrified the air.

A charged ozone smell pervaded the battlefield, signaling a presence beyond their comprehension.  Finn's heart surged with hope as he recognized the unmistakable signs of a divine arrival. It was a sensation that only a handful of beings could evoke.

"You're fucked now, whoever you are," Finn quipped, a triumphant smile gracing his face.

Then, the voice cut through the tension like a lightning bolt. "Hey you, get your hands away from the good doctor."

Rory turned, his malevolent gaze redirected. Finn followed his line of sight to the figure that stood before them—Hermes, the speedy god. Relief washed over Finn, knowing that Alex must have sent Hermes to their aid after their urgent plea.

With mocking confidence, Rory taunted Hermes, declaring his intent to make the god his next victim. Leo rushed to Finn's side, concern etched across his face. The stage was set for an epic showdown between god and demon.

"You okay, Finn?" Leo asked, his voice trembling with anxiety.

They both watched in awe as Hermes effortlessly dodged every of Rory's ferocious attacks. The god's movements were a mesmerizing dance of grace and speed, a stark contrast to the demon's malevolence.

"I'm tired of this cat and mouse fight," Hermes declared, his voice cutting through the chaos. With a swift flourish, he began to circle around Rory, creating a swirling vortex of energy in the air.

Finn could feel the surge of power as the siphon crackled with intensity. Rory's agonized scream pierced the battlefield, and for a fleeting moment, they heard Rory's desperate plea for Leo's help.

"Leo, Help me!" Rory pleaded sound like himself again.

"Rory! Hang in there" Leo said.

Leo instinctively moved to answer the call, but Finn's firm grip held him back. They could only watch as Hermes continued his relentless assault.

The siphon vanished as suddenly as it had appeared, leaving Rory's form crumpled and defeated on the ground. Hermes stood triumphant, his breath labored but victorious.

With a swift motion, Hermes scooped up Rory, his gaze shifting to Finn and Leo. The god's expression held a mixture of concern and determination.

"We need to get somewhere safe," Hermes urged, his voice a stark reminder of the ongoing danger.

Leo nodded, his gratitude toward the god evident. "Our house is the closest," Leo suggested.

Hermes wasted no time, and with Rory in tow, they made their way towards the sanctuary of Finn and Leo's home. The battle was over, but the echoes of their confrontation still reverberated in their minds, a reminder of the darkness they had faced and the divine intervention that had saved them.

# 9

# Leo

Leo's gaze remained locked onto the unconscious form of Rory sprawled across the bed. Finn stood close by, his brows knitted with worry, while Hermes, the godly figure, toiled at the edges of the room, tending to the protective wards with a meticulousness that sent shivers down Leo's spine.

The room crackled with an uneasy tension, the air electric with uncertainty. A heavy sigh slipped from Leo's lips, a sigh that seemed to carry the weight of the world. There was no room for doubt now - Rory harbored a demon within, a malevolent force that had taken residence where his brother's soul should have been.

Finn, sensing Leo's inner turmoil, dared to break the silence that hung over them like a thick fog. His voice trembled with the weight of the question that hung heavy in the room. "Did you recognize the demon?"

Leo's brow furrowed, lines of frustration etched into his face as he pondered Finn's inquiry. "No," he confessed, his voice heavy with frustration. "This demon... it was different, Finn. Stronger than any I've ever encountered."

Demon possession was a nightmare, a malevolent dance with the darkest of forces. Extracting a demon from a person required not just magical prowess but a surgeon's precision. Failure could unleash a cataclysm, a storm of anguish that would consume both the possessed and the exorcist.

Hermes, still working his divine magic on the protective wards, interjected from behind them, his tone laden with ominous weight. "You wouldn't recognize this demon because it hails from the deepest pits of Hell."

Leo's eyes widened in disbelief. Meeting a god had shattered his preconceived notions about myths and legends. Each passing second in the presence of Hermes was a testament to the unfathomable reality he now faced.

Turning toward Hermes, Leo's voice trembled with a mixture of hope and trepidation. "Do you know this demon, Hermes?"

Hermes met Leo's gaze with a solemn nod, his usually jovial countenance marred by deep concern. "The demon's name is Lyandros."

The room seemed to hold its breath as the words hung in the air. Lyandros, a name that sent shivers down the spine of even the bravest of souls. Leo couldn't help but picture the demon, a creature born of nightmares, a sinister entity that dwelled in the darkest recesses of human fear.

The protective wards, under Hermes' expert guidance, began to shimmer with an otherworldly light. It was as if the very essence of magic danced before them, a display of power that transcended mortal comprehension. The room pulsed with the energy, the walls seemingly alive with a luminescent glow.

Hermes continued his work, his hands moving with a grace that defied the laws of nature. Symbols and sigils materialized in the air, spinning and twirling in intricate patterns, as if writing a story of ancient battles and timeless struggles.

Finn leaned forward, his voice laced with urgency. "How can we defeat Lyandros, then? We can't just sit here and let him wreak havoc."

Hermes sighed, the weight of the situation evident in his expression. "I don't know, Finn, but Alex will. He and Eryx are en route to Salem as we speak. They've got a plan."

As if on cue, Justin and Harry burst into the room, their faces etched with concern. Justin wasted no time in demanding answers from Leo. "What the hell happened out there? We saw the lights and heard the commotion."

Leo took a deep breath, ready to recount the nightmarish events in the clearing. "It was a demon. It possessed Rory, and we had to fight him off. But he's not gone for good."

Harry's voice trembled with anxiety as he inquired about Rory's condition. "Is he going to be okay?"

Finn, ever the calming presence, reassured them. "He will be, for now. I'm keeping an eye on his magical signature, and it's stable. It's almost as if the demon is… taking a break."

"We can't let our guards down, though," Hermes interjected with a knowing look. "Lyandros can take control of a body he's possessed whenever he wants to. We need to be vigilant."

Harry and Justin exchanged incredulous glances. Justin, still struggling to process the surreal nature of the situation, couldn't help but blurt out his disbelief. "Are you actually real?"

Hermes chuckled, a sound that eased some of the tension in the room. "Last time I checked. Though I spend most of my time dealing with divine paperwork, I do get out once in a while." Then, with an air of authority, Hermes turned more serious. His divine aura filled the room, making it crackle with energy. "They're here. We better take this to the living room."

Harry's curiosity piqued, and he couldn't help but ask, "Who's here?"

"Alex and Eryx," Finn announced as he headed towards the door. "Come on, guys. Rory will be fine here."

Everyone nodded in agreement and followed Finn as he led them to the living room. The room, bathed in warm, inviting light, provided a stark contrast to the darkness of their recent ordeal.

As they entered the living room, Finn went to the door to greet Alex and Eryx. Hugs and greetings were exchanged, and Finn offered to help them with their bags. Alex, his expression a mix of concern and determination, wasted no time and got straight to the point.

"What do you know so far?" he asked.

Finn, ever the level-headed one, stepped forward and began to explain the situation. "Rory got possessed by a demon, and Hermes here told us that you could help."

Leo, who had been silently observing the exchange, finally stepped forward to greet their guests. "Alex, Eryx, these are my brothers, Justin and Harry."

Alex nodded at the brothers and then shifted his attention back to the matter at hand. "So, tell me everything."

Finn took a deep breath and launched into an explanation of the events that had transpired. He described the eerie possession, the battle with the demon, and Rory's current state of vulnerability.

Leo offered his guests seats as they listened intently. The living room was adorned with cozy furniture, and the walls were lined with shelves filled with books and mystical artifacts.

"Rory had no chance against the demon's power, but we managed to get him out of there. That's when Hermes intervened and brought us here." Finn continued.

"Can we see Rory?" Alex asked, his brow furrowed in concern as he glanced around the room, eager to get to the bottom of the mystery.

"Sure, but don't you guys want to rest first?" Finn suggested, his eyes weary from a long day of chasing supernatural leads.

"If my suspicions are right, Rory's case might be connected to the one in Manhattan," Alex said, his voice low and serious.

"You mean Agnes' case?" Finn asked, raising an eyebrow, intrigued.

"Yes, the patterns are similar," Alex replied, his gaze focused and determined. "And from what we've been told while you were gone, Finn, a body was sent to the morgue Leo was working the night before we were called out to Annie's coven."

Leo, sitting in a chair nearby, tensed at the mention of the body. "Something wasn't right about that body," he said, his voice carrying a hint of unease.

"Can you tell us what you found?" Eryx inquired, leaning forward with genuine curiosity.

"I felt something was wrong with the body as soon as I touched it," Leo explained. "My magic caught onto something dark. When I used my magic to examine the body, it started to act on its own."

"What do you mean?" Alex pressed, his eyes locked onto Leo.

"My magic turned red and formed a shape," Leo continued, his voice quivering with uncertainty. "But I remember feeling that it was a demon." Leo rubbed his face with a trembling hand, frustration and regret evident in his body language. "I should have realized that earlier. Fuck!"

Without hesitation, Finn rose from his seat and enveloped Leo in a reassuring hug. "You couldn't have known," Finn comforted, his voice steady. "You're here now, though."

As Finn and Leo shared a moment, Finn's sharp ears caught Alex's voice, breaking the silence and the intimacy of the scene. Alex's tone was urgent as he reminded them of the pressing task at hand. They couldn't afford to waste any more time.

"We need to see Rory immediately," Alex declared, his eyes filled with determination.

Turning to Hermes, Alex instructed him to wait in the library. Hermes nodded, rallying Justin and Harry, to accompany him.

Alex nodded in approval, his mind focused on the impending task.

Leo took charge, leading Alex and Eryx to Rory's room. Inside the dimly lit room, Alex exchanged a brief glance with Finn before addressing him in a hushed tone.

Alex proceeded to approach Rory's bed. Finn observed with a mixture of awe and gratitude as Alex summoned his otherworldly powers to assess Rory's condition. It was a power he still weren't entirely used to, but they were grateful to have it on their side.

Alex's hand began to glow with a deep and otherworldly purple hue. The light cast eerie shadows on the walls, creating a surreal, almost magical atmosphere. It was a stark reminder of the supernatural forces at play.

After what felt like an eternity, Alex's hand dimmed, the purple glow fading away. He turned to Finn, his expression grave, and delivered his assessment in a hushed tone.

"What did you find?" Leo asked.

"Someone deliberately put the demon inside of him. We need that book as soon as possible," Alex urged, his voice laced with urgency and a touch of fear.

Finn and Leo nodded in agreement, knowing that their journey was far from over. The mysteries they were unraveling were leading them deeper into the unknown, and with every revelation, the stakes grew higher.

Leo led them to the library, its shelves lined with dusty tomes and the faint scent of ancient knowledge in the air. The team gathered around a wooden table in the center of the room, anticipation hanging in the silence like a heavy curtain.

Leo went in and took the book from where he hid it back in the secret chamber.

Alex's inquisitive eyes darted toward the book Leo held. "Is that the book?" he asked, leaning in closer. Leo simply nodded, his expression tense with a mix of hope and trepidation.

With a careful motion, Alex opened the book, its pages whispering secrets of the past. Everyone held their breath as Alex flipped through the aged parchment, each page more cryptic than the last. The room was filled with a tangible sense of expectation.

Eryx, standing by Alex's side, couldn't bear the silence any longer. "What does it say?" he urged, his curiosity getting the best of him.

Alex's brows furrowed as he continued to peruse the pages. "This book," he began, his voice laced with a hint of awe, "was written using the ancient language of the underworld. Only Nyx and Hecate were fluent in writing the language, while I can only read some of it."

Eryx leaned in closer, eager for more information. "Go on."

"Whoever had this book," Alex continued, "knew the language. From what I can decipher, the writing appears to be that of Hecate herself. According to this, in order to free Rory's soul from the spirit realm, we have to find the people who put the demon inside Rory in the first place."

A heavy silence fell over the room, the weight of their task sinking in. Leo took a deep breath, his eyes flickering with resolve. He revealed, "Hecate showed herself to me when I found the book. She told me that she had been locked inside that book for a long time until I came in and freed her."

Finn, standing beside Leo, gave his hand a reassuring squeeze, a silent promise that they would face whatever challenges lay ahead together.

Justin, always one to ask the tough questions, spoke up. "Were you going to tell us this?"

Leo rubbed the back of his neck, his demeanor sheepish. "I was planning to, but we have more urgent matters to attend to."

Alex interjected with a sense of urgency. "Leo's right. We can't afford to waste any more time. Rory's soul is gradually being corrupted by the demon. When that happens, Rory will die, and his body will become a vessel for Lyandros."

Harry, his concern evident, asked, "What can we do to stop it?"

Alex didn't mince words. "There's a way to slow down this process, but I'm going to need Finn and Leo to do it."

Leo's eyes met Finn's, a silent acknowledgment passing between them. "Whatever it is, we're ready," Leo declared, determination lacing his words.

Alex nodded, appreciating their resolve. "Good. I need you two to return to the spirit realm because both of your magics are crucial to this process. Finn, your skills as a soul healer, and Leo, your ability as a soul tracker, will help safeguard Rory's soul from Lyandros's relentless pursuit. But be warned, this is risky. You could get trapped in the spirit realm forever, so you have to be careful."

Finn and Leo exchanged glances, their hands still intertwined, a silent vow to protect Rory's soul. "We're ready," they said in unison, their voices carrying the weight of their commitment.

As the team prepared to face the unknown, the library seemed to come alive with an ethereal energy. The room's ancient, dusty tomes shivered in their shelves as if sensing the impending magic. The air itself crackled with anticipation.

Alex closed his eyes briefly, focusing his energy. With a flourish, he gestured toward Finn and Leo, their forms beginning to shimmer and waver as they slowly faded from view. Wisps of iridescent light spiraled around them, like a dance of fireflies in the night.

Finn and Leo, their souls now partially detached from their physical bodies, felt a rush of energy envelop them. They hovered in a surreal liminal space, the boundaries between the mortal world and the spirit realm blurred.

With a final surge of power, Alex completed the spell, and Finn and Leo vanished from sight, leaving the rest behind.

# 10

# Finn

Finn's eyes blinked open to an eerie sight—a dark forest stretching out endlessly before him. The very air seemed to hum with an otherworldly energy. He scrambled to his feet, a mix of confusion and anxiety gripping him.

"This is the spirit realm," Finn muttered to himself, trying to make sense of his surroundings. He reached out, hoping to find Leo.

His voice cracked as he called out, "Leo! Leo, where are you?"

Only silence answered him, broken only by the haunting echo of his own voice. Finn's heart sank, realizing he was alone in this mystic world. Determination drove him forward, his footsteps crunching on the dark forest floor.

The energy in the air was palpable, like static electricity before a storm. Finn felt it in his bones, a mysterious power he couldn't yet grasp. Ignoring the unease creeping up his spine, he pressed on.

"Leo!" Finn's voice echoed through the dark trees again, but still, there was no response.

As he ventured deeper into the shadowy woods, he caught a movement out of the corner of his eye. A creature which seemed like a gryphon, lay tangled in underbrush, struggling to move. Finn hurried over, his heart going out to the poor spirit.

With a wave of his hand and a muttered incantation, Finn channeled his magic into the creature, bathing it in a soft, ethereal light. The spirit's wounds closed, and its breathing steadied. Finn watched, his heart racing, as life returned to the mystical creature.

Time seemed to stand still as Finn waited for the spirit to awaken. Hours passed, or perhaps mere moments in the spirit realm's strange flow of time. Finally, the creature's eyes fluttered open. It blinked slowly at Finn, a hint of fear in its gaze.

Finn extended his hand, offering a comforting gesture. "Hey there, little guy. You're safe now."

The spirit hesitated for a moment, then nuzzled Finn's hand with its beak. A smile tugged at the corners of Finn's lips. He gently petted the creature's feathery mane, reassuring it with soft words.

"It's gonna be alright," Finn whispered. He reluctantly stood up, preparing to continue his journey. "I've got to find Leo. You take care, okay?"

But as he turned to leave, he felt a presence at his side. The spirit had risen and was following him, its large, soulful eyes fixed on Finn.

Finn raised an eyebrow and chuckled. "You want to come with me?"

In response, the creature let out an eager, almost comical squeak.

"Alright, alright," Finn said, shaking his head in amusement. "You can tag along, but you've gotta keep up."

The spirit hopped along with a bound of excitement, flapping its wings with glee. Finn couldn't help but smile at the sight.

"Guess we're in this together, buddy," Finn said, and together, they ventured deeper into the mysterious and visually spectacular spirit realm.

The forest seemed to respond to their presence, casting ethereal glows and weaving intricate patterns of light as they moved. Trees swayed in time with their steps, and luminescent fireflies danced around them. Finn's own magic seemed to amplify, creating bursts of colorful sparks that illuminated their path.

"Wow," Finn muttered, his voice filled with awe. "This place is something else."

The spirit responded with a joyful trill, and they continued their journey through the enchanting and magical realm, Finn's determination unwavering, and his newfound companion adding a touch of whimsy to their quest.

Finn gazed at his new companion, its presence was eerie yet intriguing. "I should really give you a new name, huh?" Finn mused aloud.

The spirit emitted a happy noise, a sound that caught Finn off guard and made him chuckle. "How about Goldy?" he suggested.

The spirit scoffed at the idea, its reaction swift and disdainful. Finn sighed, undeterred. "Mhmm. How about Poofy?"

This time, the spirit squealed in delight, a high-pitched sound that resonated with an odd sense of agreement. "Poofy it is," Finn declared with a smile.

Poofy couldn't contain its joy and affection. It licked Finn's face with its long, spectral tongue, eliciting a disgusted frown from him. "It's a good thing you're cute," Finn remarked.

Finn locked eyes with Poofy, his expression becoming serious. "Look, you cute little gryphon-looking spirit, I need to find my friend Leo, and I don't really know where to start. You're from here, so if you can, please help me. That would be great."

Poofy tilted its head, considering Finn's request for a moment. Then, without warning, it began sniffing at Finn's pocket. "Hey, what are you doing?" Finn protested, laughing. "I'm ticklish in that area, Poofy!"

Poofy paid no mind to Finn's protests and pulled out a piece of jewelry from his pocket. Finn examined it closely and realized it was Leo's ring. He hadn't even noticed it had ended up in his pocket during their journey through the spirit realm.

Finn's eyes widened in realization. "Can you use this to track Leo?" he asked, his voice filled with hope.

Poofy nodded in response, a gesture that was surprisingly clear and affirmative. "Off you go, boy," Finn said, patting Poofy's head. "Lead me to Leo."

With Leo's ring in its possession, Poofy took to the air, its spectral wings carrying it effortlessly. Finn watched closely as they soared northward, the wind rushing past them. They didn't have to go far before Poofy descended to the ground, signaling Finn to follow. Finn knelt beside Poofy, giving it some well-deserved pets on the head before they continued their journey on foot.

As they ventured deeper into the spirit realm, the scenery around them began to shift and transform. The dense forest, initially shrouded in an eerie mist, gradually changed. Trees with twisted, gnarled branches stretched toward the sky, their leaves a vivid shade of iridescent blue. Strange, luminescent creatures flitted among the branches, casting an otherworldly glow.

The ground beneath their feet was soft and springy, covered in moss that seemed to pulse with a subtle, silvery light. Tiny, ethereal flowers sprouted from the moss, releasing a gentle, sweet fragrance that hung in the air.

Finn couldn't help but marvel at the beauty of this ethereal realm, even as the tension in his heart grew with each step. He knew that finding Leo in such a mystical place wouldn't be easy.

They continued on their path through the enchanted forest for what felt like hours, guided by the spectral presence of Poofy. Suddenly, Poofy came to a sudden stop, its spectral form bristling with unease. It began to emit a low, menacing growl.

Finn, feeling a shiver run down his spine, crouched down and whispered to Poofy, "What's wrong, buddy?"

He followed Poofy's gaze, and his heart skipped a beat as he spotted a pair of fiery red eyes gleaming in the darkness ahead. Finn and Poofy started backing away cautiously, and Finn reached for the magic within him, ready to defend himself and his spectral companion.

"Show yourself!" Finn called out, his voice quaking with a mix of fear and determination.

The entity stepped forward into the dim glow of the iridescent forest, revealing its terrifying form. It was a Lich, a creature of the darkest magic. Its withered, skeletal visage was framed by a tattered, hooded robe that billowed around its skeletal frame. In one bony hand, it held a staff adorned with a glowing, malevolent crystal.

Finn knew all too well the maleficence of Liches. Their touch was death, and their power over necromantic forces was unparalleled. He couldn't afford to let it get any closer.

The presence of the Lich weighed heavily on Finn, its aura suffocating him with an overwhelming sense of dread. His muscles tensed, and his heart raced as he prepared for a confrontation with this formidable foe.

Finn's voice shook but remained firm as he addressed the Lich. "What do you want?" he demanded, his hand trembling as he readied his magical defenses.

The Lich's hollow eyes fixated on Finn, and a wicked, skeletal grin stretched across its desiccated face. It spoke in a voice that echoed with the coldness of the grave. "I seek what you seek, mortal. The one you call Leo."

Finn's voice trembled as he faced the malevolent Lich. "What do you want with Leo?" he demanded, his words echoing in the eerie stillness.

The Lich's laughter sent chills down Finn's spine, a dark, hollow sound that seemed to seep into his very soul. Without warning, the unholy creature lunged at them, a nightmarish visage of death and decay.

With a quickness born of desperation, Finn summoned a shield out of thin air. It materialized just in time, a translucent barrier of shimmering magic that stood between them and the Lich's malevolent onslaught. The Lich's assaults were relentless, gnawing at Finn's magic like a starving predator, threatening to tear through his defenses.

"Poofy, fly. Get out of here," Finn pleaded, his eyes darting to his companion who stood bravely beside him, growling at the encroaching darkness. "Poofy, please. I don't want you to get hurt."

As the seconds ticked by, Finn felt his head throbbing, a searing pain that matched the intensity of his battle to hold the shield intact. The Lich's malevolence pressed against him, an unrelenting force that threatened to consume him.

In the midst of their desperate struggle, the Lich let out a final, ear-piercing scream, a sound that reverberated through the air, shaking the very ground beneath them. The scream shattered Finn's shield like fragile glass, sending him tumbling to the ground, defenseless and vulnerable.

Fear gripped Finn's heart as he lay on the cold, unforgiving ground, his senses overwhelmed by the looming specter of death. He was certain that the Lich was about to deliver the fatal blow, ending him in an instant.

But then, out of the chaos and darkness, a ray of hope emerged.

Poofy leaped forward, placing himself between Finn and the oncoming doom. Finn's voice cracked as he cried out for Poofy, his heart heavy with the thought of losing his companion.

"Poofy! No!" Finn cried out then everything turned blindingly white.

When the blinding light finally subsided, Finn blinked in disbelief at the scene before him. Poofy, the seemingly defenseless creature, floated serenely in the air, unharmed and untouched by the malevolence that had threatened to consume them both.

The Lich, on the other hand, was suspended in mid-air, its grotesque form contorted in a futile struggle against an invisible force. Finn's heart raced as he realized that Poofy had somehow turned the tables on their unholy adversary.

Summoning every ounce of his remaining strength, Finn staggered to his feet. He knew that this was their only chance to escape the clutches of the Lich.

"Poofy…" he murmured, his voice quivering with a mix of fear and awe.

With determination etched on his face, Finn raised his hands, his fingers trembling as he unleashed the last vestiges of his magic. Tendrils of iridescent energy snaked out from his fingertips, weaving and coiling around the Lich's wretched form, rendering it immobile.

Finn's breath caught in his throat as he locked eyes with the malevolent creature, a silent battle of wills raging between them. He knew that he couldn't hold the Lich for long, but it was enough to buy them precious moments.

"Poofy," Finn urged, his voice urgent and pleading. "We have to go. Now."

Poofy responded with a high-pitched squeal, a testament to their unbreakable bond. Slowly, he lowered himself to the ground, his eyes never leaving the trapped Lich.

Finn didn't need any further encouragement. He turned and fled, his heart pounding in his chest, every step a frantic dance between life and death. Poofy followed, his tiny wings buzzing with determination as they raced away from the nightmare that had threatened to consume them.

In the distance, the malevolent laughter of the Lich echoed, a chilling reminder of the darkness they had narrowly escaped. But Finn and Poofy pressed on, their bond unbroken, their determination un-wavering, as they ventured into the unknown, leaving the malevolent presence of the Lich behind them.

Finn and Poofy dashed deeper into the mystical woods, their hearts pounding in tandem. They didn't have a clear destination in mind, just a desperate need to evade the Lich's ominous presence that hung in the air like a suffocating shroud. The daylight was quickly fading, and the looming shadows of the ancient trees cast eerie silhouettes.

As the encroaching darkness enveloped them, Finn's thoughts shifted to the urgency of finding shelter for the night. He had no idea that such things existed in the enigmatic spirit realm, but he had learned that surprises lurked around every corner in this surreal place.

In the distance, a small cabin emerged from the gloom, its timeworn facade standing in stark contrast to the otherworldly forest. Finn exchanged a quick glance with Poofy, searching for any sign that the cabin's owner might be home. Poofy, however, remained oddly indifferent to their surroundings, so Finn cautiously approached the cabin and knocked on its weathered door.

With a creak, the door slowly swung open, revealing a woman who struck a chord of familiarity in Finn's mind. He couldn't quite place where he had seen her before, but there was a certain connection, a puzzle piece waiting to be fitted.

The woman regarded Finn and Poofy with a calm curiosity, her eyes revealing a depth of wisdom that transcended the ethereal realm. "How may I assist you?" she inquired, her voice carrying a soothing cadence.

Finn's words tumbled out in a rush, "We…we need shelter for the night."

A nod of understanding passed between the woman and Finn. She gestured for them to enter the cabin, a warm smile gracing her lips. "Come inside."

As they stepped over the threshold, a tantalizing aroma filled the air, teasing Finn's senses. The woman chuckled softly, as if reading his thoughts, and directed them to the cozy kitchen. "My husband is preparing dinner. Please, join us."

In the kitchen, Finn found himself face to face with a man of remarkable stature. His warm smile matched his wife's, and he extended a welcoming hand. "I'm Clint, and this is my wife, Rhea."

Finn introduced himself and then turned to Poofy, who bobbed in acknowledgment. Clint motioned for them to take a seat around a rustic wooden table.

Rhea, her eyes twinkling with curiosity, leaned forward and addressed Finn, "You're not like the others here. Your soul is whole, and your attire suggests you come from the mortal realm."

Finn blinked in surprise. "How did you know?"

Rhea's gaze seemed to penetrate his very essence. "I can sense it. Mortals have a unique presence here, and your clothing is quite distinct." She exchanged a knowing glance with Clint.

Clint, now joining the conversation, leaned in with genuine interest. "So, why do you reek of a Lich? Those abominations only exist when summoned."

Finn hesitated for a moment, weighing his trust in these mysterious hosts. He felt an inexplicable connection to them, as if they held the key to something greater. Finally, he decided to share his tale.

"We were attacked not long ago," Finn began, his voice unwavering. "Our reason for being in the spirit realm is tied to Leo, my friend. His brother, Rory, has been trapped here, possessed by a demon."

Clint and Rhea listened intently, their eyes locked onto Finn's as if they could see the very events he described. The room crackled with an eerie energy as Finn continued, his words resonating with the power of truth and desperation.

"The Lich, it wants something from us. We don't know what, but we can't allow it to get its hands on Leo. It's a race against time, and we need all the help we can get."

Clint and Rhea exchanged a solemn glance, their commitment evident.

"Tell us, what's his last name?" Rhea's voice was gentle but insistent, her gaze locked onto Finn's.

Finn, sipping his drink, couldn't help but hesitate. He swirled the dark liquid in his cup, his eyes darting between Rhea and Clint, who sat beside her, their expressions grave yet curious.

"Why do you want to know?" he finally responded, his voice tinged with unease.

"Just humor us, dear." Rhea said, her fingers tracing the rim of her coffee mug.

Finn sighed, his gaze dropping to the steaming coffee. "It's Rodriguez," he admitted reluctantly, the words escaping his lips like an unwelcome secret.

As soon as Finn revealed Leo's last name, Rhea's composure shattered. She burst into tears, her sobs echoing through the room, and she clung desperately to Clint, who enveloped her in a comforting embrace.

Clint, while comforting his wife, locked eyes with Finn. "It is him, Clint," Rhea said between her tearful gasps, her breaths labored from crying.

Finn, bewildered and anxious, couldn't comprehend the situation. "What's going on?" he asked after a moment, his voice a mix of concern and confusion.

Clint, still holding his weeping wife, regarded Finn solemnly. "We are their parents."

Finn's eyes widened in shock and disbelief. He had known Leo's parents were in Seattle. "How can that be? They are in our realm," he stammered, his mind reeling.

Rhea managed to break free from her husband's hug, her red-rimmed eyes locked onto Finn's once more. "A demon took our souls and sent them here. We've been here ever since."

Finn absorbed the astonishing revelation, struggling to wrap his head around the supernatural twist of fate that had brought Leo's parents into his life in such an unexpected manner. "So how are you guys still walking in the mortal realm if you guys are here?" he asked, his curiosity piqued.

Clint leaned forward, his expression grave. "That might be the case, but inside those bodies were other demons that work with the one who sent us here."

Finn shuddered at the chilling thought. "Then, if that's the case, I will need both of your help to find Leo and help safeguard Rory's soul. We are pretty sure that the demon will not stop until he gets what he wants, whatever that may be."

Clint and Rhea exchanged a meaningful glance, a silent understanding passing between them. Finally, they nodded in unison. "I think it's time for us to get back what we lost and reconnect with our family,"

# 11

# Leo

Leo's eyes fluttered open to a dimly lit room, the ceiling above him a blur. His mind swirled with disorientation, and he could only surmise that he lay upon a bed. The last memory he could grasp was gripping Finn's hand and being hurled into the enigmatic Spirit Realm.

As the dizziness began to ebb, Leo's surroundings came into focus. The room appeared to be fashioned from rustic wood, and the bed cradling him proved unexpectedly comfortable. Soft beams of sunlight filtered through an open window, casting gentle rays upon him.

Leo tentatively probed his body for injuries, yet to his amazement, he felt perfectly whole. A strange sense of well-being washed over him. But there was no time to revel in it; he needed to find Finn urgently, for they were both stranded in this mystical realm.

Before he could muster the strength to sit up, the creaking of a door heralded an unexpected visitor. A man, clad in nothing but a simple loincloth, strolled into the room.

"Oh hey, sugarplum, you're awake," the man greeted Leo, approaching the bedside with an affable grin. "I'm Bliss, by the way. Do you want something to drink?"

Leo nodded, still baffled by his surroundings. Bliss extended his hand, and with a flick of his wrist, conjured a shimmering glass of an otherworldly beverage. Leo marveled at the sight, wondering if this was yet another facet of the Spirit Realm's peculiar magic. He accepted the glass, brought it to his lips, and took a sip. The elixir was like a symphony of flavors, and he felt his own dormant magic stirring within him, responding to the drink's enchantment. As he drained the glass, he returned it to Bliss, his gratitude evident.

"Thank you, I am Leo. Where am I?" Leo inquired as he cautiously attempted to rise.

"You're in my humble abode. I found you unconscious on the shore of the River of Spirits," Bliss replied, his voice a soothing melody.

Leo absorbed this information, gazing at the wooden ceiling in contemplation. "How about Finn? Have you seen him with me?"

Bliss shook his head, his demeanor shifting from easygoing to an unmistakable edge. "I'm sorry, sugar, but you came in as a single package."

Leo's resolve solidified. "I have to find Finn."

Bliss, however, seemed determined to dissuade him, his tone oozing sarcasm. "It can wait, you know. It's already dark out. What's so important about finding this Finn person anyway?"

Leo's eyes gleamed with urgency as he leaned forward. "A demon named Lyandros trapped my brother's soul in the Spirit Realm. We need to safeguard his soul before it's too late."

Bliss's sassy demeanor took a drastic turn. He clenched his fists and his voice dripped with venom. "Did you just say Lyandros? That motherfucker is still alive, huh?"

Leo grimly nodded. "Unfortunately, yes. He's still out there."

Bliss heaved a sigh, realizing the gravity of the situation. "Alright, sugar. Get some rest. We'll leave at first light."

Leo's brows arched in surprise, but before he could voice his questions, Bliss sauntered out of the room, leaving him to wonder about the enigmatic character who had seemingly come to his aid.

Leo settled back onto the comfortable bed, his mind racing with questions and fears. The only thing that matters to him at this point was finding Finn.

Leo woke up some time later. He sat up in bed feeling surprisingly refreshed. He blinked a few times, still adjusting to his new surroundings. As he looked around the room, his eyes landed on the bedside table, where a plate of delicious-looking food awaited him. His stomach grumbled in response, and he wasted no time in devouring the meal. Leo couldn't help but think that the food was better than anything he could have cooked himself.

Once he'd finished eating, Leo realized that he needed to freshen up. He scanned the room and noticed a door in the corner that seemed to lead to a bathroom. Bliss's house was more spacious than it appeared from the outside, which was a relief. Leo made his way to the bathroom, took a quick shower, and emerged feeling much more human.

With renewed energy, he set out to find Bliss. Leaving the room, he entered what appeared to be a cozy living room, with wooden interiors that matched the rustic vibe of the house. Bliss was nowhere in sight, and Leo didn't want to intrude on his host's privacy by snooping around. So, he decided to step outside to see if he could find him.

As Leo opened the door, he spotted Bliss approaching the house, carrying what looked like a bow in his hands. Bliss noticed him and waved, and Leo returned the greeting.

"Hey, sugar, how are you feeling?" Bliss asked as he drew nearer.

"I'm feeling better. Thanks for the food, by the way. It was fantastic. You really didn't have to do that," Leo replied with a grateful smile.

Bliss shrugged playfully. "Well, you can't have this kind of bod without eating only the best of foods." He spun around dramatically to emphasize his point, and Leo couldn't help but chuckle.

Leo raised an eyebrow, curiosity getting the better of him. "So, where did you disappear to?"

Bliss rolled his eyes, a mischievous glint in them. "I went to gather some supplies."

Leo looked around but couldn't see any bags or supplies nearby. "Where are they then?"

Bliss let out an exasperated sigh. "Magic, sugar. It's all about the magic."

Leo blinked in surprise. "Magic, huh?"

Bliss grinned. "Yep, magic."

Leo hesitated for a moment before asking, "Are you sure you want to come with me? It could be dangerous."

Bliss waved off his concern. "Of course, sugar. Lyandros and I have some unfinished business to settle. Plus, I can't resist a chance to show off my skills."

Leo nodded, feeling reassured. "Alright then. What about your house? Who's going to take care of it while you're gone?"

Bliss smirked and leaned in closer. "Don't you worry about that, darling. The house is warded. It's not going anywhere. Now, I just need to get ready, and we can hit the road."

Leo waited patiently as Bliss disappeared into the house. He didn't have to wait long before Bliss reemerged, dressed in what looked like a modern reinterpretation of Hercules. Leo couldn't help but laugh at the sight.

"Why are you laughing?" Bliss asked, raising an eyebrow.

Leo shook his head, still chuckling. "It's just... you look like a superhero from a cheesy action movie."

Bliss grinned, striking a pose. "Well, in that case, I'm ready to save the day."

Leo chuckled again and nodded towards the road. "Let's go, superhero."

Leo and Bliss continued their uncertain journey through an otherworldly realm, their steps echoing softly in the eerie silence. As minutes turned into what felt like hours, Bliss couldn't resist poking fun at their situation.

"Do you even know where we are going?" Bliss quirked a questioning brow at Leo, his sassy tone cutting through the tension.

Leo scratched the back of his neck, his uncertainty laid bare. "Not really. We didn't really expect to be separated when we got here."

Bliss rolled his eyes, his patience running thin. "Ugh, fine. Give me your hand."

Leo hesitated but reluctantly extended his right hand. "Why? What are you going to do?"

"Stop asking so many questions, sugar. Just do what I say." Bliss waved his hand forward, and Leo felt an electric charge as their fingers intertwined.

In that moment, Leo sensed an insurmountable power coursing through Bliss. It sent shivers down his spine. "What are you?" he couldn't help but ask.

With a smirk and a mischievous wink, Bliss replied, "Let's just say that I am your guardian angel." Leo's bewilderment grew as Bliss continued, "You're a necromancer, huh? Seems fitting in this realm and all that."

"You're insane, but in a good way," Leo remarked, and Bliss erupted into laughter, his mirth echoing through the ethereal landscape.

Their connection deepened as they ventured forward, Leo growing more at ease with Bliss's peculiar yet charming demeanor. "I've been told worse things. Now be quiet, I need to concentrate," Bliss ordered, and Leo obediently hushed.

As Bliss focused his mystical prowess, the world around them began to shift and warp. The colors bled into one another, and the ground beneath their feet seemed to ripple like water. Leo tried to call out

Finn's name, but his voice faded into the dissonant symphony of the shifting reality.

Leo was disoriented as he looked around his surroundings. The world had shifted and twisted, leaving him standing in the midst of a dense, otherworldly forest. The trees loomed tall and gnarled, their bark black as midnight. Eerie, bluish mist curled around the gnarled roots, and Leo's heart pounded in his chest as he realized he was no longer in the realm he knew.

Over in the distance, Leo spotted Finn, his friend and fellow adventurer, walking cautiously through the eerie woods. His silhouette was barely visible through the haunting haze.

"Finn!" Leo called out, but his voice seemed to vanish into the thick air.

Beside him, Bliss chuckled, a mischievous grin playing on his lips. "He can't hear you, sugar. We're in a different plane now."

Leo clenched his fist in frustration, his mind racing with concern for Finn. He couldn't just stand here while his friend wandered through this strange and unsettling forest.

Bliss, with his inscrutable power, placed a reassuring hand on Leo's shoulder. "Don't worry, we'll get to him. But we need to be careful. There's more going on here than meets the eye."

Leo's eyes darted around, taking in the bizarre surroundings. The very air seemed to hum with a malevolent energy.

Finn wasn't alone. Leo could make out the shadowy forms of two others accompanying him, their faces obscured by the swirling mist.

"Who are those people with Finn?" Leo asked, his voice filled with trepidation.

Bliss smirked, his tone dripping with sass. "Well, darlin', the way this little power of mine works, it only shows us who we desire."

Leo nodded, absorbing the information. He couldn't make out the identities of the two shadowy figures, but if they were here with Finn, they had to be allies.

"Tell me, Bliss," Leo began, "do you recognize this place? Where are we?"

Bliss looked around, his eyes narrowing as he took in the eerie surroundings. "We're in the Forest of the Damned, sugar. It's a lovely little vacation spot for restless spirits and lost souls. I thought you would have known that since you're a necromancer."

Leo shivered, the name of the place sending a chill down his spine. "We need to find Finn quickly, then. If this place is as dangerous as it sounds…"

Bliss waved his hand once more. This time, the magic unfolded with an epic visual spectacle. The air crackled with energy as they stepped onto a shifting path of mist and shadows. Trees with bark like obsidian shot up around them, their leaves whispering eerie secrets. Leo marveled at the breathtaking and intimidating transformation of their surroundings.

The duo continued their journey, and Bliss couldn't resist another quip. "So, ever done something like this before? Traveling through dimensions to rescue your friend from restless spirits and all?"

"Yeah, but the only other realm I have been to other than the mortal realm is this one. Though, you're making this quite an adventure."

Bliss grinned, his confidence unwavering. "Darling, adventure is my middle name."

As Leo and Bliss ventured deeper into the otherworldly forest, the air grew thick with an eerie mist, and the trees loomed overhead like ancient sentinels of the spirit realm. Leo couldn't shake the curiosity about his unexpected ally, the sassy guardian angel, Bliss. They had a friend to rescue and a realm of restless spirits to navigate, and for now, Bliss seemed like the perfect companion.

"How long have you been living here? I know that you're not just an ordinary spirit," Leo inquired, his voice a mix of wonder and uncertainty.

Bliss flashed a mischievous smirk, his eyes dancing with an other-worldly light. "If I tell you, I'll have to kill you," he quipped, his words dripping with sarcasm. "And I've been here for a long while. I don't know how to really tell you because time here moves differently than in the mortal realm."

Leo nodded in understanding. The peculiar flow of time in the spirit realm was something he had heard of before, but experiencing it firsthand was another matter entirely. With a thoughtful expression, he decided to probe further. "So is there a reason why you're here?"

Bliss came to a sudden halt, and Leo nearly bumped into him. The playful smile that had adorned Bliss's face moments ago now turned into a thin, enigmatic line. Leo couldn't help but wonder if he had crossed a line with his question.

"Lyandros took someone who's very dear to me," Bliss confessed with a heavy sigh, his voice carrying the weight of old wounds. "I've been looking for the bastard for a long time. I've been informed that he was residing here, and all of my attempts to find him didn't work. The fucker was elusive, but we may now have a way to track him down."

Leo's temper flared at the mention of his brother being used as bait for Bliss's revenge. He clenched his fists, struggling to control his anger. "You're telling me that you're going to use my brother just so you can get revenge?"

Bliss turned to face Leo, his eyes locking onto Leo's with an intensity that sent a shiver down his spine. The guardian angel's smirk returned, more devilish than ever. "Oh, calm your dick down, sugar," he retorted, his tone unapologetic. "We'll get your brother in time. Just let me have my way with that Demon."

Leo couldn't contain his frustration, his voice trembling with anger. "If something happens to my brother, you're going to regret coming along with me," he growled.

Bliss simply patted Leo's head as if he were a child throwing a tantrum. "I'd like to see you try, sugar," he taunted, his confidence unshaken. "Now come on, we have a couple of ways to go."

## 12

## Finn

Finn strolled alongside Clint and Rhea, their voices floating on the gentle breeze like leaves on a lazy river. They had been navigating the enigmatic terrain of the Spirit Realm for what felt like hours, but time was a slippery concept here.

"Do you think that they'll ever forgive us?" Rhea's voice carried a hint of vulnerability, like a fragile wisp of cloud in a clear sky.

Finn, with his characteristic smile and a nod, didn't hesitate to respond. "I am sure that they would understand. I may not have known them long, but from what I can tell, if given the time, they would eventually give you their forgiveness."

Rhea's eyes brightened with a glimmer of hope as she considered Finn's words. "You think so?"

"Yeah, whatever the you in the mortal realm did wasn't your fault," Finn assured her with a soft-spoken sincerity. "Don't worry, I got your back."

Rhea, touched by Finn's support, reached out and gently squeezed his hand. "Leo is so lucky to have you as a friend."

Finn's heart skipped a beat at the mention of Leo, the man who occupied his thoughts like the sun illuminating his every day. "I am very lucky to have him, too."

As they continued their journey through the Spirit Realm, Finn couldn't help but feel the weight of his unspoken emotions. He missed Leo profoundly, and with every step, he promised himself that when they escaped this peculiar realm, he would finally muster the courage to ask Leo out on a date. The only thing that held him back was his relentless doubt, the nagging feeling that he wasn't worthy of Leo's affections.

The trio wandered along a trail that traced the path of a meandering river. The air grew thicker with an unspoken tension, like a storm brewing on the horizon. Clint had mentioned earlier that this place was the infamous Forest of the Damned, renowned for its danger even in the Spirit Realm.

Clint, with a skeptical squint, couldn't help but voice his concerns. "You know, Finn, they say the Forest of the Damned is a real hotbed of trouble."

Rhea nodded, her expression mirroring Clint's skepticism. "Yeah, spirits who come here are never the same. And not in a good way."

Finn scratched his head, a thoughtful grin on his face. "Oh, come on now, folks. What's the worst that can happen in a place called the Forest of the Damned?"

Clint exchanged an incredulous glance with Rhea. "Well, let's see," he began with mock seriousness, "there's the tree that tells you jokes so bad, your ears bleed."

Rhea chimed in, her tone equally deadpan. "And the river that turns your clothes into itchy wool sweaters."

Finn's laughter echoed through the eerie woods. "You two are really painting a grim picture here! But seriously, what are the actual dangers we should be on the lookout for?"

Clint leaned in, his voice hushed as if sharing a treacherous secret. "Legend has it that if you step on a crack in the path, you'll be followed by an invisible choir that sings off-key show tunes all day long."

Rhea nodded gravely. "And don't even get me started on the mischievous squirrels. They'll steal your shoelaces and leave you hopping around like a demented bunny."

Finn burst into laughter again, unable to contain himself. "You two are a riot! But really, what's the scoop on this place?"

Clint and Rhea exchanged amused glances, then turned their attention back to Finn. "Okay, okay," Clint relented, "enough with the jokes. In all seriousness, this forest is said to be a testing ground for spirits. It's filled with illusions, traps, and challenges that can mess with your mind. If you're not careful, you can lose yourself in here."

Rhea nodded in agreement. "Exactly. The Forest of the Damned preys on your fears and insecurities. It shows you what you dread the most, and if you let it, it can break you."

Finn's smile faded as he absorbed their words. "So, it's like a haunted house but on a grand scale?"

Clint shrugged. "You could say that, but the spirits here are not exactly looking to give you a good scare for Halloween. They're testing your mettle, trying to see if you're worthy of whatever it is they guard."

As they continued down the winding path, the forest seemed to grow denser, and a chill crept into the air. Finn shivered and muttered, "Well, I hope they're in the mood for a friendly chat because we're just passing through."

Finn's voice barely escaped his lips before the world around him froze. He blinked, bewildered, finding himself encircled within an intricate faerie ring. Panic welled up, but he managed to mutter a colorful expletive under his breath.

"All of you stand behind me," he commanded, his voice tinged with urgency. "Poofy, be on guard."

Their magical abilities seemed to wither within the confines of the ring. It was as if the very air conspired against them. Finn's eyes darted about, searching for the source of the unnatural energy that had ensnared them. Then, amidst the charged atmosphere, he heard the unmistakable sound of giggling.

"Show yourselves. I can hear you," Finn called out, his tone laced with both curiosity and caution.

The giggles swelled in response, growing louder, and Finn knew that whatever creatures were responsible for this enchantment were drawing near. Desperation clawed at him as he attempted to tap into his well of magic, but it remained stubbornly silent.

And then, like a playful breeze, pixies began to materialize before him. They were small, not more than a hand's width, and their ethereal forms danced with vibrant colors that defied the imagination.

Finn blinked in amazement at the sight of them. "Well, I'll be damned," he muttered, the words slipping out despite his astonishment. He'd always thought that pixies were denizens of the Fae Realm, living harmoniously with the faeries. Yet here they were, vivid and lively, in the spirit realm.

Clearing his throat, Finn addressed the pixies. "So, what's the deal here? Why've you got us trapped?"

The pixies exchanged mischievous glances, their tiny voices chiming like wind chimes. "We can't let you go," one of them sang, their words carrying an eerie, otherworldly quality.

Finn arched an eyebrow. "And why's that?"

Their response was another bout of giggles. "Our king is on his way."

Finn sighed, folding his arms. "Well, if your king's anything like you lot, I reckon we're in for a right laugh."

As if on cue, the faint echo of footsteps reached Finn's ears. He squinted toward the sound's origin and watched as a figure emerged from the luminous haze. The newcomer was of the same height as Finn, with sharply pointed ears and gossamer wings that emitted a constant flurry of pixie dust, coating everything in a shimmering veil.

Finn couldn't help but wonder if all the royal bloodlines of pixies were human-sized, but he wisely refrained from voicing that curiosity.

Poofy, on the other hand, reacted quite differently. The small, fluffy creature gave a delighted squeak and bounded toward the approaching king.

The king's lips curved into a warm smile as he spotted Poofy. "Ah, Dragor," he said, his voice as melodious as a woodland brook. "It's been too long, my friend."

Finn's eyebrows shot up. "Dragor? Seriously? That's the name you went with?"

The king turned his gaze toward Finn, his expression curious. It was then that Finn decided to take a stand.

"Poofy," he said with an air of authority, "is a much better name, don't you think?"

Poofy nodded emphatically, as though understanding every word.

The king blinked at Finn, an amused glimmer in his eyes. Clearly, he hadn't anticipated a debate over the name of his loyal companion.

As the surreal encounter continued, Finn couldn't help but marvel at the whimsicality of it all. Here he was, trapped in a faerie ring, negotiating the name of a fluffy, magical creature with a pixie king. The magic around him crackled and shimmered, a visual symphony of colors and wonder that defied explanation.

The king, with a regal sweep of his wings, spoke. "Very well, Finn. Poofy it is."

Finn grinned, feeling a strange sense of accomplishment. "Excellent choice."

The king's piercing gaze settled on Finn for what felt like an eternity. He extended a royal hand, his lips curving into a warm smile. "King Demetrius Ravenspar, and you are?"

Finn accepted the proffered hand, his grip firm. "Doctor Finn Sloane. So are you going to let us out of this ring?"

A mischievous glint sparkled in Demetrius's eyes. "Dragor, I mean Poofy here seemed to like you, so consider yourself lucky. This little baby gryphon doesn't like anyone easily." The king then turned to the pixies. "Lela, tell the guards to stand back. We'll be with them soon."

With a nod, the pixies scurried away, leaving Finn, Clint, and Rhea. Finn shot a puzzled look at Leo's parents, who stared back at him as if they had just seen a ghost.

"Do you know this guy?" Finn inquired, and they both simply nodded. His attention returned to King Demetrius, whose smile seemed eternally affixed, irritating Finn to no end.

Demetrius held out his hand, the ring's power bending to his will. Slowly, Finn could feel his own magic returning, and he breathed a sigh of relief. "Thank you. Can we get out of the ring?" he implored.

Demetrius chuckled softly. "Should be able to. The magic that's been preventing you from stepping out is now gone. Go on, try it."

Obeying the king, they stepped tentatively toward the edge of the ring. The invisible barrier had felt suffocating, but as they crossed it, they could finally breathe freely. Finn approached King Demetrius, who was still grinning. Driven by a surge of irritation, he threw a punch at the king's face.

To his astonishment, the punch had an unforeseen effect. Pain coursed through his hand as if he had just struck a brick wall. Demetrius continued to laugh uproariously, seemingly unaffected by the half-hearted attack.

"And what did we learn?" Demetrius asked between fits of laughter.

"That you're a dick who likes to trap unsuspecting people in a faerie ring!" Finn retorted, vexation evident in his tone.

Demetrius cackled loudly, his laughter echoing through the clearing. Finn couldn't help but marvel at how a king could laugh so boisterously.

"Come on, we were camping out here and felt a presence around us. You can't blame us for being too careful," Demetrius explained, still grinning.

"Why are you camping out here?" Finn asked, finally helping Clint and Rhea exit the ring.

"Let's get out of here so we can walk and talk to our camp. Shall we?" Demetrius offered.

Finn glanced at Leo's parents, concern in his eyes. "Are you guys able to walk further?"

Rhea nodded with a reassuring smile. "Yes, don't mind us."

Finn turned back to Demetrius. "Where is this camp of yours?"

With a flourish of his hand, Demetrius led the way. "This way."

As they followed the king through the enchanted forest, a playful banter filled the air. Finn couldn't help but notice the peculiar beauty of the place. Trees whispered secrets, flowers emitted radiant glows, and streams sparkled with an otherworldly light.

Finn walked alongside King Demetrius, his hand still throbbing from the ill-fated punch, but the pain was slowly giving way to a dull ache. The forest around them was both eerie and enchanting, with gnarled trees that seemed to whisper secrets to the wind. Finn couldn't help but be captivated by the surreal beauty of the Forest of the Damned.

"So, King Demetrius," Finn began, trying to make the best of the situation, "what brings you and your army to this forsaken place?"

King Demetrius smiled and adjusted the ornate crown on his head. "We received a report of a demon sighting around the Corrupted Sea. Our spies claimed to have seen a soul being trapped there."

Rhea gasped, her voice barely a whisper. "Rory..."

Finn exchanged a knowing look with her. It seemed their quests had converged, and Rory's predicament might be tied to the demon they sought.

Demetrius looked genuinely concerned. "Do you know the identity of the trapped soul?"

Finn nodded. "We were actually on a mission to find this demon and rescue the soul. It could very well be Rory."

Demetrius's eyes widened in understanding. "I see. That explains your presence in this cursed forest."

The group continued to follow Demetrius deeper into the Forest of the Damned, the trees growing denser, their branches intertwined like gnarled fingers reaching out for the heavens. The air was thick with a sense of foreboding, and the occasional eerie calls of unseen creatures sent shivers down Finn's spine.

They walked in silence for a while, the only sound the rustling of leaves and the hushed whisper of the wind. Rhea and Clint exchanged glances, their expressions a mix of excitement and concern.

Finally, they reached the campsite, hidden in a small clearing that seemed to have miraculously escaped the forest's curse. Tents were pitched, a fire crackled merrily, and soldiers were going about their duties. The entire setup was as unconventional as the king himself.

Finn marveled at the sight. "I have to say, this is not what I expected from a royal camp."

Demetrius chuckled, his laughter rich and hearty. "Well, we believe in making the best of a bad situation. And, trust me, this forest can be quite unforgiving."

As they settled around the campfire, the group shared tales and laughter, the surreal and enchanted forest becoming a backdrop to their conversation. The tension from earlier had all but dissipated, replaced by a sense of camaraderie.

Finn couldn't help but admire King Demetrius's ability to lighten the mood, especially given the grim circumstances. The king regaled them with stories of his past adventures, interjecting with dramatic gestures and comical expressions that had everyone in stitches.

Rhea, too, found herself laughing freely, momentarily forgetting her worries about Rory. Clint, usually reserved, joined in with a smile that warmed Finn's heart.

With the flicker of the campfire casting dancing shadows and the forest providing a haunting yet strangely beautiful ambiance, Finn couldn't deny the magic of the moment. He felt a renewed sense of hope that they might just succeed in their mission to rescue Rory and confront the demon.

As the night grew darker, King Demetrius leaned in closer, his voice hushed. "Now, let's talk about your quest and how we can join forces to rescue your friend. I have resources and knowledge that may prove invaluable."

Finn nodded, grateful for the unexpected turn of events. In the midst of the Forest of the Damned, beneath the starlit canopy and surrounded by newfound allies, their shared mission began to take on a more hopeful and epic quality.

The fire crackled, casting its glow on their faces, as they plotted their course of action, united by a common goal and a touch of the fantastical in this mystic forest.

As the night wore on, and the others began to make their way to their respective quarters, Finn and Leo's parents, being the elder couple, were given the first pick of the cots. They exchanged tired smiles and grateful nods with their fellow campers before shuffling off towards their sleeping arrangements. It was a gentle, almost choreographed exit from the campfire circle.

Finn, however, was not so eager to retreat to the comfort of his cot just yet. He was the kind of guy who found solace in the crackling flames and the night's cool embrace. As the others vanished into their tents, he remained perched on a weathered log, one hand propped on his knee, the other holding a tin cup of something that sparkled in the firelight.

Finn took a deep sip, and the warmth spread through him like a supernova, sending ripples of delight down to his very toes. He let out a low whistle, leaned back, and gazed into the roaring campfire, which danced with fervor, casting flickering shadows across the campsite.

While the campfire crackled and sent its flickering tendrils of light dancing into the night, Finn sat alone, gazing into the heart of the fire. The flames wove a tapestry of warmth and memories. It was there, amidst the comforting embrace of the fire's glow, that Finn's thoughts drifted to a chapter of his past, a painful memory etched into his heart.

Finn recalled the first time he met Jonathan, a man whose presence had once shone like the campfire, bright and promising. They had crossed paths at a fundraising event, a swirl of voices and clinking glasses, but amidst the chaos, Jonathan's eyes had found Finn, and something in them had ignited.

"Hey there," Jonathan's voice, smooth and inviting, had been the first notes of their story. Finn remembered the thrill in his chest when he turned to meet those green eyes, twinkling with curiosity.

The memory unveiled itself further. "I'm Finn," he had introduced himself.

"Jonathan," the man replied, offering his hand. "I couldn't help but notice you from across the room."

As Finn continued to watch the fire, he couldn't help but let the weight of that memory press down on him. The recollection of their first meeting was a bitter reminder of the beauty they had once shared.

"Jonathan was great," Finn mumbled to the flames. "He was the light in my life."

In the memory, the two had shared countless laughs, explored the city together, and celebrated each other's victories. Life with Jonathan had been a whirlwind of joy and companionship, and Finn had felt like he was living in a fairy tale.

"We were happy," Finn sighed, the warmth of the campfire mirroring the warmth of his recollections.

But as the memory unfolded, a shadow crept over the flames of his thoughts. Finn remembered how he had hidden his magic from

Jonathan, concealed it like a deep secret, fearing the rejection and disdain he knew would come. Jonathan had made it clear from the beginning that he had no tolerance for supernaturals or magic users. It was a truth Finn had chosen to ignore in the name of love.

"Finn," Jonathan had once said, his tone heavy with disapproval, "I can't stand people who mess with that supernatural crap. It's all nonsense, and it just causes trouble."

And yet, despite the growing chasm of secrets between them, Finn had continued to love Jonathan, believing he could change his mind, bridge the divide, and make Jonathan see beyond the magic. The memory portrayed Finn as an optimist in the face of inevitable heartache.

"We were in love, and I thought love could conquer anything," Finn murmured, his voice heavy with the weight of his memories.

But the memory didn't end there. It continued to unravel, each scene drawing Finn deeper into the abyss of his past. The campfire illuminated the scenes as if they were playing out before him.

Then, in a moment that still sent shivers down Finn's spine, he remembered the day someone had revealed his secret to Jonathan. He recalled the look on Jonathan's face, contorted with shock and betrayal, as the truth of Finn's magic came to light.

"You lied to me!" Jonathan's voice echoed in the memory. "All this time, you hid this from me? You're one of them!"

Finn's heart ached as he remembered the pain in Jonathan's voice, the raw hurt that had torn their love apart. Jonathan's newfound knowledge had twisted his affection into something unrecognizable. The love that had once flowed freely had withered, replaced by resentment and anger.

"You don't know what you're talking about," Finn had tried to reason, desperation creeping into his voice. But the argument had escalated, accusations flying like sparks from a fire.

Then, in the memory's darkest chapter, Jonathan had crossed a line that Finn had never thought possible. The campfire's flames mirrored the flames of rage that had consumed Jonathan, who had gone so far as to hire someone to harm Finn, to snuff out the light that had once brightened his world.

As the memory reached its devastating climax, Finn remembered the searing pain, both physical and emotional, that had coursed through him. He had awoken in a sterile hospital room, the antiseptic scent of the place mingling with the acrid taste of betrayal.

"I couldn't believe he had done it," Finn whispered, his voice trembling with the weight of that fateful night. "He tried to end me."

The memory had left him broken and wounded, physically and emotionally, the flames of his past still licking at his soul. Finn's parents had been there, their tears mirroring the shimmering campfire's glow, as they had nursed him back to health, both in body and spirit.

Finn continued to stare into the fire, tears glistening in his eyes, knowing that the scars from that memory would never fade. The campfire whispered its warmth, a silent companion to his painful recollections, as he sat alone in the quiet night, lost in a world of love lost and a heart forever scarred.

"He sounds like someone not worthy of your love then," a voice, gentle and understanding, broke through the stillness. Finn turned to find King Demetrius standing by the tree, his gaze fixed on him.

Finn's surprise was evident in his eyes as he asked, "How long have you been there?"

King Demetrius wore a soft, remorseful smile. "Been here a while. I was going to ask if you wanted to take a walk but didn't want to disturb you. I apologize, I didn't mean to eavesdrop."

Finn nodded, feeling the weight of his past bearing down on him. "It's okay. It's been years since it happened."

Demetrius stepped closer, his eyes reflecting empathy. "Is it okay if I sit here?"

Finn shifted to make room for the king, a silent invitation to share the shade and his burden. "Sure, go ahead."

Demetrius took a seat beside him and, with the air of someone who had faced similar pain, he began to speak. "Before I met my beloved, I was engaged to another. I don't know if you know anything about the cultures of pixies, but we tend to get engaged by those our parents wanted us to marry."

Finn listened, his eyes attentive, giving Demetrius his full focus. "Then what happened?"

Demetrius exhaled deeply, as if exhaling the ghosts of the past. "Then I met my Rion. You see, Finn, my parents didn't like the idea of me marrying another man, as we wouldn't produce an heir. Rion is a human, which also disappointed my parents."

Finn couldn't help but interject, his curiosity getting the best of him. "Aren't you worried that his lifespan is not as long as yours?"

A hint of a playful smile graced Demetrius's lips. "Who's telling the story here?" They both chuckled, and Demetrius continued, "I met him in the mortal realm while I was on a mission, and when I saw him, it was over. We got to talking and went out on a few dates. At first, I was hesitant to tell him my true nature, but I had to tell him. In the beginning, I thought that he would resent me, but he proved me wrong. From that point on, our love blossomed, and I brought him to our palace."

Finn was drawn into the story, his own pain momentarily pushed aside. "What happened then?"

Demetrius's eyes glistened with the memories of a love story forged in defiance of tradition. "As soon as we got out of the portal, we were attacked. We survived, but Rion barely did. I had to bind our souls together for him to live, which, in turn, changed his lifespan. Later on, I found out that Remua, my supposed partner, ordered the attack after she found out about us. I was about to end it as soon as I introduced Rion to my parents."

Curiosity piqued once more, Finn inquired, "What happened to Remua?"

Demetrius's expression darkened briefly. "She was sentenced to death, and my parents apologized to me for not listening to what I needed. We got married not long after that."

Finn couldn't help but feel a glimmer of hope as he asked, "Is Rion here with you?"

Demetrius's face lit up with affection. "Yes, he's at home with our son. We managed to find a way to have children, though that's a story for another day."

Finn looked at Demetrius with gratitude shining in his eyes. "Thank you for telling me the story."

Demetrius stood, and as he left, he gave Finn's shoulder a reassuring squeeze. "You're welcome. Just remember that someone will come for you, Finn."

Finn contemplated the words of the king. Demetrius's tale had given him a newfound perspective on love and the complexities of relationships. He thought of Leo, his own feelings, and wondered if Leo was the one meant for him. Finn couldn't wait to find out, and for the first time in a long while, a glimmer of hope ignited in his heart.

# 13

## Leo

Leo's labored breaths echoed in the stillness of the mountain as he and Bliss continued their ascent. The sun's relentless rays bore down upon them, turning Leo's face a rosy shade of exhaustion. Bliss, on the other hand, moved with an effortless grace.

"Why are we hiking up a mountain again? You said the forest was nearby," Leo panted, his words barely finding the strength to escape his parched lips.

"Sugar, I never said that. Besides, we're incredibly close now," Bliss replied, a mischievous smile playing on his lips.

Leo wiped the sweat from his brow and managed a weak chuckle, "You said that a while ago, and I'm starting to think you're taking me out here to murder me."

Bliss chuckled in response, the sound as melodious as it was unnerving, "If I was, then you'd have been dead before we even started."

A bead of sweat trickled down Leo's temple as he pushed on, determined to uncover the secrets of this mysterious forest. "How far do we still have to go?" he sighed, coming to a halt.

"Just a couple more," Bliss assured him, his voice holding a note of unwavering determination.

Leo was about to retort when Bliss abruptly stopped in his tracks. "What's going on?" Leo asked, his voice trembling with a mixture of fear and fatigue.

"I feel something. Are you still good to fight over there?" Bliss said, his eyes fixed on a point in the distance.

"Yeah, I can still fight," Leo replied, reaching deep into the well of magic within him, feeling it respond with a gentle hum.

"I know you're here. I can feel you, Wendigo," Bliss growled, his stance shifting into a battle-ready position.

Leo's eyes widened in alarm. "You couldn't have told me that sooner, Bliss? A fucking Wendigo?"

Bliss shot him a withering look, his voice dripping with sarcasm, "Well, I would have thought that you noticed since, I don't know, you're a fucking necromancer!"

Leo didn't want to admit it but Bliss was right. He was a fucking necromancer and he should have sensed the vile creatures.

The very trees surrounding them seemed to wither and decay, their leaves turning to ash, and their branches curling into grotesque shapes.

The Wendigo emerged from the shadows, its form shifting and twisting with an otherworldly grace. It stood tall, its emaciated body covered in mottled, ashen skin. Its eyes, a malevolent shade of crimson, bore into Leo's soul, sending shivers down his spine.

Bliss swiftly notched an arrow in his bow, and it began to glow with a radiant golden light. "Leo, you need to conjure a weapon. Do it now!"

Leo's heart raced as he stammered, "I'm not that strong, Bliss. I can't conjure my own weapon."

Bliss shot him a knowing look, his eyes locked onto Leo's, "You can, Leo. I sense an insurmountable amount of death magic within you. Use it to conjure your own weapon."

Nodding with determination, Leo closed his eyes and reached deep into his core. He visualized the darkness within him, the well of death magic that pulsed with untapped potential. With every ounce of willpower, he drew it forth.

In a surge of power, Leo conjured a sword from the depths of his being. It materialized in his hand, a shimmering blade swirling with dark mist. He could feel the weight of the weapon in his grip, the surge of energy coursing through him.

Bliss shot him an approving grin, his lips curling with sassy confidence. "Good job, sugar. Now, let's show this Wendigo what we're made of!"

As Bliss and Leo faced off against the Wendigo, the tension in the air was palpable. The supernatural showdown had begun, and Leo could feel the weight of his newfound abilities. With every swing of his conjured sword, the dark mist trailed behind, leaving a haunting and ethereal mark on the world.

Bliss moved with uncanny grace, his enchanted arrows finding their mark with deadly accuracy. He let out a low whistle as he took aim and fired, a mischievous gleam in his eye. "Right in the kisser, big guy!" The arrow sailed through the air, trailing a golden shimmer, before striking the Wendigo in the face. The beast howled in agony as the golden light of Bliss's arrows pierced its ashen flesh.

Leo's sword cut through the air like a shadowy specter, leaving a trail of darkness in its wake. He grinned back at Bliss. "This is some freaky sword action, ain't it?"

Bliss chuckled, his voice dripping with sarcasm. "You have a way with words, Leo."

The battle raged on, a dance of life and death, magic and malevolence. Leo's heart pounded in his chest as he fought alongside Bliss, the two of them a formidable force against the Wendigo's relentless onslaught.

Through it all, the mountain seemed to hold its breath, and the very earth quivered with the power of their magic. The Wendigo snarled and swiped its razor-sharp claws at them, but Bliss nimbly dodged and taunted the creature. "Come on, big and ugly, you'll have to do better than that!"

Leo lunged forward, his sword slicing through the air. The dark mist clung to the blade as it cut into the Wendigo's leg, eliciting a guttural growl from the beast. "How about you pick on someone your own size?"

Bliss loosed another arrow, this one glowing with an ethereal fire. "Don't you know it's rude to crash a party, Wendigo?"

The arrow struck the creature's chest, and it stumbled back, its movements becoming sluggish. Leo seized the opportunity, swinging his sword with all his might. The blade cut through the Wendigo's flesh, sending a spray of dark mist into the air.

The Wendigo howled in agony, its once fierce eyes now filled with fear. Bliss's eyes twinkled with mischief. "Feeling a bit frosty there, buddy?"

Leo didn't miss a beat. "Guess the heat's too much for you!"

Their banter was relentless, and their attacks even more so. Leo's sword slashed through the air, while Bliss's arrows rained down like a celestial storm. The Wendigo fought back, but it was clear that it was no match for this dynamic duo.

With a final, powerful swing of his sword, Leo struck the decisive blow. The dark mist swirled around the Wendigo as it let out a deafening howl. Bliss couldn't resist a parting shot. "Better luck next time, frosty!"

The Wendigo crumbled to the ground, defeated and dissipating into a cold breeze. Leo and Bliss stood triumphant, chests heaving with exertion. The mountain, having held its breath, seemed to sigh in relief, and the earth stilled.

Bliss grinned at Leo, his sassy tone not missing a beat. "Not bad for a newbie, sugar."

Leo couldn't help but smile, the rush of the battle still coursing through his veins.

Bliss and Leo lowered their weapons, their eyes fixed on the towering Wendigo before them. Its ghastly form loomed in the dim, eerie light of the forest of the damned. The air was thick with an unsettling wrongness, and it sent shivers down their spines.

"What do you think brought it here?" Leo inquired, his voice barely above a whisper.

Bliss, with a sardonic smirk, replied, "Lyandros knows we're here. And if this Wendigo attacked us, I'm pretty damn sure something similar happened to your friend. We gotta hurry." Leo nodded in agreement, the urgency of the situation pressing upon them. They needed to reach Finn and ensure his safety, no matter what.

Bliss, undaunted by the ominous creature, crouched down to examine something near the Wendigo's decaying corpse. In his hand, he held a pulsating red crystal, its glow fading as they watched.

"What is that?" Leo asked, genuine curiosity etching his features.

"A Blood Crystal," Bliss answered, his voice hushed. "It seems like Lyandros is not working alone." He carefully wrapped the Blood Crystal and tucked it into his bag. "Let's go. We're close, I can feel it."

As they descended further, reaching the depths of the forest of the damned, the atmosphere took a sinister turn. The spirits that resided in this wretched place were restless, and the very air seemed to resist their intrusion.

Bliss broke the heavy silence. "Tell me about Finn. What's he like?"

Leo's eyes lit up with warmth as he began to talk about his friend. "Finn... he's wonderful, you know? The kindest person I've ever met. Always helping others, never asking for anything in return." He shared stories of their adventures and the countless times Finn had stood by his side, a steadfast companion.

Bliss chuckled at Leo's heartfelt words, breaking the tension that hung in the air. "Seems like you've got quite the soft spot for him, huh?"

Leo grinned, his heartfelt reply filled with affection. "You have no idea. He's more than a friend to me."

Their laughter resonated through the eerie forest, a brief but welcome respite from the ominous surroundings. Leo realized that, despite the dire circumstances, he was starting to appreciate Bliss's company more and more.

As they continued deeper into the forest, Leo unwittingly stepped on something solid. He glanced down to discover a familiar pin half-buried in the decaying leaves and soil.

Bliss, noticing Leo's find, asked, "Do you know whose pin that is?"

Leo nodded, his voice trembling with a mixture of excitement and concern. "It's from Finn."

Without hesitation, Leo sprinted forward, his heart pounding with a singular purpose. Bliss called out to him to wait, but all Leo could think of was reuniting with Finn.

In the depths of the forest, Leo came to a sudden halt at an intersection, his heart pounding in his chest, consumed by anxiety. He clutched a small rainbow pin in his trembling hand, its significance heavy on his mind. Bliss, his companion, eventually caught up to him, his presence announced by a low, growling voice.

"What the heck do you think you're doing?" Bliss's words were laced with irritation.

Leo's voice was strained with worry as he responded, "Finn never takes this pin off his person." He met Bliss's eyes, desperation etched across his face.

Bliss took a deep breath, attempting to quell Leo's rising panic. "Will you calm down? We won't find him any faster if you keep acting like this."

Leo's brows knitted, but his grip on the pin loosened slightly. "You don't understand, Bliss. If something happens to Finn…"

Before he could finish, emotion overcame him, choking his words.

The fear for his friend was becoming unbearable.

"Trust me, I understand, Leo. Can I have a look at the pin?" Bliss asked, his tone softening.

Leo studied the rainbow pin for a moment, his fingers caressing it as though it held the key to Finn's safety. Finally, he handed it over to Bliss.

"What are you going to do with it?" Leo asked, still anxious but willing to consider any hope of finding Finn.

Bliss held the pin delicately, his fingers brushing over the small, colorful curves. "I will try and sense his magical signature from this and use it to track him down," he explained, determination in his eyes.

Leo watched with bated breath as Bliss began to work his magic. Bliss's hand started to glow with a bright yellow light, and a feeling of raw power emanated from it, causing Leo's eyes to widen in awe. The glow extended to the pin, causing it to levitate in mid-air.

With a voice barely above a whisper, Bliss recited an incantation, a cryptic string of words that felt as ancient as the forest itself. Then, with a swift, precise motion, Bliss threw the pin into the air. Panic surged through Leo; he feared it might shatter into pieces.

However, his concerns were unfounded. The pin exploded with a dazzling burst of multicolored light, rays scattering in every direction like a fireworks display. Bliss, unruffled by the spectacle, began to manipulate the radiant beams.

The rays, once chaotic and disordered, started to converge, fusing together as one. Leo couldn't tear his eyes away from the mesmerizing spectacle; it was as though Bliss was orchestrating a celestial ballet.

Bliss then extended his hand forward, and the concentrated ray of light obeyed, forming a luminous path that unfurled before them, twisting and winding as if it had a mind of its own. It was a surreal sight, the kind of magic that legends were made of.

Bliss, his voice steady and his confidence unwavering, raised his hand higher, and the pin, encased within the radiant path, slowly descended into his open palm. He held it there for a moment, his gaze locked on Leo's, a small but reassuring smile tugging at the corner of his lips.

Leo accepted the pin, his fingers trembling, and examined it closely. It remained unscathed, not a single scratch or dent to mar its vibrant surface.

Bliss chuckled softly, a hint of amusement in his eyes. "Don't worry, it's not damaged," he reassured Leo.

Leo couldn't help but be overcome with curiosity. "What did you just do?" he asked, his voice filled with a mixture of awe and confusion.

Bliss, still grinning, responded, "Sometimes, Leo, it's best not to ask too many questions. Just follow the light, and everything will be fine." He laughed.

Leo nodded, deciding not to pry any further, and gazed at the path of light Bliss had created. It stretched out before them, a brilliant trail leading the way. He felt a sense of hope and determination wash over him as they embarked on their journey to find Finn in this maze of a forest.

The forest was dark and eerie, and Leo felt a shiver crawl up his spine as he and Bliss followed the glowing trail of magic. It led them to what appeared to be a faerie ring, a perfect circle of toadstools nestled in the heart of the shadowy woods. The radiant path abruptly halted there, leaving Leo baffled.

"Why did the trail stop?" Leo inquired, glancing around at the mysterious surroundings.

Bliss knelt down beside the faerie ring, his brows furrowing. "It means that his magic was trapped here temporarily," he explained, his voice laced with concern. He inspected the circle closely, his eyes narrowing as he took in the details. "This faerie ring looks like it was used recently, and I'm not sensing any wards on it. But I can see footprints heading north from here. I'm willing to bet that he was taken somewhere."

Leo nodded, his anxiety building. "Who do you think took Finn?"

Bliss let out a disgruntled sigh. "If I had to guess, the only one I know who uses faerie rings like this is an annoying and insatiable king."

Confusion flashed across Leo's face. "Is Finn going to be safe from this king?"

Bliss grumbled, his irritation evident. "Probably. If he doesn't kill him with his smugness."

They set off, following the footprints that meandered northward. Leo couldn't help but notice the peculiar beauty that still lingered in the Forest of the Damned. He turned to Bliss and spoke in awe, "This place is beautiful."

Bliss cast a quick glance at Leo, offering a rare moment of sincerity. "The forest used to be one of the most sought-after areas in the spirit realm because of its beauty. But when the restless spirits claimed it as their own, it started getting corrupted. Yet, you can still see some of the beauty beneath the decay."

Leo nodded in understanding and continued to admire the hauntingly beautiful, twisted trees and ethereal glows that occasionally peeked through the gloom as they followed the footprints.

Their journey led them deeper into the heart of the forest, and as they pressed on, the tension in the air grew palpable. Leo was brimming with questions, but he kept his inquiries to himself, instead focusing on the mesmerizing but eerie landscape.

Finally, the trail of footprints ceased, and Leo spotted smoke wafting through the trees. Bliss and Leo trailed the ethereal smoke until they encountered a group of human-sized pixies adorned in royal army regalia. The diminutive soldiers, with their minuscule swords and serious expressions, presented an absurdly tense sight.

Bliss, undaunted by the bizarre encounter, stepped forward and addressed the guards with a snarky tone. "Alright, you pint-sized warriors, where's King Demetrius?"

One of the guards recognized Bliss, his features softening as he realized who was addressing him. He exchanged a few words with his companions before turning back to Bliss and nodding. "Follow me. The king is waiting."

Leo followed Bliss and the pixie guards as they made their way deeper into the forest, his heart pounding with a mix of anxiety and hope. He couldn't help but wonder if Finn was safe and what kind of eccentric ruler King Demetrius might turn out to be.

# 14

# Finn

Finn was sprawled on his cot in the makeshift camp, the cold, hard ground beneath him a far cry from a comfortable bed. The absence of proper tents meant that he could hear and see everything that happened around him. It was a restive night, but the real excitement was yet to come.

The distant hum of activity pulled Finn from his attempts at sleep. He sat up, rubbing his eyes, and surveyed the camp. His eyes settled on Demetrius, who was darting towards the camp's entrance. With a groggy determination, Finn rose and followed in Demetrius' footsteps.

"What's going on?" Finn inquired as he reached Demetrius.

"One of the guards on the perimeter just reported an unexpected guest," Demetrius explained.

Finn squinted at Demetrius, who seemed more than just upset. "Why the foul mood? Are we in danger?"

Demetrius shook his head. "No, just follow me."

With that, he quickened his pace, leaving Finn bewildered but eager to know more. The closer they got, the more Finn heard. The man's voice was incessant, and Finn couldn't ignore the overpowering presence emanating from the intruder. It was a power Finn had only sensed once before, that of a god. He wondered what kind of god would wander in the spirit realm, and he was about to find out.

"Finally, what took you so long?" The man's voice cut through the air, and before Finn could register the sight, his eyes landed on Leo.

"Leo…" Finn whispered, his heart pounding as he sprinted toward his friend, launching himself at Leo for a heartfelt hug.

"Finn?" Leo sounded as dazed as Finn felt but soon embraced him tightly.

"Leo," Finn sighed, their friendship reaffirmed.

However, their reunion was short-lived, as someone nearby cleared their throat. Finn's gaze shifted to a god-like figure who was smiling at them. While Finn didn't know the god's identity, he decided not to pry.

"Aren't you going to introduce us, sugar?" the man inquired.

"Of course," Leo said, beaming. "Bliss, this is Finn. Finn, meet Bliss, the one who saved me and helped me find you."

Finn extended a hand, but Bliss surprised him with a warm hug. "I know you can sense what I am," Bliss whispered in Finn's ear. "But let's keep it under wraps for now."

Demetrius intervened, ushering Bliss away for a private conversation. Finn expressed his gratitude before watching the two disappear into the night.

With the distractions gone, Finn and Leo retreated deeper into the woods, finding a secluded spot where they could converse without prying ears.

Leo turned to Finn, his voice trembling. "I was so scared, Finn. I thought I'd lost you."

Finn tenderly brushed away the tears forming in Leo's eyes. "You'll never lose me. We're in this together, remember?"

Leo looked guilt-ridden. "I'm sorry, Finn, for getting you involved in all of this."

Finn's brows furrowed in frustration. "No need to apologize, Leo. We chose this path together, and we'll see it through together."

Leo nodded, and their eyes locked, the unspoken bond between them speaking volumes.

Finn leaned in slowly, capturing Leo's lips in a gentle, heartfelt kiss. The world around them disappeared, and all that mattered was their reunion and the shared promise of the journey ahead.

Finn gazed into Leo's eyes, and for a moment, time seemed to stand still. They were deep in the heart of the enchanted forest, surrounded by ancient trees and a soft, mossy carpet beneath their feet. The whispers of the leaves and the hum of unseen magical creatures filled the air.

Leo's voice was a low, husky whisper, filled with longing. "Finn," he said, his words almost a plea. "I can feel it too, that hunger inside me. It's like an ache that only you can soothe."

Finn's heart pounded in his chest, and he couldn't deny the truth in Leo's words. The attraction between them had been building for so long, and now it was impossible to ignore. "Leo," he confessed, his voice equally filled with desire, "I've never wanted anyone like I want you right now."

The forest seemed to lean in, lending its silent approval to the burgeoning connection. The air was charged with anticipation as they moved closer, guided by an unseen force, their bodies drawn together as if by a powerful magnet.

Their lips met, and it was like the collision of two stars. Their kiss was electric, passionate, and so full of longing that it threatened to consume them both. Their tongues danced in a fiery waltz, exploring each other with a fervor that left no doubt about their desire.

Leo pulled back slightly, their breaths mingling in the cool forest air. "What do you want, Finn?" he asked, his voice still husky from their kiss.

Finn's eyes glistened with a mixture of desire and fear. "I'm scared, Leo," he confessed. "Scared of how much I want you."

Leo's voice was tender, reassuring. "You don't have to be scared, Finn. Not if you're with me. Just say the words, and I'm yours."

Tears welled up in Finn's eyes, threatening to spill over. "I don't want to be hurt again," he admitted, his voice trembling.

Leo's response was swift and filled with determination. "I promise, Finn, that I'll take care of you. No one will ever hurt you again. I won't allow it."

Finn felt the weight of Leo's promise, as if it were a magical bond between them. "I want you, Leo," he said, his voice filled with certainty. "It's been you since the moment we met."

Leo didn't need any more encouragement. He kissed Finn again, more aggressively this time, as if sealing their pact with every passionate embrace.

The forest, in all its ancient wisdom, seemed to come alive with the magic of their connection. The leaves overhead shimmered with an ethereal glow, and fireflies danced around them, casting a soft, enchanting light on the scene. The very ground beneath their feet seemed to pulse with the rhythm of their desire, echoing the beating of their hearts.

As they continued to kiss, the world around them transformed. The trees swayed in time with their passion, and the mossy carpet below seemed to ripple like a gentle wave. It was as if the forest itself celebrated their union, showering them with its silent blessings.

They shed their clothes, revealing their naked forms to each other. The moonlight caressed their skin, casting an ethereal glow upon them. The forest floor became their sanctuary as they tumbled down, their limbs entangled in a symphony of desire. They moved together, their bodies finding a rhythm that was both primal and transcendent. The forest echoed with their moans and their gasps.

Finn's hand went down to Leo's pants and start undoing all of the buttons. Once they were off, Finn's hand found Leo's long hard cock that was he felt that was already leaking. Finn started stroking slowly and then gradually pick up speed as they grind on one another.

With a firm grip, Leo claimed control of Finn's arousal, his fingers gliding along his length with purpose and authority. His eager response fueled my hunger, and their bodies moved in sync.

"Leo," Finn moaned, his voice filled with fervor and submission. "Make me yours completely." The forest bore witness as Leo's touch intensified, his strokes expertly navigating the terrain of Finn's desire

"You are mine, Finn," Leo growled, his voice dripping with dominance. "Your pleasure is mine to command, and I will take you to the edge and beyond." With each stroke, Leo asserted his control, relishing in the power he held over him.

"Yes, Leo," Finn gasped, surrendering to Leo's dominance. "Take me, claim me as your own." Their bodies moved with a fervent urgency, merging dominance and submission in a symphony of passion.

"You crave my dominance, Finn," Leo asserted, his voice laced with authority. "Submit to me completely, and I shall grant you what you want." Their connection deepened, the forest echoing their uninhibited desires, amplifying the intensity of their union.

Their bodies lay intertwined on the moss-covered ground, the moonlight casting ethereal shadows upon them, the primal energy between Finn and Leo grew with every passing moment. A wicked grin played upon Leo's lips as he positioned Finn on his hands and knees, his exposed vulnerability fueling my hunger for control. With deliberate intent, Leo prepared his eager entrance, his fingers tracing circles around his quivering opening.

"Leo," Finn whispered, his voice laced with a mix of longing and submission, "please, take me, claim me with your cock." Finn moaned. Finn eagerly offered himself to Leo, his body a canvas for Leo to explore and conquer. "Yes, Leo," Finn moaned, his voice filled with need, "fuck me with your hard cock."

Leo's grip tightened on Finn's hips, his fingers digging into the flesh. With a primal growl, he plunged his rock-hard member into Finn's waiting heat, the force of his thrusts igniting a fiery passion between them.

Waves of pleasure washed over Finn as Leo claimed him, his cock filling him completely, stretching him to the limits. "Oh, Leo," Finn cried out, his voice a symphony of pleasure and surrender, "fuck me harder, make me yours."

The sound of flesh meeting flesh filled the forest as Leo obliged, his thrusts growing more forceful and commanding. "You belong to me, Finn," Leo declared, his voice dripping with dominance, "feel the power of my cock as it possesses you."

Lost in a haze of ecstasy, Finn surrendered to the depths of Leo's dominance, his body a vessel for Leo's insatiable desire. "Leo…" Finn moaned.

"You are mine to fuck, Finn," Leo growled, his voice filled with possessiveness and triumph. With every thrust, he reveled in the control he held over Finn, his cock driving them both towards the pinnacle of pleasure.

"Yes, Leo," Finn gasped, his voice a symphony of submission and pleasure, "dominate me with your cock, make me scream." The forest bore witness to their unfiltered connection, their bodies moving in harmony, guided by their unrelenting passion.

Leo and Finn found themselves engulfed in a crescendo of pleasure. With each thrust, their bodies trembled in unison, teetering on the edge of ecstasy.

Overwhelmed by pleasure, Finn's body convulsed beneath Leo's commanding touch. His moans filled the air, a symphony of surrender and satisfaction. Sensing Finn's impending release, Leo intensified his movements, driving them both towards the brink of ecstasy. With one final thrust, Finn's body tensed, and he cried out in rapture as his orgasm washed over him.

Waves of pleasure crashed over Finn, his body shuddering with the intensity of his release. He gasped for breath, lost in the euphoria of his climax. As Finn's pleasure subsided, Leo continued his relentless movements, savoring the power he held over Finn. With a final, primal roar, Leo reached his own climax, his release marking the pinnacle of their shared desire.

As their bodies trembled with the aftershocks, Leo and Finn lay entwined, their breaths mingling in the stillness of the forest.

Leo's dominant aura softened, and he held Finn in his arms, their bodies basking in the warmth of their connection. "You are mine, Finn," Leo whispered, his voice a mixture of possessiveness and tenderness.

With a contented smile, Finn nuzzled against Leo's chest, basking in the afterglow of their intense encounter. "And you are mine, Leo," Finn murmured, his voice filled with a sense of belonging.

The forest bore witness to their uninhibited desires, both their bodies and souls entwined in a dance of dominance and surrender.

They lay there on the ground, a tangled mess of limbs and sweaty skin. Finn rested his head on Leo's chest, the rhythmic rise and fall of Leo's breath comforting against the backdrop of the dense forest.

"Are you finally going to tell me what happened to you?" Leo's voice cut through the stillness after a while.

Finn sighed and propped himself up on his elbows. He met Leo's concerned gaze and began to recount the harrowing events that led him to help Poofy and face the malevolent Lich. "The Lich, Leo, it was after you. It wanted you, but it found me instead."

Leo's arms tightened around Finn. "I'm damn glad you got away from that creature. But if that fucker ever dares to hurt you again, I won't hold back."

Finn's heart swelled with the fierce protectiveness in Leo's eyes. "You know, I can take care of myself, right? In fact, before I even came to Salem, Alex asked me to join their team full time."

Leo leaned in, his lips brushing Finn's forehead. "I know you can, and I'm proud of you. But creatures like that Lich fall under my domain of magic, and they are my problem. I can't stand the thought of you getting hurt, especially when I could do something about it." He paused, his voice softening. "What else did you and your new friend discover?"

Finn hesitated, unsure of how much to reveal. "After we fought off the Lich, we stumbled upon a hidden cabin deep in the forest. And Leo, I swear, the people who took us in…they were your parents. I can tell because your resemblance to your dad is uncanny."

Leo's eyes widened in disbelief. "What? That can't be, Finn. My parents are in Seattle," he said, his voice quivering with uncertainty.

"I don't think it's my place to tell you everything, Leo. It should come from them," Finn said gently.

"Where are they?" Leo asked, his curiosity overcoming his doubt.

"They're back at the camp," Finn replied. "They came with us because they wanted to see you and explain everything once they found out what we were doing here in the Spirit Realm."

Leo nodded slowly. "We should find somewhere to wash up."

Finn was relieved for the change of subject. "Yeah, let's do that."

They got up from the ground, brushing leaves and twigs off their sticky skin, and decided to look for a nearby lake where they could wash up.

The lake shimmered in the dappled moonlight filtering through the tall trees. Its surface was like a sheet of glass, reflecting the vivid green canopy above. Leo and Finn waded into the cool, refreshing water, laughter bubbling up as they splashed and played with each other.

They reveled in the simple joy of the moment, their connection growing stronger with each shared laugh and gentle touch. As they finished washing up, they stood on the shore, facing each other with goofy grins.

Finally, they dressed and decided it was time to head back to the camp. They walked hand in hand, their fingers intertwined, occasionally sneaking glances at each other, their smiles mirroring those of teenagers who had just experienced a milestone in their relationship.

As they approached the entrance to the camp, Finn turned to Leo. "Are you ready for this?"

Leo took a deep breath, his expression resolute. "Let's get this over with."

# 15

# Leo

As soon as they got back into the camp, Finn led Leo to the campfire, where he found the two people he was dreading to see. He really hadn't believed Finn at first about his parents being in the spirit realm. For all he knew, these people were not his real parents, but he needed to find out what was going on.

His parents were holding each other lovingly, which was so far from what he was used to back at home. The two of them stopped just out of sight.

"Do you want me with you there?" Finn asked.

Finn was holding Leo's hand, and Leo appreciated it. He gave Finn's hand a gentle squeeze. "Do you mind if I talk to them alone for now?" Leo turned to see a smiling Finn.

"Of course. Just remember that I am just around the corner if you need me," Finn said before leaning in and giving him a peck on the lips.

Finn gave him one last hug before joining Demetrius and Bliss nearby. Leo took a deep breath and headed toward his parents.

His parents looked up and saw him walking, and Leo saw his mother start to tear up. He didn't know how to feel about it, but somehow, he was struck by it. He reached them and sat on the log in front of them.

"Leo," he heard his father say.

"Dad, Mom. Is it really you?" Leo asked hesitantly.

"Yes, it is us. Leo, we missed you and your brothers," his mother said, who was still leaning on his father.

"Tell me everything and don't leave anything out," Leo said.

"What did your brother tell you?" his father asked.

"Only that you guys went to help a pride member and came back different. That's all there was to it," Leo said.

His father nodded. "Yes, that was the case. The night before that, we were contacted by one of our pride allies about one of their pride members being possessed.  Though they left out one big piece of information – that the member was possessed by a demon.  We managed to take the demon out, but it put up a fight. We didn't realize it at first, but as the demon took shape and spoke, that's when all hell broke loose. It was the king of the demons, Lyandros, and before he escaped, Lyandros trapped our souls here, and we've been here ever since."

"If that's the case, then who's inside your bodies in the mortal realm?" Leo asked after processing, though he was finding it difficult to do so.

"We assumed that Lyandros put two of his demon workers to use our bodies to do his dirty work," his mother said.

"So that was why you guys were extremely cold when it comes to me and always made me feel like I don't belong," Leo said somberly, not looking his parents in the eye.

"Leo, you have to understand. Whatever we ended up doing wasn't our fault," his father said.

"Please, Leo. You have to understand," his mother said.

"I'm not going to lie. Whatever those demons have done did a number on me, and I don't think it can be fixed after one night. It will take me some time for me to be able to see you as my parents again," Leo said after a while.

His parents nodded. "We will take whatever you will give us," his mother said.

Leo nodded. "I can't speak for any of my brothers, but I'm pretty sure they will forgive you better than I did." Leo looked at his parents thoughtfully. "I don't know how much Finn has told you, but we're here because we want to safeguard Rory's soul, and we need to get to him fast before Lyandros can get to him."

"Yes, that's why we went with Finn. Once he said your names, we started hoping again," his mother said.

Leo nodded again. "For now, get some rest. I'll have a talk with Finn and see where we are at." His parents nodded and stood up and walked toward their cot.

The campfire crackled, casting flickering shadows across the faces of those gathered around it. Leo sat for a moment, taking in the warmth of the fire and the surreal conversation he'd just had with his parents.

Finn returned to his side, and their eyes met. There was a silent understanding between them, a connection that went beyond words. Leo felt grateful for Finn's presence, even if he couldn't fully express it.

Finn leaned in, his lips brushing against Leo's in a tender kiss. "We'll figure this out together," he whispered.

Leo managed a faint smile, appreciating Finn's unwavering support. "Yeah, we will."

As they sat by the campfire, Leo couldn't help but notice the mystical energy that seemed to dance in the air. The flames took on an otherworldly blue hue, and the shadows cast by the fire seemed to twist and elongate, creating an eerie but mesmerizing spectacle.

"Here, I believe this ring belongs to you," Finn said, extending his hand, revealing a gleaming silver ring with an intricate design.

Leo's eyes widened as he recognized the ring. It was his, a precious gift from his late master, Ryland Creed. He didn't even realize he had lost it and was glad that Finn found it. "Thank you. How did you manage to find it?" Leo asked, a mix of surprise and gratitude in his voice.

Finn grinned, his eyes gleaming with an unusual confidence. "I didn't, Poofy did."

"You've been talking about Poofy a lot. Where is the fella?" Leo asked, his curiosity piqued.

Finn proceeded to call Poofy, and Leo was taken aback by what he saw. Poofy was no ordinary spirit gryphon like Finn had described before. The creature had an ethereal quality, its body shimmering with a translucent, ever-shifting glow.

Leo couldn't help but smile as he observed Poofy's presence. "Do you know what Poofy is, Finn?" he asked after a while.

Finn shook his head. "No, Demetrius said that Poofy was a rescue and never really got along with everyone other than me."

Leo chuckled and gave Finn's hand a squeeze. "He's a spirit familiar. They are extremely rare, and they only attach themselves to those they find worthy. It seems like Poofy has chosen you."

Finn continued to stroke Poofy, who was clearly enjoying the attention. "Demetrius said I can have him, but I'm not quite sure how I'm going to be able to take him to our realm."

"Well, you can't have him out in the mortal realm for a long time," Leo explained. "Their energy will deplete quickly if they aren't connected to the spirit realm in some capacity."

Finn's curiosity got the better of him, and he asked, "How do you know all of this?"

Leo turned to Finn, a soft smile on his face. "My master, Ryland, taught me how to control my magic. He was the greatest and the most patient teacher I've ever known."

"He sounds like an amazing teacher," Finn said. "What happened to him?"

Leo's gaze turned distant as he remembered the years he spent with his master, the bond they shared, and the training that molded him into the necromancer he had become. Ryland had been a tall, imposing figure with sharp features, a salt-and-pepper beard that reached down to his chest, and piercing, storm-gray eyes that held the wisdom of centuries.

"He passed away not that long ago," Leo said, his voice tinged with sadness. "You know that us necromancers have a shorter lifespan the more we use our magic. That's what happened to him. His magic took him in the end."

Finn listened with genuine sympathy in his eyes, understanding the heavy burden that came with the mastery of dark arts. "Are you... are you scared that your magic will do the same to you?"

Leo's expression grew solemn, and he took a deep breath. "I'd be lying if I said I wasn't scared, Finn. It's a risk that comes with the kind of magic we wield. But it's also the price we pay to understand the mysteries of life and death, to protect those we care about, and to ensure that the balance is maintained."

The crackling campfire continued to cast its eerie, dancing shadows, and the magical energy in the air seemed to intensify, as if emphasizing the weight of Leo's words.

Finn's voice was filled with empathy as he reached for Leo's hand. "I'm here for you, Leo. Just as you've shared your knowledge with me, I'll stand by your side, no matter what."

Leo's eyes met Finn's, and a deep sense of gratitude welled up within him. "Thank you, Finn. It means more than you can imagine."

Leo gently stroked Poofy's ethereal form, feeling a warm, tingling sensation as his hand passed through the spectral fluff. He was grateful that the familiar allowed him this contact. Finn watched, his curiosity piqued.

"Do you know how we can take Poofy home?" Finn's question broke the silence.

Leo continued to pet Poofy, his mind whirring with an idea. "I have an idea, but I'm going to need your help," he said, looking at Finn.

Finn leaned in, eager to assist. "What are we going to do?"

Leo toyed with a ring on his finger, its intricate design glowing softly. "I'm going to try and put Poofy's spirit in this ring. You see, this is not just an ordinary ring; it's an artifact that can be used to home creatures that couldn't walk in the mortal realm. You don't have to worry about anything; Poofy will be fine. This will only be temporary until we find a way to keep Poofy permanently out in the open," Leo explained.

Finn gazed at Poofy, who looked like an adorable, ghostly pet, its tongue wagging in delight. Finn turned to the spectral furball. "What do you think, Poofy? You want to come home with me?" Poofy squealed and playfully licked both Finn and Leo, sparking chuckles from the two friends.

With their hearts set on the plan, Leo took charge. "Come on, let's talk to Demetrius and find out where we can do the ritual." Finn nodded in agreement.

The trio made their way to the camp's center, where King Demetrius and his soldiers watched over the camp with an air of vigilance. Demetrius spotted them approaching and signaled for them to join him.

Demetrius regarded Leo and Finn with a curious expression. "What's going on?" he asked.

Leo hesitated for a moment before asking Demetrius for a suitable location to perform the ritual, explaining their intention to seal Poofy within the ring so they could take it home.

Demetrius regarded them with his piercing eyes, taking a moment to ponder their request. Eventually, he nodded. "There's a clearing not far from here," he said.

The king led them through the forest, his steps echoing with authority, until they reached a secluded glade, a sacred space within the Forest of the Damned. The area thrummed with the power of lingering spirits, most of which remained docile, but Leo knew they couldn't afford to be complacent. They had to be careful.

Taking charge, Leo drew a precise circle on the ground, marking the boundary of their ritual space. Finn stood just outside the circle, King Demetrius at his side.

With the circle prepared, Leo motioned for Finn to join him in the center. Finn obliged, standing in the marked space. Leo pulled out a gleaming blade from his jacket, its edge shining with an otherworldly light. He turned to Finn, holding the blade out.

"I just need a little bit of your blood," Leo said, his voice a gentle whisper, carrying the weight of the moment. "This is the key to making this work."

Finn nodded, unwavering, a resolute expression on his face. He extended his hand, offering it to Leo, who accepted it with care. With a practiced, almost imperceptible motion, Leo drew the blade across Finn's palm, causing a thin, precise cut. A few drops of blood fell into the center of the meticulously drawn circle on the forest floor. The blood merged seamlessly with the intricate patterns Leo had etched into the earth.

As the crimson drops made contact with the symbols, the circle began to shimmer with an eerie, ghostly light. Its lines and curves seemed to come to life, pulsing with an ethereal energy. At the heart of it all lay a simple, unadorned ring, unremarkable in appearance but brimming with latent magic. It absorbed the energy emanating from the circle.

Leo closed his eyes for a moment, centering himself, then began to recite the ancient incantations, words that resonated with the spirits of the forest and the forgotten magic of ages past. *"Spiritus, veni ad me,"* he intoned, his voice carrying the weight of centuries.

The ring, once mundane, pulsed with newfound power. It seemed to breathe in harmony with Leo's incantations, gradually drawing in Poofy's essence, the spirit familiar who had taken the form of a gryphon. Poofy had been their faithful companion, a guardian and guide in this magical world. And now, they were attempting to bind Poofy's spirit to the ring, to hold onto their beloved friend even after the gryphon's physical form had departed.

Finn's eyes remained closed, his face a mask of serenity, as he channeled his energy into the ritual. Leo, with his own eyes closed, began to see the strings of magic that connected Finn and Poofy. These ethereal threads wove an intricate tapestry, binding the two together on a profound, metaphysical level.

With each whispered word of the incantation, Leo reached out to these threads, like an expert weaver working with the finest silks. He could feel the essence of both Finn and Poofy, their unique magical signatures. This was the moment, the culmination of years of study and preparation.

In the realm of deep focus, Leo gently touched the threads that connected Finn and Poofy, his fingertips tingling with the sensation of raw magic. He marveled at the connection between man and spirit, a bond that transcended the physical world. It was a union of souls, an unbreakable link forged through shared experiences and a deep, unspoken understanding.

As Leo reached the climax of the incantation, the forest around them seemed to hold its breath. The air was charged with an otherworldly energy, and the circle of symbols blazed with a mesmerizing light, like the faint glow of distant stars. The ring at the center of the ritual absorbed this newfound power, its simple design transformed into a vessel of ethereal radiance.

"*Spiritus, veni ad me,*" Leo repeated, his voice unwavering, the Latin words carrying the weight of their collective hope.

Finally, as the last syllable left his lips, a brilliant burst of light erupted from the circle. It swirled and danced, taking on the form of a majestic gryphon, its feathers shimmering with a myriad of colors and its eyes glowing with intelligence and love before fading away.

"You can opened your eyes now, Finn." Leo said and Finn did.

"Did it work?" Finn asked.

"Yes. Now I want you to try and call Poofy out of the ring."

Finn closed his eyes and held the ring out in front of him. A hushed stillness fell over the clearing. Moments passed, each one feeling like an eternity. Then, like a gentle breeze, Poofy emerged from the ring, unharmed and as lively as ever. It was an awe-inspiring sight.

If you two are done," Demetrius interjected from where he was standing, "we need to go back to camp so we can plan what we are going to do."

Finn and Leo looked at each other, their hands still entwined, and chuckled before taking each other's hand and following Demetrius back to the camp.

Back at the camp, Demetrius led them to one of the roofed tents where a table was in the middle. Leo's parents sat at the table, and Bliss was there, too, his charm and wit on full display. They were all laughing and smiling, caught up in the magic of the moment. Leo couldn't help but smile, too. Perhaps, he thought, they could be a proper family again once all this was over.

Bliss noticed their arrival. "Are you two lovebirds just going to stand there and stare at my beauty?" he teased with a smirk.

Finn and Leo chuckled. "Was he like this when you met him?" Finn asked.

Leo nodded. "Yeah, pretty much." He tugged Finn's hand and moved closer to the table where a map lay spread out.

Demetrius cleared his throat, taking charge of the situation. "Is everyone here?"

One by one, the members of their party nodded in agreement.

"Now," Demetrius continued, "I already briefed Bliss on what's going on, but we still need all of your input."

Leo spoke up, determination in his eyes. "Whatever you need."

Demetrius turned to Finn. "Like I told Finn before, we received some information about an unusual magical signature in the middle of the Corrupted Sea. And from what Finn told us, Leo, you were looking for the soul of your brother. Is that correct?"

Leo took a deep breath and nodded. "Yes. I also have something that may add to your plans."

Demetrius encouraged him to continue.

Leo glanced at his parents, finding their anxious but supportive faces. Finn's hand squeezed his, grounding him. "As you all know, I am a necromancer, though my ability lets me track souls when needed." He paused for a moment, taking in the gasps of surprise from his parents. He needed to finish what he started. "I managed to track Rory's soul, but it led me into a tower of some sort. Rory was alone and scared, but he told me to get out and pushed me back into the Spirit Realm. From what we knew, Rory didn't have any sort of magic, but at that point in time, I felt that he was more powerful than me."

Demetrius absorbed this information and nodded. "If that's the case, then we're going to need you to track him down inside the tower. My suspicions tell me Rory is being held in the Tower of Spirits, where all the dark spirits reside."

The group fell into a thoughtful silence, processing the implications of Leo's revelation.

Leo's mother finally spoke, her voice trembling. "We have to save him, no matter what."

Leo's father nodded in agreement, his eyes filled with resolve. "We'll do whatever it takes."

The rest of the group expressed their determination to rescue Rory, and Bliss flashed a confident smile. "We're in this together, then."

With a united purpose, they began planning, their words and ideas flowing like a river, filling the tent with the electric buzz of anticipation and hope.

Demetrius outlined the mission with clarity, and Leo and Finn absorbed every detail. They discussed strategies, potential challenges, and contingencies. The atmosphere in the tent was charged with a sense of purpose and the unshakable bond that had brought them all together.

As they planned, the campfire outside crackled, casting long, dancing shadows on the tent's walls. The night air was alive with a sense of magic, as if the very world conspired to aid their cause.

They sorted through supplies, checked their magical protections, and reviewed Leo's knowledge of the Tower of Spirits. The urgency and importance of their mission were tangible in every spoken word and every shared glance.

The map on the table became a canvas for their dreams and determination, as they marked out the path they would take, the dangers they would face, and the ultimate goal they would reach.

Leo and Finn sat side by side, their fingers occasionally entwining, reminding each other that they were in this together.

# 16

# Finn

Morning's arrival found Finn waking up with Leo by his side, their bodies intertwined in a cozy embrace. The day they had eagerly anticipated had finally dawned, and Finn couldn't quite put his finger on how he felt about it. Gratitude washed over him because they finally had a plan, but beneath the surface, fear lurked – the fear of not measuring up when the time came for battle.

"You're thinking way too loud again, Doc," Leo grumbled sleepily, his arm draped protectively over Finn.

Finn snuggled deeper into Leo's chest, seeking solace. "How did you know?"

"I don't have to be magic to know that you always think a lot." Leo's chuckle rumbled through his chest as he turned to face Finn.

A playful grin tugged at the corners of Finn's lips. "You're such a dick. But yeah, I suppose I should stop, huh?"

"Tell me what's going on in that smart head of yours." Leo's smile remained soft, and his eyes held the warmth of their affection.

"I'm just worried that I won't be able to pull my weight when it comes to the fight," Finn confessed, his vulnerability on display.

"Sweetheart." Leo's voice was gentle, and the endearment sent shivers down Finn's spine. "I've seen you fight, and you can hold your own. And think about it, Alex wouldn't have put you on his team permanently if he didn't sense the power in you." Leo's reassurance was a soothing balm to Finn's anxiety.

"Thank you. I needed that." Finn beamed a grateful smile at Leo, his heart swelling with affection.

Leo cupped Finn's cheek and leaned in to press a soft, reassuring kiss to his lips. "I'll be with you all the way."

Bliss's voice interrupted their tender moment. "Alright, boys, stop making us all feel bad and get up and eat."

They both chuckled, their bond strengthened by shared laughter. "Come on, if Bliss cooked, it'll be great," Leo said, offering Finn a hand to help him up.

Hand in hand, they walked toward the center of the camp, where the tantalizing scent of food hung in the air like an invisible symphony of flavors. The aroma beckoned with the promise of a delicious meal.

Finn's nose detected the distinct blend of herbs and spices, the rich scent of roasted meat, and the earthy undertones of freshly baked bread. Each inhalation teased his senses, making his mouth water with anticipation.

Bliss and Leo's parents, their faces radiant with love and pride, served food to the gathering crowd. Leo's parents had been a source of strength and support throughout their journey, and the sight of them was a heartwarming reminder of the family he left back home.

Leo and Finn joined the line, and it wasn't long before it was their turn to receive their portions of the delectable feast. Finn offered a heartfelt "Thank you" to Bliss, who winked mischievously at him, causing Finn to blush with embarrassment and affection.

With their plates filled with Bliss's culinary delights, Leo led Finn to a quiet corner of the camp where they could savor their meal in tranquil solitude.

The camp was a bustling hive of activity, with warriors sharpening their weapons, mages practicing spells, and healers tending to the wounded. Despite the impending battle, there was an air of camaraderie and determination among the diverse group of allies.

After everyone had eaten their fill, King Demetrius called for everyone to gather around. His voice carried a weight of authority and experience, and his words resonated deeply with those who had chosen to follow him.

"Today, we stand on the precipice of a great challenge," King Demetrius began, his voice unwavering. "We face a formidable enemy, but we do not face it alone. Together, we are strong, and together, we will prevail."

He went on to share stories of their collective struggles, emphasizing the bonds they had forged and the sacrifices they had made. His words were simple but heartfelt, a testament to the unity and determination of the group.

As King Demetrius continued his speech, the sun hung low in the sky, casting a warm golden glow over the camp. The magic in the air seemed to respond to his words, shimmering with an ethereal energy that wove through the gathered warriors. The very earth beneath their feet seemed to pulse with anticipation.

The sky above darkened, and the first stars began to twinkle, their light piercing the canvas of the fading day. At King Demetrius's signal, the mages among them raised their hands, and their magic infused the atmosphere. The air crackled with power, and the entire camp was bathed in a soft, otherworldly light.

The magic coalesced into a breathtaking display, a celestial dance of colors and patterns that painted the night sky. Arcane symbols and sigils of protection and courage hung suspended in the air, casting a protective shield over the assembled warriors.

Finn and Leo exchanged a glance, their hearts filled with a sense of purpose and unity. They were part of something greater than themselves, bound together by a shared mission and a deep, unbreakable love.

In the midst of this magical spectacle, King Demetrius concluded his speech with a resounding cry. "To the Tower of Spirits, my friends! Let our courage light the way, and our unity be our strength!"

With a chorus of cheers and raised weapons, the warriors of the camp prepared to embark on their fateful journey to the Tower of Spirits. The night had fallen, but their spirits were ablaze with determination, and the magic that surrounded them served as a visual reminder of the power of their unity and resolve.

The Tower of Spirits awaited, and with each step, they moved closer to their destiny, ready to face whatever challenges lay ahead.

Finn and his companions, King Demetrius, Leo, and Bliss, walked alongside the through the eerie landscape of the Forest. Leo's parents followed, accompanied by Poofy. Finn had released Poofy from the ring, and his spirit familiar now hovered nearby.

"Do you think Lyandros would be there?" Leo asked, breaking the silence with a hint of uncertainty in his voice.

"Knowing him, he would be waiting and biding his time," Bliss replied confidently. "Lyandros wouldn't let someone he thinks is powerful slip out of his control."

"We also don't know how many of his minions are lurking around the Corrupted Sea. So we need to tread carefully. One mistake can be fatal," King Demetrius cautioned.

Bliss turned to Leo. "Do you have any idea what your brother's magic might be?"

Leo shook his head. "No, everything happened so quickly when he kicked me out of the spirit realm."

"I have an idea of what he could be, but everything I know is just an assumption at this point," Bliss admitted.

Curiosity piqued, Leo pressed further, and Finn could sense Leo's parents listening intently as well. "What do you think he could be?"

Bliss began to reveal a piece of hidden history. "In the annals of history, when the mortal realm was first exposed to magic and it began to spread, there was always someone assigned to guard the doors between realms. That person was simply known as the Guardian, and only one person could be the Guardian at any given time. I'm willing to bet that Lyandros is using your brother's magic to jump into other realms easily."

Finn couldn't help but interject, his voice laced with concern. "You think Rory is the Guardian?"

Bliss nodded solemnly. "Yes, we need to reach him swiftly before Lyandros fully corrupts his soul."

As their conversation continued, the group made their way toward the shore of the Corrupted Sea. The journey was not swift, and the anticipation weighed heavily on their shoulders. It took them a while to get to the shoreline, the path fraught with eerie sights and sounds.

The Corrupted Sea unveiled a haunting, surreal world as they approached. The air was thick with an otherworldly fog that wrapped itself around them, shrouding the surroundings in an unsettling embrace. The stench was foul and unmistakable, a putrid odor that stung their nostrils and lingered in the air.

The sea itself was unlike any body of water Finn had ever seen. It glowed with an eerie, unnatural purple hue, casting an unsettling radiance. The waves moved with an almost sentient purpose, whispering dark secrets with their gentle but menacing lapping against the shore. The water seemed to pulse with a malevolent energy that sent shivers down their spines.

Amidst this surreal landscape, they could see the spirits of the departed, floating aimlessly in the purplish water. These ethereal forms drifted like lost memories, their presence lending an otherworldly quality to the already haunting scene. They paid no heed to the living souls in their midst.

At the heart of the Corrupted Sea rose the Tower of Spirits, an imposing structure that seemed to defy gravity. It reached up into the fog, its spires disappearing into the shroud that obscured the upper reaches. The tower was a grotesque amalgamation of twisted architecture, a testament to the corruption that had seeped into this realm.

Finn couldn't help but gawk at the spectacle before them. The visuals were beyond anything he had ever imagined, and the tension in the air was palpable. He knew the fate of Leo's brother rested on their shoulders, and the task ahead was daunting.

The group continued on their path, the atmosphere tense and heavy. But even in the face of impending danger, there was a touch of the absurd in the situation. Finn couldn't help but notice the comedic aspect of their strange company. Here they were, a young man, a king, a mysterious magic user, and a Poofy, all on a mission to save Rory.

Leo, breaking the silence again, couldn't help but add a bit of levity to the moment. "I never thought I'd see the day when I'd be walking into the Corrupted Sea with a floating furball by my side."

The tension in the group seemed to momentarily dissipate, replaced by a nervous chuckle. Even Bliss, with his enigmatic aura, cracked a small smile. King Demetrius gave a hearty laugh, his royal worries momentarily forgotten before addressing every

The group finally arrived not long after that. King Demetrius stopped in front of everyone and addressed the crowd. "Alright, you all know your jobs. All I ask is that you stay safe and alive after this is over. Take your positions now!"

Finn saw every pixie, spirit and royal guard moving into position. Pixie dust filled the air, which Finn thought would annoy him, but not as much as it did Leo, who was currently trying not to sneeze. Finn chuckled and Leo looked at him, which made Finn laugh even more.

"Hey, this pixie dust can kill, you know?" Leo said once he was done with his sneezing fit.

"Sure, sure. Come on, lover boy. Let's go." Finn held out a hand to Leo and dragged him towards the corrupted sea water where Bliss and King Demetrius stood.

"Where are my parents?" Leo asked.

"They're with some of my guards. They barely have any magic left in them, so I thought it wise to have them join my guards, who can protect them better," King Demetrius answered.

"We should have just left them back at the camp then," Leo said tightly.

"We tried to dissuade them, but they were as stubborn as someone else I know," Bliss teased.

"How are we getting to the Tower? You said you had a contact," Finn asked.

"He's close by. Though knowing him, he's always fashionably late," Bliss said and King Demetrius grumbled in agreement.

Finn was going to ask more questions, but the air suddenly became charged. They all felt it, and Leo looked around, but Finn knew only a god could change the atmosphere like burning ozone. Finn wondered about that since Bliss didn't give off that effect, but he shrugged it off for now. Bliss and Demetrius looked annoyed and impatient.

"Oh, stop with the dramatic entrance, Than. We need the boat!" Bliss said.

Suddenly the fog lifted just a little and a guy in a tailored suit riding a boat emerged.

The guy, Than, looked at them before glancing back at Bliss and King Demetrius. "Bliss, how many times do I have to tell you that looking this good takes time." Than said before addressing the King, "Demetrius, it's been a while."

"Thanatos, enough dramatics. Are you going to lend us the boat or not?" King Demetrius growled.

"Calm down, old friend. I just want to issue a warning. Lyandros is inside the tower, though I believe his army is lurking around in and out of the waters. Caution is key." Than said.

"Aren't you going to help us?" Finn asked.

"I wish I could, but no. I am not allowed to tamper with what's going on with the spirits in the spirit realm. I can only guide them." Than explained. "Don't worry Doctor, Alex knows what's happening. He asked me to watch over you and your friend."

"Just what are you?" Finn heard Leo ask.

"Oh, don't be naive, my little necromancer. You definitely know who I am, so don't pretend you don't," Than answered before smiling and vanishing in a puff of black smoke.

"Was that really Thanatos?" Leo asked Bliss and the King.

"Yes, now we don't have time for this. Get on the boat and get your magic ready," King Demetrius said.

They were on their way to the Tower of Spirits using the boat, but in the middle of their journey, Finn saw something in the distance. It was a Kraken.

The massive creature emerged from the corrupted waters, towering over their small boat. Its long tentacles lashed through the air as its giant eye focused on them.

"A Kraken!" Leo yelled. "I thought those were just myths!"

"Clearly not," Finn said grimly, bracing himself.

King Demetrius drew his sword as the Kraken approached. "Be ready to fight!"

The Kraken let out an ear-piercing shriek as it loomed over them. Its tentacles slammed into the water, creating huge waves that rocked the boat violently.

Leo struggled to keep his balance. "How are we supposed to fight something that big?"

"Together," Bliss said. "Focus your magic and look for a weak spot."

Finn eyed the Kraken warily as it circled them. Its scale-covered body provided ample protection, but its eye looked vulnerable. "Aim for the eye!" he shouted.

King Demetrius took flight and dove straight for the Kraken's massive eye, sword poised to strike. Leo and Bliss unleashed blasts of magical energy as Finn steered the boat, trying to evade the creature's flailing tentacles.

King Demetrius, flew over head and hovered above the raging sea. His iridescent wings shimmered as he raised his hands, conjuring crackling balls of pixie magic.

"Alright, you overgrown calamari!" he shouted at the Kraken. "Get ready for a pixie-sized can of whoop-ass!"

He hurled the magical spheres at the creature's gigantic eyeball. They exploded in bursts of light, making the Kraken recoil with an angry bellow.

On the boat below, Bliss drew back his engraved bow, an ethereal glow surrounding the mystical weapon. "Try some of this, ugly!" His arrow flew straight and true, piercing the Kraken's rubbery hide.

Leo's hands were outstretched, purple wisps of necromantic energy swirling around him. "Have a taste of the grave, freakshow!" Skeletal arms burst from the water, grappling at the creature's thrashing tentacles.

Finn stood at the helm, his own magical aura shining white. "We can take this monster!" he yelled encouragingly.

The Kraken smashed an enormous tentacle down on the boat with a crack. Wood splinters flew, and the vessel nearly capsized. Finn and the others struggled to stay upright.

"Whoa!" Leo yelped, pinwheeling his arms. "Let's not get too cocky yet!"

King Demetrius zipped around the Kraken's head, unleashing more pixie blasts. The explosions stung its eye, making it shriek in irritation. "We need to blind this ugly brute!" he called to the others. "Aim for the eye!"

"I'm on it!" Bliss rapidly fired two arrows at once, sunk deep into the Kraken's slit-shaped pupil. It bellowed furiously, dark blood weeping from the wounds.

Leo sent more undead hands to clamber over the beast. "Man, this thing smells like low tide!" He gagged dramatically.

"Now Finn!" shouted King Demetrius. "Hit it with everything you've got!"

Finn focused his energy, aiming his palms at the Kraken's face. His magic manifested as blazing rays of light, searing into its injured eye.

The Kraken thrashed violently, nearly upending the boat again. It clutched its smoking, ravaged eye in agony. With an earsplitting wail, the gargantuan creature began to sink below the churning waves.

"Yes!" Leo pumped a fist in victory. "Bwahaha! Not so tough now, are you Squidface?"

King Demetrius fluttered down and landed lightly on the boat that was now magically fixed. "Well done, everyone! We make a good team."

Finn let out a relieved breath. "That was touch and go for a minute there. I really thought we were going to end up as Kraken chow."

Bliss chuckled, stowing his bow. "All part of the job when you're battling giant sea monsters."

Leo nudged Finn with a grin. "Gotta admit though, our magic kicked that thing's butt!" He gesticulated wildly.

Finn laughed. "Yeah, we were pretty awesome back there." He high-fived Leo.

King Demetrius' expression became serious again. "Let's not celebrate too soon. We may have defeated the Kraken, but the Tower still awaits." He gazed ahead at the hazy outline of the imposing structure.

Bliss put a hand on the king's shoulder. "We'll stop Lyandros too. He doesn't stand a chance against all of us together."

Leo cracked his knuckles. "Yeah, we'll knock that punk's block off! Right, Finn?"

"You know it," Finn said with a decisive nod. "Let's finish this quest and save the Spirit World."

King Demetrius took hold of the tiller. "Full speed ahead to the Tower of Spirits!"

The group steeled themselves as the boat cut through the shrouded sea toward the looming tower and the final confrontation awaiting them there. But together, they knew they could overcome anything, even the lord of the dead himself.

As they approached the tower, an oppressive gloom seemed to settle over them. The corrupted water turned dark and oily, sloshing against the sides of the boat. Strange whispers echoed from unseen sources.

Leo shivered. "Geez, creepy much? This place gives me the heebie-jeebies."

King Demetrius' expression was grim. "Lyandros' evil power grows stronger the closer we get. Be on your guard."

Finn felt the hairs on his neck stand up. The air itself felt heavy with dark energy. "We can do this," he said, trying to psych himself up. "It's just some creepy whispers and shadows."

Suddenly, ghostly faces appeared in the water around them, mouths gaping in silent screams. Bliss drew back in alarm. "Fucking dark spirits."

The anguished visages swirled around the boat, clawing at the edges. Their mournful wailing grew louder.

Leo covered his ears. "Make it stop!"

King Demetrius slashed at a nearby specter with his sword, but it had no effect. "Foul spells will not halt us!" he declared, though his voice shook slightly.

Finn strengthened his resolve, magic glowing brighter to pierce the darkness. "Stay with me, guys. The tower's right there."

Together they weathered the storm of phantoms, determined not to let evil consume them. Lyandros would pay for his cruelty.

# 17

## Leo

Leo could hear everyone fighting in the background and hoped everyone on their side would come out okay.

"Leo and Finn, head on up. We'll take care of everything down here," King Demetrius said as they countered another attack from the corrupted spirits. "Go, we'll be right behind you."

Leo saw another spirit hurl a spirit globe at them and he countered it with his own magic, conjuring a necromantic shield that intercepted the attack. It exploded on impact.

"That should help block their attacks for a while. Don't get out from under it," Leo said. Demetrius and Bliss nodded in response. Leo took Finn's hand, who was still using his magic to shield them from behind. "Finn, let's go."

Finn dropped his shield and took Leo's hand. Together they entered the Tower of Spirits. Inside, the atmosphere felt suffocating, which was new. Something wasn't right and they had to stay alert.

"Can you feel that?" Finn asked.

Leo nodded. "When I tell you, put up your shield."

They moved cautiously through the shadowy interior. Strange whispers echoed around them, sending chills down their spines. The evil presence was palpable.

Leo felt the hair on his neck stand up. "Be ready, Finn. I sense something coming."

Finn tensed, ready to summon his magic. "I've got your back."

Without warning, dark apparitions swirled around them, spectral faces contorted in anguish. Their sinister wailing reverberated off the walls.

"Now, Finn!" Leo yelled.

Finn called on his power, enveloping them in a glowing shield. The phantoms shrieked and recoiled from its light.

"We've got to keep moving," Leo said. "Lyandros knows we're here."

As Leo and Finn ascended through the Tower of Spirits, an oppressive gloom permeated the curved stone walls around them. Strange whispers echoed from unseen sources, sending chills down their spines.

The Tower's interior was a mesmerizing blend of ancient, weathered stone and ethereal, otherworldly beauty. The walls bore intricate, ghostly carvings that seemed to writhe with life, depicting scenes of spirits in various states of existence. Faint, otherworldly glows emanated from the carvings, casting surreal patterns of light and shadow that danced along the spiraling staircase.

Leo squinted through the dim light. "Man, I can barely see a thing in here. You'd think the Lord of the Demons would install some mood lighting."

Finn chuckled nervously. "No kidding. This place gives me the creeps."

They emerged onto the first floor and were immediately set upon by a pack of shadowy wolf spirits. Their eyes glowed crimson as they stalked toward Leo and Finn, fangs bared.

Leo quickly summoned a protective barrier while Finn launched bolt after bolt of glowing energy, disintegrating the ghostly canines one by one until none remained.

Leo wiped his brow. "Whew, that was a close one! Nice shooting."

"We make a pretty good team," Finn said with a grin. But his smile faded as more sinister sounds echoed from above. "Let's keep moving. Something tells me that's just the welcome wagon."

The next floor enveloped them in an icy mist. Shambling forms emerged from the fog, their bodies gaping black holes.

Finn recoiled. "What the heck are those things?"

"Hungry ghosts," Leo said ominously. "Don't let them touch you or they'll drain your life force."

He fired off arcs of green lightning, scattering the creepy spirits. Meanwhile, Finn picked them off at a distance with targeted beams of energy. But the onslaught was relentless.

Leo panted from exertion. "Man, these dudes do not let up!"

"We can't keep this up forever," Finn worried. "Sooner or later we'll run out of juice."

"Chin up, dude. We've got this," Leo replied, though he was definitely starting to feel drained. He rallied his strength and pressed forward.

The third floor brought an even greater threat - a colossal dragon wreathed in shadow. It reared back and spewed scorching darkness from its maw.

Leo hastily threw up a shield. "Hit it with everything you've got!" he yelled to Finn over the roaring flames.

Finn focused his power, hands glowing bright. He hurled volleys of concentrated energy bolts, pounding away at the shadow dragon's hide. It shrieked in pain and fury, lashing its spiked tail.

"Keep that shield up, Leo!" Finn shouted, not letting up his magical assault. "This ugly worm is going down!"

Leo gritted his teeth from the effort of maintaining the protective barrier against the dragon's flames. "You...got it!" he grunted. "Fry this freak!"

Finn bombarded the beast relentlessly until it finally collapsed in an explosion of shadow. Panting, he gave Leo a weary thumbs up. "Another baddie bites the dust."

Leo let the shield drop with a gasp of relief. "Remind me to bring a bazooka next time. My arms feel like limp noodles." He shook them out with a tired grin.

Pressing forward, they finally reached the top of the tower. An ornate door barred their way to the roof where Lyandros awaited.

Leo steeled himself. "Let's finish this."

But as they moved to open the door, more spectral beings emerged from the walls around them. Their hollow eyes and mournful wails made Leo's skin crawl.

"Not more of these freaks!" he groaned. Finn looked drained, his motions slowing.

The shadowy hordes pressed in, sapping their energy. As Finn struggled to keep his shield intact, Leo knew they were in trouble.

Mustering the last of his power, Leo linked his magic to Finn, sharing his waning strength. The influx of energy allowed Finn to expand the shield, driving back the attacking spirits. But both boys were flagging.

Just then, a blaze of light shattered the darkness. Bliss stood before them, bow drawn and gleaming. "Need a hand, sugar?" he quipped with a sassy grin.

Despite their dire situation, Leo couldn't help an eyeroll. "About time you showed up."

Finn flashed Bliss a relieved smile. "Boy, are we glad to see you."

As they caught their breath, Leo asked Bliss, "Where's King Demetrius? Thought he'd be with you."

"Still outside playing ghostbuster," Bliss replied, leaning casually on his engraved bow. "Said he'll handle the baddies out there and join us shortly."

Finn wiped sweat from his brow. "That shadow dragon took everything I had. Please tell me there's not more of those things upstairs."

Leo shook his head. "Nah, that overgrown lizard didn't have the real gravitas of a dragon. No offense to it." He pantomimed tipping a hat to the fallen beast.

Rolling his eyes, Bliss headed for the ornate door leading to the tower roof. "Come on, we've got a demon to take down."

But before they could reach it, a bloodcurdling shriek came from above. A winged creature with fiery hair and blazing eyes dropped from the shadows.

"Down!" Bliss yelled, knocking Finn and Leo flat as lethal claws swiped the air where their heads had been.

"What fresh hell is this?" Leo cried, getting an upside down view of the winged monster as it perched on the door. Its gaze oozed madness and malice.

Bliss scowled, drawing his bow and notching a gleaming arrow. "Tisiphone. One of the Furies." He spoke the name like a curse. "Nasty creatures. We need to take it out fast."

As Bliss traded shots with Tisiphone, Leo's mind raced. She looked human, not like a creature at all. But her identity was unmistakable - one of the Greek Furies of vengeance.

Tisiphone appeared as a strikingly beautiful but severe looking woman. She had long, dark hair that whipped around her face like serpents. Her eyes were a piercing, icy blue that seemed to cut right through to one's soul.

She wore black leather armor studded with silver spikes across her shoulders and gauntlets. A blood-red sash was tied around her waist, over black leggings and boots. Strange symbols glinted along the edges of her armor in silver thread.

An ornate dagger with a twisted black handle was gripped in her claw-like gloved hand. The obsidian blade seemed to drink in the dim light around it.

Though she seemed human, there was something chilling and otherworldly about her presence - an undeniable menace that was nearly palpable in the air around her. She moved with preternatural speed and precision, her beauty masking the deadly nature within.

When she screamed, it was like the tortured wails of the damned in the deepest pits of the underworld. This was no mere mortal they faced, but a dangerous agent of vengeance and destruction.

"Little help here!" Bliss called out. Leo shook off his shock and readied scintillating bolts of necromantic energy.

Nearby, Finn was breathing hard, magical reserves running on empty. They had to end this quick.

Bliss said in a low voice, "Listen close. When I say go, run for the door. I'll deal with Tisiphone."

Finn started to protest, but Leo cut him off. "Dude, you're toast. Just be ready for Lyandros. We've got this."

Seeing Leo's resolute look, Finn reluctantly nodded.

Bliss unleashed a rapid volley of spirit arrows, forcing Tisiphone back. "Ready boys? Go!"

Finn sprinted for the exit. Tisiphone screeched in rage, but Leo hit her with a necromantic blast that knocked her into the wall.

"Bliss, finish her!" Leo yelled.

With a final arrow, Bliss struck Tisiphone down. They then hurried to join Finn, ready to confront Lyandros.

As Leo and Finn entered through the door, they found Rory's soul floating in the center of the room.

Leo carefully approached his brother and called out to him, but Rory didn't respond. His head moved slowly to look at Leo, but there was no recognition in his vacant eyes. It broke Leo's heart to see his vibrant brother reduced to this empty shell.

Still, Leo persisted, moving closer while Finn cautioned him to be careful. But Rory remained unresponsive, his blank stare aimed right through Leo.

Then suddenly, in a chilling, distorted voice, Rory spoke. "Leave… now…" he warned hauntingly.

Leo shook his head. "Rory, we're here to help you. Just hang on."

But Rory shouted again, his voice a twisted mockery of itself, "I said LEAVE!"

"Leo!" Finn shouted in warning.

Leo looked up to see a dark figure emerge - the demon Lyandros, looking like a mafia boss with a jagged scar running down his face. He smirked cruelly. "So good of you to finally join us."

Leo clenched his fists. "What do you want with my brother, you monster?"

Lyandros clicked his tongue. "Now, now, that's no way to speak to your host. As for dear Rory here, his soul will be the key I need to unleash chaos on both the spirit and mortal realms."

The demon's dark power thickened the air. But Leo stood defiant. "We're taking my brother back."

Lyandros chuckled. "I'm afraid neither of you will be leaving here alive."

Lyandros' body contorted, horns erupting from his head as his form became monstrous. Power rolled off him in crushing waves.

With a guttural roar, the demon lunged at Leo. Throwing up a magical barrier just in time, Leo gritted his teeth from the force of the impact.

"You pathetic worm!" Lyandros snarled, hammering against the shield. "You stand no chance against my might!"

Sweat beaded Leo's forehead as he poured all his energy into maintaining the barrier. But his magical reserves were running on empty. Still, he had to hold on for Rory.

Nearby, Finn hurled spheres of glowing energy that exploded against Lyandros like grenades. But the demon seemed unaffected, continuing his assault on Leo's faltering shield.

"It's no use!" Leo yelled over the deafening crashes. "Physical attacks aren't hurting him!"

"There has to be a way!" Finn shouted back. With a massive blow, Lyandros shattered Leo's barrier and sent him flying.

Hitting the ground hard, Leo coughed blood. Every inch of his body screamed in pain. Lyandros loomed over him, grinning cruelly.

"Pathetic fool. You thought you could challenge me?" The demon grabbed Leo by the throat, hoisting him up.

Leo clawed uselessly at the iron grip cutting off his air. Spots danced before his eyes. Suddenly, Finn tackled Lyandros from behind.

"Let him go!" Finn blasted the demon at point blank range, finally making him drop Leo.

Leo gasped for breath. "Thanks, I owe you one."

"What are friends for?" Finn quipped, though he was looking rough. Blood dripped from multiple cuts and contusions.

Lyandros laughed, a horrible guttural sound. "I'll thank you for saving me the trouble of killing you separately."

He charged, brutally swatting Finn aside before renewing his assault on Leo. The blows came relentlessly, reducing Leo to a ragged, bleeding mess.

Through swollen eyes, he saw Finn struggling to rise. They were both running on empty, hope fading fast. But they had to keep fighting, for Rory's sake.

Leo managed to shoot a distress signal out the tower window. "Bliss…help…" he croaked, before Lyandros seized him again.

"Still clinging to hope? There is none!" The demon squeezed mercilessly. "Now die!"

Leo's vision darkened. This was it. But suddenly Finn was there, smiling reassurance even as blood dripped from his mouth. A blinding aura surrounded them.

When Leo could see again, ghostly tendrils connected his and Finn's magic. Trusting his instincts, Leo combined their power. A shockwave of energy exploded outward, sending Lyandros flying.

Leo rose, filled with renewed strength. He stopped the demon's charge with an upraised hand.

"No more. This ends now." Leo's voice echoed with power. He blasted Lyandros with a concentrated beam, forcing him back to human form.

"This…isn't over…" the demon hissed.

"Yes it is." Leo's next attack drove Lyandros away in defeat.

With the threat gone, Leo rushed to Rory's side. "Rory! Are you okay?"

His brother gave a tired smile. "Thanks to you. But I can't leave yet." His voice was back to normal.

Finn nodded. "We should put safeguards around his soul." Together, they wove protective enchantments.

"Thank you both." Rory's smile saddened. "But now I need you to go." Mustering his last dregs of power, he teleported them away.

They found themselves suddenly back on the shore, the Tower of Spirits disappearing behind them. Leo got unsteadily to his feet, heart heavy but still hopeful they'd see Rory again someday.

"What the hell just happened?" Bliss asked, looking around in confusion. "How'd we end up here?"

"Rory used the last of his power to kick us out once we safeguarded his soul," Leo explained, bitterness in his tone. "Had to be the hero."

He did a quick check of the others. "Is everyone alright? Bliss, King Demetrius?"

Bliss rolled his neck with a few cracks. "I'll live. Tisiphone was one nasty hellcat, but I've survived worse."

King Demetrius sheathed his sword. "Just some minor wounds. What of Lyandros?"

Leo shook his head. "The coward got away when I blasted him. But we did what we came to do."

Finn spoke up, "Where do you think he scurried off to?"

"If I had to guess, back to our world," Leo replied. "We need to get back and report what happened."

He turned to King Demetrius. "Can you have your guards regularly check on Rory's soul? Just want to be sure he's safe."

The king put a hand on Leo's shoulder. "You have my oath he will be protected. I shall patrol the area myself."

Leo gave a grateful nod then looked to Bliss. "You coming back with us or staying here?"

Bliss flashed a wicked grin, conjuring his ghostly bow. "And miss a rematch with that demon scum? I'm in."

With that settled, Leo went to find his parents, who were huddled together nearby. He managed a tired smile. "Ready to head home?"

His mother grasped his hand, eyes glistening. "Oh yes, my dear." His father put an arm around them both.

Leo led them back to the others, relief flooding him. This ordeal was finally over.

Finn gave Poofy an affectionate pat before returning the puffball to his ring for safekeeping. "So what's the plan when we get back?"

"We find Lyandros and take him down for good this time," Leo said vehemently.

King Demetrius raised his hands, summoning a swirling portal back to their world. "I can travel between realms easily. Call if you need reinforcements." He embraced each of them before they left.

Steeling themselves, the group stepped through, leaving the Spirit World behind. They emerged into a thankfully calm night in their own world.

# 18

## Finn

The portal took them directly into the living room of Leo's home. Leo was still right next to his parents trying to help them out of the portal while Bliss was already looking around the room.

"It is good to be back here. Damn, sugar, your house is massive." Bliss said and his smile was massive.

"Yeah, yeah. It is just a house." Leo chuckled then turned to his parents. "Are you guys okay?"

"Thank you, son. We are just glad to be back home." His father said and Finn saw that Leo was smiling. Finn thought that it was about time that Leo get some closure and have the family that he always wanted.

Finn heard footsteps that were rushing towards their general direction. Not a moment later, Eryx's head popped up in the corner and Finn smiled. He missed his friend, his relationship with Finn had come a long way since they first met.

Eryx's eyes darted between a smiling Bliss and Finn but just shrugged it off and went directly to Finn and hugged him tightly. "Oh, I am so glad you're back. We've been worried that you're going to get stuck there forever."

Give it to Eryx to go all melodramatic on him so Finn just chuckled. "How long have we been gone? And where's everyone?"

"You've been gone for about a couple of hours. And the other are on their way. How did it go in there?"

"Let's wait for the others, but first Eryx, meet Bliss. Bliss, meet Eryx." Finn introduced the two together.

Bliss smirked as the two shook hands. "I never thought this day would come but yet here we are." Bliss hugged Eryx tightly who was currently stunned but slowly hugged Bliss back. "I've miss you, Apollo."

Just then, Finn felt Alex's presence nearby and that's when Alex entered the room. Alex stopped when he spotted Bliss who was had Eryx on a one armed hug. "Eros?" Alex said and the name resonated with Finn as he tried to remembered who Eros was in the pantheon of gods.

"Hi uncle, its been a while." Bliss said.

"What are you doing here?" Alex said then growled. "Your father, do you know where he is?"

Bliss shrugged, "I honestly don't know, uncle. I haven't talked to him since I left home and at this point I couldn't care less about the old fart."

"Alright guys, come on, let's take this to the kitchen where we can talk properly." Leo interjected and turned to his parents. "Mom and dad meet Eryx, and Alex."

Leo's parents suddenly fell to the ground Finn could see that Leo's parents corporeal form was fading fast.

Alex immediately rushed towards the two and crouched down to assess the situation. "Finn, I am going to need your help. I need you to lend me a sliver of your magic." Alex asked Finn while still looking at Leo's parents.

Finn nodded and closed his eyes to tap on his magic that gave him a gentle hum. Alex stood up and faced Finn. Alex raised his hand and took some of the magic that resides inside Finn which glowed a whispy white. "Is that my magic?" Finn asked.

"Yes, don't worry, I'll give it back." Alex went back to look at the couple of stood over them. Alex raised another hand and conjured up his own magic. Everyone watched intensely as the two globes of magic started to float above Leo's Parents. The two orbs circled around each other.

"Mom, Dad? What's going on?" Finn heard someone way. He took his gaze away from what was going on in front of him and saw that the voice came from Justin who had Harry in tow.

Finn saw Leo walk towards his brothers and give them a brief of what's going on.  Finn went back to observing knowing that The brothers will be okay.

In front of him, The two orbs now rotating at each other at tremendous speed the all of a sudden it dropped down to the couple and they started glowing. The glow was only visible for less than half a second before dying down. Finn saw Alex take the two orbs out of their bodies and without missing a beat went, Finn's magic went back to him and the same goes for Alex.

"What just happened?" Leo asked.

"I used your healing magic and combined with mine to help them be last longer in their corporeal form in this realm.  Than told me everything and we need to find their bodies fast." Alex explained.

Leo nodded before he and his brothers helped their parents stand up. "Come on, let's talk somewhere comfortable."The portal swirled with energy, and in the blink of an eye, Leo, Bliss, and Finn found themselves in Leo's spacious living room.  Bliss wasted no time in taking in the surroundings, his eyes wide with amazement.

"It is good to be back here. Damn, sugar, your house is massive," Bliss exclaimed, his smile infectious.

"Yeah, yeah. It's just a house," Leo chuckled, turning to his parents who were still emerging from the portal. "Are you guys okay?"

"Thank you, son. We're just glad to be back home," Leo's father replied, and Finn couldn't help but notice the joy in Leo's eyes. It was about time Leo got the family he had always wanted.

The sound of hurried footsteps approached, and a familiar face popped into the corner of the room. Finn grinned as he saw Eryx, his long-time friend. Their relationship had come a long way since they first met.

Eryx's eyes darted between Bliss, Finn, and their smiles, but he shrugged it off and rushed to Finn, wrapping him in a tight hug. "Oh, I'm so glad you're back. We've been worried you were going to get stuck there forever."

Finn chuckled at Eryx's melodramatic welcome. "How long have we been gone? And where's everyone?"

"Only a couple of hours," Eryx replied, his grip not loosening. "The others are on their way. How did it go in there?"

Finn decided to wait for the rest of their friends, starting with the introductions. "First things first, Eryx, meet Bliss. Bliss, meet Eryx."

Bliss smirked as their hands met. "I never thought this day would come, but here we are." He pulled Eryx into a tight hug. "I've missed you, Apollo."

Just then, Finn felt another presence nearby, and Alex entered the room. He paused as he spotted Bliss, who had Eryx in a one-armed embrace. "Eros?" Alex said, his words triggering a distant memory in Finn as he tried to place the name within the pantheon of gods.

"Hi, uncle. It's been a while," Bliss said nonchalantly.

"What are you doing here?" Alex questioned, a growl underlying his words. "And your father, do you know where he is?"

Bliss shrugged, his demeanor indifferent. "I honestly don't know, uncle. I haven't talked to him since I left home, and at this point, I couldn't care less about the old fart."

Leo interjected, "Alright, guys, let's take this to the kitchen where we can talk properly." Leo then turned to his parents. "Mom and Dad, meet Eryx and Alex."

Finn noticed that Leo's parents were rapidly losing their corporeal form and slowly falling to the ground. Alex immediately rushed to their side, crouching down to assess the situation. "Finn, I'm going to need your help. I need a sliver of your magic," Alex requested, still focused on Leo's parents.

Finn nodded and closed his eyes, tapping into his magic, feeling it hum gently. Alex stood up, facing Finn, and extracted a bit of his magic, which emitted a faint, wispy glow. "Is that my magic?" Finn asked.

"Yes, don't worry, I'll give it back," Alex assured him. He then turned his attention back to the couple. Alex raised his hands, conjuring his own magic. The two orbs of magic, one from Finn and one from Alex, floated above Leo's parents, their glow mesmerizing. The orbs circled around each other in a breathtaking display.

"Mom, Dad? What's going on?" a voice piped up, and Finn turned to see Justin, who had Harry in tow.

Leo walked over to his brothers, providing them with a brief explanation. Finn returned his focus to the enchanting spectacle in front of him, knowing that Justin and Harry would be okay.

The two orbs spun faster and faster, until suddenly they descended onto Leo's parents, bathing them in a brilliant, but fleeting, light. Finn watched in awe as Alex removed the two orbs from their bodies, his and Finn's magic returning to them seamlessly.

"What just happened?" Leo inquired.

"I used Finn's healing magic, combined with mine, to help them remain in their corporeal form in this realm a bit longer," Alex explained. "Than told me everything, and now we need to find their bodies fast."

Leo nodded and, with his brothers, helped his parents stand. "Come on, let's talk somewhere comfortable."

The group made their way to the kitchen, Finn reflecting on the magical display he had just witnessed and he couldn't help but feel that their journey was far from over.

Gathered around the cozy kitchen, the motley crew of warriors shared a moment of unity. Finn, leaning comfortably next to Leo, stole a sidelong glance at him, his usual grin playing on his lips. The rest of the group occupied various spots, some standing, others seated around the worn wooden table. It was time for a serious conversation, but even in the direst of times, humor found its way into their midst.

Alex leaned forward, his piercing gaze locking onto each of them in turn. His deep voice cut through the air with a sense of purpose. "Has Rory's soul been safeguarded?" He got straight to the point, wasting no time on formalities.

"Yeah, it is done. What's going to be our next step?" Leo chimed in, his brow furrowed with anticipation.

"We need to capture Lyandros. Thanatos told me that you guys managed to take Lyandros out but fled. Is that correct?" Alex inquired, his voice laced with urgency.

"Yes, we believe that he fled over here to the mortal realm, but we're not sure if that was the case," Finn answered, his eyes reflecting the uncertainty of their predicament.

Alex nodded in understanding, then shifted his gaze to Leo. "From what I've gathered, Leo, the bodies of your parents have demons inside them, and they need to be returned back." Leo nodded, his expression somber.

"Yes, that's what we believe happened. A body cannot walk around the mortal realm without a soul inside them. But there's one thing that we forgot to tell you, Leo." Rhea said.

Curiosity filled the room, and all eyes turned to Rhea. "What is it?" Leo asked.

"The body that a demon possesses slowly dies if they go unchecked," Clint, another member of the team and Leo's father, revealed, concern etched on his face.

Leo's brows knitted together as he processed the grim information. "Is there a way to prevent this from happening?"

Rhea's voice was soft, tinged with hope. "There might be a way, but we have to do some research. This hasn't happened for centuries, and the books that our predecessors wrote may have some answers."

"Harry," Alex instructed, "I want you to help your parents look for that book. I've already informed the team in New York about the whereabouts of the demons. They'll contact me if something comes up. But if nothing comes up, we head to plan B."

Bliss, a member who had remained silent, couldn't resist interjecting. "Is it going to be fun and explosive?"

Alex ignored Bliss's attempt at humor and continued with determination. "We lure them in."

Leo's concern bubbled to the surface. "Damn it, Alex. We can't risk that. We can't risk my family being casualties in all this."

Alex's voice was firm. "Do you have any other ideas? Whatever we do, someone will get hurt. We're fighting against the leader of the Demons." He silenced Leo with a stern look. "Are we clear?"

Leo nodded reluctantly, the weight of their mission pressing heavily upon him.

"Leo, Alice Peterson told me that she's open to cooperating with us and will be visiting tomorrow," Justin added, offering a glimmer of hope.

Leo's expression softened. "Good, she could probably help us with some missing pieces."

With the night's pressing matters laid out on the table, Alex gave the order to disband. "Alright, everyone, get some rest. We'll reconvene tomorrow morning."

As the group dispersed, Leo turned to Finn with a lighthearted glint in his eye. "Finn, you want to sleep in my room tonight?"

Finn's face broke into a wide smile, his voice filled with playful eagerness. "Sure, why not? Your snoring can't be worse than Bliss's bad jokes."

They chuckled, the weight of their mission momentarily forgotten in their shared camaraderie.

As Finn and Leo entered Leo's room, the door shut tight, sealing them off from the world. Leo's eyes burned with raw desire as he lunged at Finn, attacking his lips with unbridled passion.

"Ffffuck, Leo!" Finn groaned, his voice heavy with need. "You had me craving you so fucking bad."

Leo's hands gripped Finn's body possessively, his touch sending sparks of ecstasy dancing along Finn's skin. Their bodies writhed together, a dangerous dance of primal desire. Finn's breath came in ragged gasps as Leo's kisses trailed down his neck, marking him as his territory. "Leo, please…" Finn panted, his voice straining with desperation. "I needed you inside me, filling me up."

Leo's eyes gleamed with lust as he ripped off Finn's clothes, baring his delicious body for his pleasure. Finn shivered under his intense gaze, feeling utterly exposed and vulnerable. Leo's voice was a low growl in his ear as he whispered his desires. "You were mine, Finn. I fucked you so hard, made you scream my name."

Finn's heart pounded in his chest as Leo positioned himself at his entrance, teasing him with the promise of pleasure. With a forceful thrust, Leo plunged deep inside Finn, claiming him as his own. Finn cried out, a mix of pain and ecstasy, his body arching to meet Leo's powerful strokes. "Yes, Leo! Keep fucking me, harder!"

The room filled with the sounds of their moans and gasps, a symphony of pleasure and desire. Finn's senses were overwhelmed as Leo's relentless pace drove him closer to the edge. "God, Finn! You felt so fucking good!" Leo grunted, his voice strained. "I will never let you go."

Finn's mind was consumed by the overpowering sensations, his body a vessel of pure pleasure. He clung to Leo, his nails digging into his back as waves of pleasure crashed over him. "I am gonna cum, Leo! I am so fucking close!"

Leo's grip on Finn tightened, his thrusts growing more urgent. With one final, mind-shattering thrust, Finn cried out in ecstasy as his orgasm washed over him. Leo followed close behind, filling him with his hot release, their bodies trembling with the intensity of their passion.

They collapsed onto the bed, breathless and spent, their bodies tangled together in a post-orgasmic haze. Finn's voice was a whisper as he spoke. "That… that was fucking incredible, Leo."

Finn and Leo lay entangled on the bed, their breathing slowly returning to normal. Leo's fingers traced lazy circles on Finn's bare skin, sending delightful shivers down his spine. "You are insatiable, Finn," Leo murmured, his voice filled with satisfaction. "But I am done with you yet."

A mischievous grin danced across Leo's lips as he trailed his fingers down Finn's body, teasing every sensitive spot along the way. Finn's body responded eagerly, his nerves on fire with anticipation. "Leo, what are you planning?" Finn asked, his voice dripping with curiosity.

Leo's eyes gleamed with a wicked glint as he leaned in close, his lips brushing against Finn's ear. "I want to explore all your dirty little fantasies, Finn," he whispered seductively. "I want to take you to places you've only dream of."

Finn's breath hitched, his heart racing with a mixture of excitement and nerves. He couldn't help but surrender to Leo's intoxicating presence, knowing that he was about to experience something wild and unforgettable. "Leo, show me… show me everything," Finn pleaded, his voice filled with a desperate longing.

Leo's touch became bolder, more possessive, as he trailed his fingers down to Finn's throbbing length. He stroked him slowly, his touch sending jolts of pleasure through Finn's body. "I am gonna make you mine, Finn," Leo hissed, his voice dripping with dominance. "You are gonna beg for more."

As Leo expertly worked Finn's body with his hands and mouth, Finn couldn't help but become lost in a whirlwind of sensation. His moans filled the room, blending with the sound of skin slapping against skin. "Leo, fuck… harder," Finn gasped, his voice a plea for more.

Leo's thrusts became faster and more relentless, driving Finn to the edge of pleasure once again. Finn's body arched, meeting Leo's every movement, as they both chased their release. "Leo, yes! Just like that!" Finn screamed, his voice a melody of pure ecstasy.

Their bodies moved in perfect sync, their passion burning hotter with every passing moment. Finn could feel the familiar coil of pleasure building within him, ready to explode. "Leo… I am gonna cum," Finn moaned, his voice strained with anticipation.

With one final, powerful thrust, Finn succumbed to the overwhelming intensity of his orgasm. Pleasure washed over him like a tidal wave, his body convulsing with pure bliss. Leo followed suit, their bodies joining in the symphony of release. "Fuck, Finn… you're incredible," Leo gasped, his voice filled with awe.

As they lay there, their bodies still entwined, Finn's mind raced with the possibilities of what was to come. The night was far from over, and they had only scratched the surface of their deepest desires.

# 19

## Leo

Under the soft duvet, Leo slowly awakened from his slumber, unaware of the sinful surprise that awaited him. As his senses came alive, he felt a tantalizing warmth enveloping his manhood, sending electric shocks straight to his core.

Leo's eyes fluttered open, and his breath caught at the sight before him. Finn, his lips wrapped around Leo's throbbing length, worked tirelessly to bring him pleasure. The room was filled with muffled moans and the wet sounds of Finn's expert mouth, intertwined with the sweet symphony of their desire.

Leo's body tensed with a mixture of desire and anticipation. He gripped the sheets, his knuckles turning white as Finn's talented tongue danced along his sensitive flesh. The sensations were almost too much to bear, a sweet torment that drove him to the edge of sanity.

"F-Finn," Leo stammered, his voice laced with need. "Fuck, you know how to start the day."

Finn glanced up at Leo, a mischievous glimmer in his eyes as he continued his sinful assault. He teased Leo's tip with the tip of his velvety tongue, savoring the taste of him.

Leo's hips involuntarily bucked, seeking more of Finn's intoxicating mouth. His fingers tangled in Finn's tousled hair, urging him on. Every flick, every suction was a symphony of pleasure, threatening to shatter Leo's composure.

"God, Finn," Leo groaned, his voice strained. "You're gonna make me explode."

Finn hummed around Leo's shaft, intensifying the vibrations and pushing Leo further towards the brink. The sensations flooded Leo's senses, his body trembling with indescribable pleasure.

Leo couldn't hold back any longer. The mounting pressure within him became too much, building into a crescendo that demanded release. He arched his back, his muscles coiling like a taut spring.

"Finn!" Leo cried out, his voice filled with ecstasy. "I'm gonna… I'm gonna cum!"

With one final, mind-blowing suction, Finn brought Leo to the edge and beyond. Waves of pulsating pleasure crashed over Leo, consuming him entirely. His body convulsed, his release cascading into Finn's eager mouth.

As the aftershocks of his orgasm rippled through his body, Leo collapsed onto the bed, breathless and satiated. Finn, still holding Leo's gaze, licked his lips, the taste of Leo lingering on his tongue.

Leo's heart pounded in his chest as he tried to catch his breath. His mind was a haze of bliss, his body humming in the aftermath of their passionate encounter.

"Finn," Leo panted, his voice filled with a mix of satisfaction and desire. "We should… w-we should shower and get ready."

Finn grinned, a wicked gleam in his eyes. "Oh, Leo," he purred, crawling up the bed to hover over Leo's naked body. "Don't think for a second that our adventures are over. The day has just begun."

As they embraced, the steamy bathroom awaited them, a playground for their renewed passion. Their bodies glistened under the hot spray of water, their whispers of desire mingling with the steam.

After showering, Leo and Finn headed downstairs. In the kitchen, Leo found his brother Justin nursing a cup of coffee.

"Hey man, where is everyone?" Leo asked.

Justin looked up. "Oh hey guys. Alex and Eryx are in the library having some kind of meeting. They want you there too."

"Thanks, we'll head over," Leo replied, giving Justin a quick hug. Justin hesitated then squeezed back tightly.

"You better get going before Alex flame broils me for stalling you," Justin joked weakly. Leo chuckled and patted his brother's shoulder before leaving with Finn.

In the library, Alex and Eryx were gathered around a table with two others - Gabe and Olivia, Leo recognized. Alex's top strategist and arcane mage.

Alex waved them over. "Good timing. We've got important updates."

Leo and Finn sat down next to each other. Under the table, Finn gave Leo's hand a subtle, comforting squeeze.

Gabe tapped the futuristic device on his wrist. "We've tracked the demons in your parents' bodies. They're hours away, heading for Salem."

"What's the plan for dealing with them?" Leo asked.

"We'll lure them somewhere safe first. The cemetery nearby should work," Gabe explained.

Finn looked uneasy. "You're expecting a big fight then?"

Alex nodded grimly. "They're demons who serve Lyandros. They won't go quietly."

"With no one around, they can't jump into new hosts either," Leo added. Finn seemed to accept that logic.

More taps on his device and Gabe showed them two dots - one red, one purple - moving across a map. "Marcus is shadowing them already. We'll be ready."

Eryx turned to Finn. "We need you here, protecting Justin, Harry and Leo's parents."

Finn immediately protested. "But I can help fight too!"

"Having you here as backup is strategic," Olivia reasoned gently. "We can't leave everything undefended."

Reluctantly, Finn agreed. Leo felt bad but knew it made sense.

Alex looked at Leo. "You'll join us. Your skills will be critical to expelling the demons."

Leo set his jaw firmly and nodded. He would do whatever it took to free his parents.

The team suited up in lightweight armor that Gabe and Olivia enchanted for protection and concealment. Meanwhile, Leo helped Finn ward the house against potential threats.

"I should be going with you," Finn insisted again.

Leo cupped his cheek. "I need you here, watching my family's back. I'll be okay." He pulled Finn into a fierce kiss before joining the others.

Alex opened a shimmering portal. "Let's move."

They emerged outside the wrought iron gates of the cemetery. Gabe and Olivia immediately set complex trap spells along the perimeter. Leo could feel the magic thrumming in the air.

"Bait's arriving," Alex muttered, peering down the road. A sleek black car approached.

Leo's gut twisted with anticipation. He thought of his possessed parents, trapped and helpless. Not for much longer.

The car stopped and two figures stepped out - a man and woman with dead, soulless eyes. The demons inhabiting Leo's parents. Rage simmered inside him.

"Remember, restrain and contain them only. We want those bodies intact," Alex commanded.

The demons stalked closer, smiling coldly. "This is your ambush? Pathetic," they sneered in unison.

Leo confronted them. "Tell us where to find Lyandros and we'll consider going easy on you."

Leo's necromantic magic surged through him as he hurled crackling bolts of violet energy at the demons. They screamed in rage as the attacks seared their flesh, the sickly sweet smell of burnt demonic essence filling the air.

The demons fought back ferociously, slashes of inky darkness streaking toward Leo. He rolled and dodged, the blackness tearing through tombstones and gouging smoldering craters in the earth. Leo returned fire, explosions of purple flame bombarding the demons.

One demon deflected a blast off its obsidian claws, then charged Leo with preternatural speed. He hastily raised a shield, straining as the demon pounded relentlessly against the magical barrier. Sparks flew as long fissures spread across its surface like spiderwebs.

With a roar, the demon shattered Leo's shield, the force of the blow hurling him backward. He tumbled limply across the ground. The demon loomed over him, murder in its fathomless eyes, and raised a razor-sharp claw for the killing strike.

A blur intercepted the attack and Alex had the demon by its corded throat. His eyes were pits of hellfire as he squeezed mercilessly. The demon clawed and flailed in his unbreakable grip, jet trails of inky magic evaporating in the air.

But finally one demon landed a crushing blow, sending Leo flying. He hit the ground hard, blood filling his mouth. The demons rushed to finish him.

Suddenly Alex was there, catching the demon's arm before it could strike. "Back off," he growled, eyes blazing.

The demon laughed mockingly. "Come to protect this pathetic human? Too late!" It broke Alex's grip, swiping at him.

Alex deflected the blow almost lazily. Nearby, Gabe wrapped the second demon in glowing bindings of earthen magic. It thrashed and spat curses.

"Enough games," Alex commanded. "Surrender or face oblivion." Dark power rolled off him in waves.

But the demons only cackled louder. "You cannot stop what comes, oh mighty Hades! Your reign ends soon."

Rage boiled up in Leo. Ignoring his injuries, he hurled another sphere of energy. It slammed into the demon attacking Alex, driving it back with a scream.

The other demon broke Gabe's bindings and rushed straight for Alex's unprotected back.

"Behind you!" Leo yelled in warning.

Alex glanced back, almost bored, and froze the demon in mid-air. Inky bands of magic wrapped around the paralyzed demons.

The demon's claws raked towards Alex's back with lightning speed, aiming to rip his spine from his body. But Alex whirled with inhuman quickness, catching the demon's hand inches from his flesh. The demon hissed and spat, writhing in Alex's iron grip.

"You dare raise a hand against me?" Alex thundered, his eyes flashing with crimson fury. The air crackled with gathering power as he called upon his ancient magic. The demon wailed in sudden terror, realizing its fatal mistake.

Alex's hand began to glow red-hot on the demon's wrist, searing its putrid flesh. The demon howled and thrashed, trying futilely to break free. But Alex only tightened his hold, face carved from stone. Flames erupted where he gripped the demon, consuming its arm in a matter of seconds.

The demon's screams rose to unearthly pitch, echoing across the blood-soaked battlefield. But Alex showed no mercy, continuing to burn the vile creature as it begged for death. Finally the flames reached the demon's body, bursting forth to engulf it completely. It fell to the ground, nothing but ashes and echoes of suffering.

Alex stood unchanged, his eyes still bursting with wrathful fire. The message was clear - he would show no quarter to those who dared challenge him or threaten those under his protection.

"Enough games," Alex commanded. "Leo, banish these wretches, now!"

Gritting his teeth against the pain, Leo began the ritual. Arcane words spilled from his lips as he drew complex signs with glowing fire.

*"Et interiere in infernum. Emissa maligna potestas!"*

The demons shrieked, writhing in agony. Ghostly shapes emerged from the possessed bodies, still howling curses. With a final burst of power, the demons fled out of the bodies of his parents.

"Bon voyage, assholes," he grunted. The shadowy spirits were sucked away into oblivion.

Leo sank to his knees, completely spent. But he smiled in weary triumph. His parents were free.

Alex placed a hand on his shoulder. "Well done. Couldn't have banished them better myself."

Despite his exhaustion, Leo flushed with pride. Praise from a god wasn't given lightly.

Marcus kept watch as Gabe and Olivia helped Leo's parents into the back of an unmarked van. They would be safe at home until fully recovered.

Alex's expression was grim. "Those demons confirmed Lyandros is planning something big. We need to find and stop him immediately."

Leo met his gaze firmly. "I'm ready to end this, once and for all."

Returning home, they found the others anxiously awaiting news. Leo quickly reassured them that his parents were safe and demon-free.

Finn pulled Leo into his arms, tension melting from his body. "I knew you could do it. Are you okay? Anything I can heal?"

"I am okay, just burnt out. We need to place my parent's body somewhere safe first. If you can, please check them for any signs of demonic activity." Leo said.

All of them took his parents to the master bedroom, and he could feel Gabe put up a ward that was stronger than he could ever make, and he was grateful for it.

"Where's Bliss anyway, I haven't seen him around at all today," Leo wondered. His friend should have been with them in the fight.

"I ordered Bliss to track down Lyandros' movements. He will be back once he's got something." Alex explained, and Leo nodded.

"They'll be fine for now. I don't sense any demonic activities in their souls. But their bodies are slowly fading; the demons have taken a lot from them. We need to get your parents' souls back into their original bodies," Finn said.

"Have you found anything in the library?" Leo asked.

"Nothing yet, but your mother said that we are close, so expect the solution to come soon," Finn said. "You guys should go and rest; I'll look after them."

"Leo, can I talk to you in private?" Alex asked softly, and Leo nodded.

Leo gave Finn one tender kiss before leaving the room with Alex.

"Come on, Olivia and Marcus, let's go to the library and help," Gabe said, and the three of them left Leo and Alex alone.

"Is there a place where we could talk?" Alex asked.

"Yeah, come with me," Leo said, and Alex followed.

In the quiet of the back garden, the air was filled with the soothing scent of blooming flowers, a symphony of colors and life that stood in stark contrast to the recent battle. Every plant was meticulously arranged, creating an oasis of calm amidst the chaos of their supernatural struggles. A soft breeze rustled the leaves and carried with it the faint, earthy fragrance of the soil.

Leo and Alex leaned against the ornate railing of the viewing deck that overlooked the enchanting garden. The afternoon sun painted long, lazy shadows across the meticulously manicured lawns. It was a welcome change from the tension and exhaustion of the day.

"How are you holding up?" Alex asked Leo, his earlier aura of authority giving way to a softer, more compassionate tone.

Leo looked out at the garden, his eyes tracing the path of a tiny, iridescent hummingbird as it flitted from flower to flower. "I'm holding better than I could ever hope for," he admitted, but the weight of their situation hung heavily in his gaze. He turned to Alex, his expression a mix of curiosity and incredulity. "So, you're Hades, huh?"

Alex nodded, his gaze steady. "Yes. I hope that doesn't change how you view me as a person."

Leo let out a rueful chuckle, "Not gonna lie to you, Alex, it's a lot to process. Before I went back home, I never really knew gods existed. I thought they were just myths."

Alex arched an eyebrow, genuinely interested. "What changed your mind?"

Leo's face relaxed into a thoughtful expression. "When I was looking for the book to help Rory, I met Hecate. She said that my parents, or probably the demons, trapped her in the book. When I released her, I felt her give some of her magic to me."

Alex's eyes lit up with realization. "Then we might have a way to trap Lyandros."

Leo couldn't help but be a bit mischievous. "Can't you just zap that bloody demon to the underworld? I mean, you're a god after all."

Alex's response was tinged with regret. "I wish, but no. As long as I'm not in the underworld, my magic is limited, and tapping into it takes a toll on my body."

"I see. So, you were saying?" Leo encouraged Alex to continue.

"Bliss told me that he had the Blood Stone from the Wendigo that you guys fought. A Blood Stone needs a lot of power for it to be used. Having a sliver of Hecate's magic inside you can change that. Hecate's blessing can only be used once, and you'll have a small window of time to trap Lyandros inside the stone," Alex explained.

Leo absorbed this information, his eyes reflecting a mixture of determination and concern. "Is it going to cost me?"

Alex's voice carried the weight of their uncertain future. "I don't know. Hecate rarely gives out her blessings, so there's nothing for me to go on." He paused and then met Leo's gaze squarely. "Does Finn know?"

The question hit Leo with a pang of guilt. "Does Finn know that my magic is eating away my life force? I don't know."

Alex's concern deepened, and he offered a reminder. "You realize that you're going to have to tell him at some point, right?"

"Yeah, I know," Leo admitted, his voice heavy with the weight of his secret. "I just need to find the right time for it." As he spoke, Leo suddenly felt his vision blur, and his legs gave way beneath him.

"Leo? Are you okay?" Alex's concern was immediate, and he rushed to Leo's side, his powerful presence now focused entirely on his fallen comrade.

"I..." Leo struggled to respond, but his strength failed him, and the world around him spun into a dizzying whirl of colors and shapes. Before he knew it, Alex was rushing towards him, their connection stronger than ever in that critical moment.

# 20

# Finn

Finn had just finished making tea in Leo's cozy kitchen, grateful that Olivia had taken over watching Leo's parents. He needed this moment for himself and maybe, just maybe, a chance for some alone time with Leo. They had a conversation about their relationship that they both knew was looming on the horizon, but Finn had been adept at dodging it. He understood, though, that he couldn't evade it forever.

As he stirred his tea, he heard the familiar, somewhat clumsy footsteps of his friend, Alex, approaching. Finn couldn't help but chuckle at Alex's aura, which always seemed to announce his arrival with unmissable enthusiasm. Alex entered the kitchen right on cue.

"Hey, I'm just making some tea. Want some coffee?" Finn offered, a friendly smile on his face.

"Yes, please, thank you," Alex replied, taking a seat at the table behind Finn.

The house was a haven of coffee and tea varieties, and Finn admired it. It wasn't his home, though. His heart belonged to Manhattan, and he hoped that one day he and Leo would share a home together. But one step at a time, he reminded himself.

Finn prepared a cup of coffee for Alex, filling it with dark, aromatic coffee beans before pouring hot water from the kettle. He joined Alex at the table, holding two steaming cups.

"Where's Leo? Didn't you guys talk?" Finn inquired, taking a soothing sip of his tea.

"He fainted while we were talking, so I carried him into his bedroom," Alex explained before taking a sip of his coffee.

Finn's eyes widened, and his annoyance was genuine. "And you didn't think to call me, of all things?"

"Relax," Alex said, trying to calm Finn. "He was magically burnt out from the fight. It took a lot out of him. But I'm worried."

Finn's concern deepened. He wanted nothing more than to go to Leo and take care of him. "Why? What's going on with Leo?"

Alex held Finn's gaze, his expression intense. "You'll have to ask him."

Before Finn could respond, the doorbell rang. Justin rushed to answer it, appearing out of nowhere, and brought a disheveled woman into the kitchen.

Justin introduced the woman as Alicia Peterson. She was the other necromancer who had been with their parents the night of the possession, all those years ago. Finn felt something peculiar about her, a sensation that pricked at the edge of his consciousness, but he kept his observations to himself.

He glanced at Alex, expecting him to pick up on the odd vibe as well, but Alex's face remained impassive. It left Finn feeling like he'd missed a memo in the conversation.

Alex instructed Justin to take Alicia to the library, where they would meet them. Finn turned to Alex, his curiosity piqued.

"Do you sense anything unusual about her?" Finn whispered to his friend, furrowing his brow. Alex just shook his head and Finn didn't know what that meant..

Finn couldn't quite place the strange feeling he had about Alice Peterson, so he decided to let it go for the time being.

After finishing their drinks, they headed to the library, their steps taking them down a corridor adorned with ancient tapestries and mysterious artifacts. The library itself was an opulent chamber, with towering bookshelves that seemed to stretch into infinity, filled with tomes on magic, history, and the occult.

As they entered, they found Justin and Alicia deep in conversation. Alicia's eyes, like Alex's, held an inscrutable intensity, but Finn couldn't quite figure out what it meant. He decided to focus on the matter at hand.

Alex cleared his throat to get their attention. "Alicia has some information about our parents and the night they were possessed. She believes there's more to the story than we know."

Finn leaned forward, intrigued, and prompted, "Go on, please."

"Shouldn't we wait for Leo?" Harry asked.

"Leo is resting, we'll update him later. Now please, Alicia, tell us what you know," Alex urged.

Finn didn't know where Leo's parents were, but he could sense them around. They were probably listening, not showing themselves to Alicia. Finn could still feel something unusual with Alicia's soul.

"You have to understand that it was a long time ago, and I don't know if I still remember most of the details, but I will try to remember," Alicia sighed. "Before that night, I got a call from the pride alpha, and he told me that one of the omegas had been acting strangely, and they had been informed by their elder that the omega was possessed. My then coven leader told me to go and investigate."

"Who was your coven leader?" Justin asked.

Alicia looked at Justin and smiled at him softly. "Tera Sinclair."

Finn saw the shock on Justin's face. "Is it true that she lived more than two millennia?"

"Who is she?" Finn inquired.

"Tera was said to have lived the longest amongst necromancers. The others desired to know how she did it, but unfortunately, she took that secret to her grave not long ago," Alicia explained.

"How did she die?" Justin asked.

"She was attacked by a demon in her sleep and wasn't able to defend herself in time," Alicia said, and Justin nodded.

"What happened after you were told to investigate the omega?" Alex urged Alicia to continue her story.

"When I got there, the energy in the pride was thick with something dark. It was almost as if the energy was being drained from the inside. I was taken by the Alpha to the place where the omega was being held, and as soon as we got inside, the thick, dense air became cold and thin. I approached the omega and was hit with a strong demonic energy coming off her, and trying to get it out was impossible, and I wasn't strong enough. That's when I decided to approach your parents, Justin, and you probably know the rest," Alicia continued.

Alex nodded and addressed everyone. "Alright, it seems like we got everything for now. Justin, can you please take Ms. Peterson to her room so she can get some rest? Ms. Peterson, please let us know if you remember anything else." Justin took Alicia out of the library.

"Do we believe her? 'Cause I'm not buying everything that she was saying," Olivia asked.

"No, I know you noticed it too, Finn. Go on, tell us what your senses told you," Alex urged Finn.

Finn nodded and started talking. "My magic tells me that there's something wrong with her soul. I was able to tell that she was trying to hide it, but she probably didn't know my ability to sense souls."

"How about Rory? How are we going to free his soul and return it back to his body?" Harry spoke up after a while.

"Once Lyandros is trapped in the blood stone, his powers are going to be temporarily disabled, and we can get Rory out," Alex answered Harry before turning to Finn. "Finn, you should go and check on Leo. Eryx should be there with him."

Finn nodded and stood up to leave.

The room fell into a thoughtful silence, each person lost in their own contemplation of the revelations. Olivia couldn't help but frown, skepticism written all over her face. "This whole situation is just too bizarre, you know? Possessions, demonic energies, long-dead necromancers. It sounds like a bloody soap opera."

Alex chuckled, his eyes reflecting the weight of the situation but still holding a hint of amusement. "You're not wrong, Liv. It's like a supernatural drama, and we're the unwilling stars."

Finn added, "Well, if we are, we should at least make sure we get top billing."

Harry, who had been uncharacteristically quiet, finally spoke up. "Top billing or not, we've got a lot of work to do. And it sounds like we can't entirely trust Alicia. We need to be cautious."

Olivia crossed her arms. "I agree with Harry. And what's with her and Justin? Did you see the way she looked at him?"

Justin reentered the room, and all eyes turned to him. He gave an exasperated sigh. "Guys, let's not jump to conclusions. We have enough mysteries to solve without creating more drama among ourselves and besides, I am not into women like that."

Alex nodded. "Justin's right. Let's focus on what we can control and find a way to get Rory back."

Finn couldn't help but smile at the banter and oddity of their situation. As the group began strategizing, he slipped out of the room, intent on checking on Leo and Eryx.

Entering the quiet bedroom, Finn saw Eryx sitting in a chair nearby, nose buried in a heavy book. Finn greeted him softly, not wanting to disturb Leo's rest.

Eryx started violently, accidentally tossing the book into the air. It came down with a thump as Eryx scrambled to grab it, shooting an embarrassed grin at Finn.

Finn just chuckled. "Didn't mean to scare you. How's our patient doing?" He moved closer to the bed, gazing down at Leo's sleeping form.

"He seems stable, his magic is slowly returning too," Eryx said, coming to stand beside Finn. "I've been monitoring him closely, like Alex showed me."

Pride swelled in Finn's chest, seeing how skilled Eryx had become with his healing abilities. "You've gotten really good control over your magic now. I'm impressed."

Eryx flushed at the praise. "Thanks, I've been practicing a lot. Just want to help however I can."

Finn clasped his shoulder warmly. "You have been a huge help. Thank you for watching over Leo for me."

"Of course, anytime." Eryx leaned in for another quick hug before stepping back. "I should give you two some privacy. Alex was looking for me earlier."

Finn nodded. "We'll come find you later. Go see what scheme our dear leader is cooking up now."

Eryx grinned and headed for the door. He paused and added softly. "I'm really glad you're both back safely. We were so worried." His eyes shone with sincerity.

Finn's throat tightened. "It's good to be home."

With a small wave, Eryx slipped out, leaving Finn alone with Leo. Moving to the bedside, Finn gently brushed a curl off Leo's forehead, heart swelling with love and relief. After everything, they had made it through together.

Leo's eyes slowly fluttered open, focusing on Finn's face. A tired but happy smile spread across his lips. "Hey you," he rasped.

Finn carefully sat on the bed's edge, taking Leo's hand. "Welcome back. You had me worried for a bit there."

"What's a little magical drain between friends?" Leo joked weakly. But his grin faded. "Did we win? Is everyone else okay?"

"Thanks to you, it's over and we're all fine," Finn reassured him. "Just focus on recovering now."

Finn didn't mean to fall asleep in the chair next to Leo's bed. But the stress and fatigue finally caught up with him. He was roused some time later by a gentle hand combing through his hair. Blinking awake, he found himself gazing into Leo's beautiful eyes.

Finn smiled sleepily back at him. "Hey, how are you feeling?" he asked, sitting up straighter.

"Much better," Leo said, voice still a little raspy. "Come lay down with me?" He tugged Finn's hand in invitation.

Unable to resist, Finn carefully climbed onto the bed. Leo immediately curled against him, head coming to rest on Finn's chest. Finn wrapped an arm around him, savoring his closeness.

After a few moments of contented silence, Finn knew he had to broach a difficult subject. Taking a deep breath, he said "Leo, I think we should talk…about us."

Leo tensed slightly before sighing. "Yeah, you're probably right." He lifted his head to meet Finn's gaze. "So where do you see this going? Do you want to keep doing…whatever this is between us?"

Finn's heart ached at the uncertainty in Leo's voice. "I know I'm happy right now. I care about you so much. I guess I'm just worried I'm not good enough for you." Leo looked down, chewing his lip anxiously.

"Hey, none of that." Finn gently tilted Leo's face back up. "You are more than enough. More than I ever dreamed I'd find. I really think we could have an amazing future together."

Leo's eyes glistened with tears. "I want that too. But it scares me. I don't know if I can stop myself from falling completely in love with you." His voice shook with emotion.

Finn tenderly wiped a stray tear from Leo's cheek. "Nothing wrong with that. With you I feel safe, like I'm home. I think on some level I already love you."

A brilliant smile broke across Leo's face. "I love you too," he whispered. "So much." He leaned in and captured Finn's lips in a searing kiss.

Eventually they had to come up for air, both grinning like fools. Finn caressed Leo's face, thinking his heart might burst from sheer happiness.

But Leo's expression gradually grew serious again. "Finn, there's something else we should discuss. It's about my magic."

Finn's joy dimmed slightly from his solemn tone. But he just nodded for Leo to continue.

"Using my powers so much lately, it's put a massive strain on me. It's…it's shortening my lifespan." Leo's voice caught on the words.

Though Finn had suspected it, hearing the truth was still a punch to the gut. He clasped Leo's hand tightly. "Whatever happens, we'll face it together. I'm not going anywhere."

Leo's eyes shone with wonder. "How did I get so lucky to find you?" He leaned in for another lingering kiss.

When they finally broke apart again, Finn said "So what'd I miss while you were napping the day away?" He kept his tone playful, hoping to lighten the mood.

Leo chuckled, rolling his eyes. "Fine, Mr. Social Butterfly, catch me up."

So Finn did. He told Leo about Alicia's arrival and what she revealed which was not much. Leo listened intently.

"I want to meet her." Leo said.

"You will, but not now. You're still recovering." Finn said and Leo nodded.

"Stay with me for a while?" Leo pleaded.

"I will not go anywhere." Finn said and kissed Leo's forehead before Leo put his head on Finn's shoulders.

Finn lost track of time resting with Leo when the door suddenly opened. Marcus stood there, glancing between them.

"Alex wants you both in the master bedroom now," he informed them gruffly. "It's about your parents."

Leo was already trying to get up at the mention of his parents. Finn helped steady him as they followed Marcus down the hall.

Inside the opulent bedroom, they found Alex and Eryx waiting with Leo's brothers, Harry and Justin. After quick greetings, Leo asked "What's going on?"

Eryx stepped forward eagerly. "I think I've figured out how to return your parents' souls to their bodies, using both your magics combined."

Leo and Finn shared an excited look. This was the breakthrough they'd desperately hoped for.

"Just tell us what to do," Leo said. Eryx guided them over to the bed where Leo's comatose parents lay. Finn could see their souls, Rhea and Clint, hovering anxiously nearby.

Leo addressed them directly. "Are you ready for this? To be whole again?"

Clint nodded firmly. "It's time." Rhea clasped his hand, eyes glistening with anticipation.

Following Eryx's instructions, Leo and Finn stood over the bodies. They joined hands, magic swirling between them. Light grew, bathing the room in its warm glow.

Eryx narrated the process. "Focus on combining your energies… good, now visualize the souls reuniting with their vessels."

Brow furrowed in concentration, Leo guided the swirling mass of magic. It slowly enveloped Rhea and Clint's spiritual forms before absorbing into the physical bodies. A pulse seemed to travel through them.

After long moments, Eryx told them to stop the flow. An expectant hush fell over the room. Then, miraculously, Leo's mother took a shuddering breath, her chest starting to rise and fall. His father did the same seconds later.

Leo nearly collapsed in relief into Finn's arms. Joyful laughter and shouts erupted around them. The spell had worked! Leo's parents were restored.

It was several minutes before they finally awoke. The tearful reunion that followed was filled with laughter, gratitude and amazement. Leo kept both parents wrapped in a tight hug, Finn's arm around his shoulders.

"I don't know how we'll ever repay you boys," Clint said, voice thick with emotion. Rhea just kissed their cheeks soundly, too overcome for words.

Later, after many more jubilant celebrations, Leo and Finn collapsed exhausted together in bed. Leo nuzzled close to Finn with a contented sigh.

"Have I mentioned how amazing you are lately?" he murmured sleepily.

Finn smiled into Leo's curls, euphoria still bubbling through him. "We make a pretty great team." Together they had achieved the extraordinary against all odds. And that gave him hope for whatever trials still awaited. With Leo by his side, he could conquer anything.

Finn woke parched in the middle of the night. He padded down to the shadowy kitchen for some water. But as he entered, he realized he wasn't alone. Alicia sat at the table, regarding him strangely.

"Fancy meeting you here," Finn said lightly. "Midnight snack?"

"I was waiting for you, actually," Alicia replied. Something in her tone made Finn tense.

"What's going on?" he asked carefully.

Alicia's mouth twisted in a gruesome approximation of a smile. "He promised me great power if I deliver you and that brat Leo."

Before Finn could react, Alicia's form began distorting, limbs stretching grotesquely. Finn threw up a radiant shield just as she unleashed a blast of shadowy magic. It collided explosively with the barrier.

Alicia let out an ear-piercing shriek of rage. "You will not stop my ascension!" She battered Finn's shield with pulses of dark power.

Finn gritted his teeth, the strain already showing. With his free hand, he returned fire, blasts of light forcing Alicia momentarily back. But her strength was monstrous.

Laughing wildly, she vanished, reappearing across the room. "No one can save you now, little hero." Her voice echoed mockingly around Finn.

Desperately, Finn tried sensing where she would strike next. But his magic was running on fumes. He couldn't keep this up much longer.

"Where are you, witch?" he growled in frustration. Alicia's mad cackle answered.

A blur of movement was Finn's only warning before Alicia materialized behind him, dagger poised. As it arced down, a familiar voice shouted his name. Then everything went black.

## 21

### Leo

eo woke up to an empty pillow next to him. Panic surged through him as he scanned the room, finding it empty of Finn. His eyes darted to the nightstand, where Finn's phone and Poofy's ring remained undisturbed. Something was wrong, and Leo could feel it deep in his bones.

With a sense of urgency, Leo hastily pulled on some clothes, his fingers trembling as he slipped the ring into his pocket and clutched Finn's phone. As he reached for the doorknob, he collided with someone in the hallway. Startled, he looked up and found Bliss standing there, a look of distress etched across his face.

"Bliss? What's going on? Why are you rushing?" Leo's voice quivered with concern.

"It's Finn, Leo. She took him," Bliss replied urgently, his eyes filled with worry.

Leo's blood ran cold as he processed the words. "Who took him, Bliss? Tell me!" Leo's voice held a note of desperation.

"It was Alicia. I tried to stop her, but they vanished into thin air," Bliss explained, his voice tinged with frustration.

"Gather everyone and tell them to meet in the living room," Leo growled, his mind racing with worry and fear. Bliss nodded and hurried off to relay the message.

Leo moved through the house, his steps echoing in the tense silence. In the kitchen, he found a scene of chaos, as if a battle had taken place. Yet, there were patches of the room untouched, and Leo couldn't help but think that Finn had tried to minimize the damage to their home. The destruction spoke of a struggle, and Leo knew that there must have been noise, but it hadn't been enough to wake him.

Finally, he reached the living room, where he didn't have to wait long for everyone to gather. Alex was the first to arrive, followed by the rest of their team, Leo's brothers, and their parents. The room buzzed with a mix of concern and determination.

"Alex, I want you to lead. I can't do this alone. If anything happens to Finn, I wouldn't be able to forgive myself," Leo said, his voice heavy with emotion.

"Calm down, Leo. We will get him back," Alex assured him, his tone firm and unwavering. He turned to Bliss. "Bliss, tell everyone what you know."

Leo stood close to his parents and brothers, seeking comfort in their presence as they offered hugs and silent support.

"As you all know, I was tracking Lyandros down. I thought it was going to be easy, but he gave me a hard time tracking his magical signature. Then, yesterday, I heard whispers that a demon was making promises to unsuspecting magic users who wanted more power and immortality. I followed one of the people who accepted his offer and took control of his mind. That's when I saw a name – Alicia Peterson. I remembered Justin saying something about her, so I rushed here right away, but I was too late. Lyandros had embedded demons inside the souls of the people who accepted his terms, and Alicia was no different," Bliss explained.

"Didn't Finn say there was something wrong with her soul?" Gabe chimed in.

"Yes, he did, but I felt it too. I was waiting for her to make a move, but she outsmarted all of us," Alex added.

"You knew, and you still didn't do anything? Is that what gods do? Stand around and do nothing while someone gets hurt? Is that it?" Leo's voice was laced with anger and frustration.

"We didn't know what she would do at that point, Leo. We also couldn't do anything while you were incapacitated. Think, Leo. You're better than this, and don't let your emotions cloud your judgment. If you want to save Finn, you need to get your act together!" Alex's tone was stern, and he held Eryx's gaze for support.

Leo watched as Eryx placed a calming hand on Alex's shoulder, their bond evident in the subtle exchange. "Bliss, do you have any ideas on how to track him down?" Eryx asked, his voice calm and rational.

"Poofy. Finn's familiar. He's connected to Finn and can track his magical signature way easier than any one of us can," Bliss suggested.

Leo reached for the ring that held Poofy's spirit and stared at it, his eyes focused and determined. "How can we summon Poofy without Finn here?" he asked.

"You put him in there, Leo, so I'm pretty sure you can get him out. Poofy recognizes your magical signature, and you're also connected to Finn. Just focus on your connection with Finn," Bliss explained.

Leo took a deep breath, his heart pounding in his chest. He held the ring close, closed his eyes, and began to search for that deep connection he shared with both Finn and Poofy.

The tether that bound them together, almost like a parental bond, became clear to him. He could feel the warmth of their connection, and it fueled his determination.

Opening his eyes, Leo allowed his magic to flow through his veins, creating a swirling vortex of purple flames that enveloped his hand. With intense concentration, he whispered for Poofy to come forth, his voice filled with urgency.

In a matter of moments, Poofy emerged from the ring, but he appeared different. His ghostly, ethereal form had transformed into a magnificent creature. Poofy now sported wings that blended the colors of white and purple, reminiscent of Leo and Finn's magical auras. His coat had darkened to pure black, and his beak gleamed white.

Poofy's eyes opened, and upon seeing Leo, he greeted his master with joyful licks and affectionate headbutts. Bliss had mentioned that merging their magic together in the ring had enabled Poofy to manifest in this enhanced form.

Leo paused the excited gestures, looking into Poofy's eyes with a sense of urgency. "Poofy, we need your help to find Finn. Can you do that for us?" he asked.

Poofy responded with another series of enthusiastic licks and nuzzles before Poofy pressed their heads together.

Abruptly, Leo saw through Poofy's eyes - a summoning circle, Finn's faint heartbeat pulsing. And a familiar sigil, one Leo knew meant Finn was at his old mentor's home.

The vision cut off as Poofy released the connection. "I know where he is now," Leo announced to the others' expectant looks.

Alex immediately issued orders. "Gear up, we mobilize in five.Leo, lead the way when we're topside." His tone left no room for argument.

In no time they were armed to the teeth and dashing through a portal, Poofy circling overhead. Leo focused on Finn's location, allowing his magic to guide them.

They came upon a sprawling manor flanked by dead, twisted gardens. Cruel memories assaulted Leo, threatening to overwhelm him. This was the dark mage who had taken him in after his parents' murder.

Alex placed a steadying hand on his shoulder, grounding Leo in the present. "Stay with me, kid. We've got you." Leo took a shaky breath and nodded. Finn needed him.

The team stormed inside, weapons blazing. Shrieks and unearthly roars told Leo his old master had been experimenting again. He shuddered, pressing forward.

They encountered a hulking, misshapen beast that let loose an earsplitting howl and charged. Leo reacted on instinct, blasting it into oblivion. Panting, he met Alex's approving gaze.

"You can do this. Trust your instincts," the god encouraged. Heartened, Leo led them deeper through the grisly maze.

More nightmarish creatures barred their way, but were no match for the team's combined skill. Leo drew on reserves of power he never knew he had, desperate to reach Finn.

At last they burst into the ritual chamber. Alicia stood over Finn's bound form, dagger raised for a killing blow. With a feral cry, Leo unleashed thc full fury of his magic.

22

# Finn

The first thing Finn became aware of was a pounding ache resonating through his skull. He cracked open his eyes with a low groan, blearily taking in his surroundings. The room was shrouded in eerie gloom, its dank stone walls covered in ominous symbols etched deep into the cold surface. Thick restraints, like iron serpents, pinned his arms and legs in place on a raised slab at the room's center. Finn tugged at his bonds, but his feeble struggles proved futile.

Alicia, a sinister figure cloaked in shadows, emerged into view, her presence casting a chilling aura over the chamber. She regarded Finn with a cruel smile, her voice dripping with malevolence. "Finally awake, I see. Good. The sacrifice requires you conscious."

Finn jerked against his bonds once more, his voice hoarse with desperation. "Alicia, why are you doing this?"

She trailed a sharp nail down his cheek, leaving a cold, lingering sensation in its wake. "Don't take it personally, darling. I'm merely claiming what I'm owed."

Before he could demand answers, quick, heavy footsteps reverberated through the chamber. Two hulking forms, the same ogre-like guards from the ambush back home, took up positions on either side of the slab. Alicia moved to stand over Finn, a dagger glinting malevolently in her hand. "Let us begin."

Finn fought wildly as she cut into him, his cries and pleas drowned out by her haunting chant in a strange, guttural tongue. Blood flowed from his wounds, pooling and snaking along intricate grooves in the stone surface. He was weakening fast, his energy sapped.

Then, an ominous violet light suffused the etched markings on the stone, casting eerie, dancing shadows. Alicia's eyes turned solid black, her face contorted in demented ecstasy. "Yesss…I can feel his power flowing into me!"

She seemed to grow taller, her frame distorting as clawed, taloned hands reached for Finn, who, now completely drained.

Finn thrashed futilely against his restraints as the vile ritual continued. He could only pray his friends would find him before it was too late. And despite his longing to see Leo again, part of Finn hoped would remain far away from this nightmare.

Eventually Finn blacked out from the agony and violation. When he came to, the chamber was empty. Finn weakly struggled against the bindings chaining him upright, but it was useless in his exhausted state.

He tried summoning his magic to aid his escape. But it was like grasping at air - his power had been drained away. Despair threatened to crush what little hope remained.

Finn's thoughts turned to Leo, picturing his rakish smile and bright amber eyes. Leo was probably worried sick right now. Finn desperately wished he could reassure his friend that he still lived.

The thought of causing him more pain to Leo was unbearable. But try as he might, Finn saw no way out of this dire predicament. Unless his friends arrived soon, he was trapped.

Finn was so lost in despairing thoughts that he didn't notice the chamber door opening. Clawed fingers gripped his chin, turning his face up. Through blurred vision, he saw Alicia leering down at him, back in her glamorously human facade.

"Poor thing, you look dreadful," she mocked, trailing a sharp nail almost gently down his battered cheek. "Don't worry, we're nearly done."

Rage sparked within Finn at her callousness. "You'll never...touch Leo," he rasped defiantly, glaring at her with every ounce of hatred he could muster.

Alicia just laughed. "That passionate loyalty of yours is so adorable. But once I finish draining you, your beloved Leo is next on my list."

Summoning the last of his strength, Finn spat in her face. "Over my dead body!"

Alicia backhanded him casually, licking the blood from her nails. "That can certainly be arranged. But know your suffering is not in vain - the power I gain from it will change everything."

Her words sparked a desperate question in Finn's mind. "The attacks in the spirit realm - were you behind those too?"

Something like unease flickered across Alicia's face before her expression smoothed over. "No, that business was my master's doing. I merely...assisted him."

Finn's foggy mind raced as pieces clicked into place. "It's all been part of some grand scheme of his, hasn't it? What does he want with me and Leo?"

Alicia glanced away, almost nervously. When she looked back, her eyes were cold. "You've asked enough questions."

She pressed a glowing hand to Finn's forehead. "Sleep." Against his will, blackness engulfed Finn once more. But his spirit clung desperately to this new information. If only he could get word to Leo...

After an unknown stretch of unconsciousness, Finn was again woken by agonizing magical drainage. He thrashed weakly, crying out.

"Hush now, we're nearly finished," Alicia crooned. There was an edge of strain in her voice.

Finn forced his eyes open to glare at her. "You'll pay for this..." he rasped.

Alicia just chuckled. "Brave words. But your life force is nearly spent." To Finn's disgust, she caressed his face almost tenderly. "I take no pleasure in this."

"Liar," Finn bit out, recoiling from her touch. "Hurting people is your purpose now."

Alicia's expression twitched with what looked like regret. But it was gone in an instant. "We all have our roles to play. Try not to take it personally."

She resumed the ritual, ignoring Finn's fragmented pleas. He was on the brink of oblivion when shouting arose somewhere outside.

Alicia's concentration broke. Eyes narrowing, she strode from the chamber to investigate the commotion. Finn sagged limply in his chains, hovering at the edge of consciousness.

The noises drew closer - shrieks and inhuman howls mingled with the unmistakable sounds of combat. Disoriented hope stirred in Finn's heart.

With an almighty crash, the doors exploded inward. And through the settling debris strode the most welcome sight imaginable. Leo, wreathed in avenging violet flames, his face etched with fury and fear.

"Finn!" he cried, rushing forward to cup Finn's battered face. "I'm so sorry...just hold on..."

Finn managed a faint smile. "Knew you'd come," he whispered hoarsely. Through everything, that faith had stayed strong.

Leo's eyes shone with relieved tears. But their reunion was short-lived. A vortex opened, heralding the monstrous arrival of Lyandros himself.

Leo gently laid Finn down before turning to face the demon

alongside Alex and the others. Weak as he was, Finn silently cheered their crusade on. Light would triumph over this evil. Hope remained.

# 23

# Leo

As the monstrous Lyandros emerged, Leo turned to confront the vile demon. "Back for more already? You should've just asked for a rematch."

Lyandros let out a distorted, grating laugh. "Foolish boy. You cannot comprehend what's coming." His body began contorting, horns erupting from his head as his power grew.

Leo called over his shoulder, "Handle Alicia! Lyandros is mine!"

Bliss protested, "You can't face him alone!"

"Then help me finish this bastard for good," Leo shot back. Bliss cracked his knuckles with a wicked grin.

Amidst the sounds of his friends battling Alicia's forces, Leo asked Bliss, "You still have the bloodstone?"

Bliss nodded, holding up the glowing red crystal. "Gonna trap him inside it?"

"You know it. Hecate's blessing shouldn't go to waste," Leo replied.

As Lyandros attacked, the very air seemed to ignite with corrupted power. Bolts of shadow streaked toward Leo like black lightning. Crossing his arms, Leo wove a shield of violet flames to counter the dark barrage.

The force of each blow resonated through him painfully. Lyandros was stronger than their previous encounter - much stronger. The flames flickered as Leo gripped his magic tightly, refusing to yield any ground.

This battle was for those he loved, his home, all who had suffered by the demon's hand. Leo embraced that purpose, his soul burning with defiant resolve. He would give anything to protect them.

Magic glowed brighter within Leo, power thrumming through every fiber of his being. "Is that the best you've got?" he taunted Lyandros. "I'm just getting warmed up!"

With a guttural snarl, Lyandros intensified his assault. The blackened blasts crashed against Leo's shield like a tempest sea against coastline cliffs. Leo's boots slid back across the stone floor, muscles straining.

Mustering his strength, Leo went on the offensive. Flaming missiles spiraled toward Lyandros in a ceaseless barrage, trailing purple contrails. They detonated in a dazzling display, engulfing the demon in constant blossoms of violet fire and thick smoke.

Lyandros loosed an enraged roar, tattered wings beating away the choking fumes. Leo pressed on, weaving walls of spiritfire that encircled his foe, tightening the trap.

With reckless abandon, Lyandros barreled straight for the flaming walls. At the last second before impact, Leo nimbly rolled aside.

The demon smashed headfirst into the barrier with a resounding clang. Leo swore he could see stars circling Lyandros' skull. Shaking off the collision, the demon whirled, eyes ablaze with fiery hatred.

Dark lightning erupted once more, tendrils streaking toward Leo. Crossing his arms, Leo manifested crackling blades of purple energy just in time. Blinding sparks cascaded as the powers collided in a sizzling deadlock.

Leo could feel his teeth vibrating from the resonance. This was the most power he had ever summoned at once. Sweat poured down his face with the monumental effort of maintaining this mystical onslaught.

But one had to give way eventually. Gritting his teeth, Leo poured everything he had into one explosive push. His violet blades overpowered the shadowy lightning, severing them in a blaze of light.

Panting, Leo immediately went on the attack again. He hurled spheres of ghostly fire that detonated violently against Lyandros' torso, singing his molten flesh. The demon howled, swiping angrily at the stinging embers.

Sensing his foe's defenses faltering, Leo pressed his advantage relentlessly. With a flick of his fingers, a whip of spiritfire lashed out to snap around Lyandros' legs.

The demon crashed heavily to one knee with a grunt. Leo kept the pressure on, lashing the fiery whip over and over. Lyandros' roar of agony echoed throughout the chamber.

Whip marks smoldered across the demon's broad back, his leathery skin cracking from the heat. Lyandros thrashed violently, but Leo's hold was unbreakable. Leo bared his teeth savagely, rage and power thundering through his veins.

But abruptly the whipping ceased. Chest heaving from exertion, Leo instead began slowly contracting the flamed coils, inch by inch. Lyandros was forced lower, the burning bands constricting like anacondas.

Walking a wide circle around his captive foe, Leo manifested a fresh barrage of violet fireballs. Rather than throw them, Leo mentally guided the crackling orbs to encircle Lyandros in a dizzying ring.

With a savage gesture, Leo sent them spiraling inward all at once. They bombarded the demon from all sides in brilliant succession, pummeling his constrained form relentlessly.

Smoking craters pockmarked Lyandros' body as his defenses were pounded away bit by bit. But still the proud demon refused to yield, snarling curses through bloodied fangs.

Leo had one more ace up his sleeve. Drawing deep from within, he accessed the strange new well of power awakened during his magical evolution.

Incandescent flames wreathed his hands, growing until Leo held a massive fireball, dense with pure energy. Lyandros' eyes blew wide, sensing the deadly intent radiating from it.

With an incoherent battle cry, Leo hurled the supernova-like projectile with all his might. It impacted Lyandros head-on like a falling meteor, exploding in a blinding shockwave that shook the foundation itself.

When the dust settled, Leo saw that the blast had finally forced Lyandros to one knee. The demon swayed, eyes dazed and flickering. It was time to end this.

"Now, Bliss!" Leo roared hoarsely. And Bliss hurled the glowing bloodstone high into the air toward them...

Bliss lobbed the glowing bloodstone. Snatching it from the air, Leo raised the crystal high. "Hecate, grant me your power!" he intoned.

Leo's hand ignited with violet light that engulfed the stone. Lyandros' eyes blew wide in realization and sudden fear. He thrashed violently against Leo's hold.

Putting the blazing bloodstone directly in front of the demon's face, Leo unleashed the stored magic. Like water down a drain, Lyandros' monstrous form was sucked into the crystal to be sealed away.

A guttural scream tore from the demon's throat before ending abruptly. Leo collapsed to his knees, spent but triumphant. It was over.

Bliss whooped exuberantly, clapping Leo's back. "We freaking did it! Lyandros is history!" Leo just nodded wearily, too exhausted to celebrate yet.

But after catching his breath, Leo got to his feet, resolve hardening.

Their friends still battled Alicia and time was short.

Leo met Bliss' gaze. "I have to help the others." Bliss' expression sobered as well and he hefted the prisoned demon.

"I'll take care of it. Go kick some ass!" With a jaunty salute, Bliss disappeared through a portal with Lyandros.

Steeling himself, Leo rejoined the fray against Alicia and her corrupted followers. They fought on, but Lyon's toxic influence over them was broken. Together, Leo and his allies would defeat this evil for good.

In the end, it was Alex whose power overwhelmed Alicia, purging the darkness from her. "Find the light again," he told her sadly before teleporting away.

Alicia and her remaining forces retreated for now, but they knew this war was far from over. Though exhausted, Leo refused to rest until Finn was safely home.

Leo rushed over to where Finn lay, his heart pounding in his chest as he joined Finn's parents who were desperately trying to keep him breathing. The grim reality hung heavy in the air.

"How is he?" Leo asked, his voice trembling with fear and desperation.

"He's fading fast, Leo, I am sorry. Finn had lost a lot of blood," his mother said, her eyes reflecting the anguish they all felt.

Leo couldn't bear the thought of losing Finn. It was too soon, too sudden. They had just begun, and it couldn't end like this. Panic gripped his heart; he had to do something, but he was no doctor like Finn. His mind raced as he felt utterly helpless.

Then, in the distance, he heard hurried footsteps. He turned to see Eryx sprinting toward them, a glimmer of hope in the form of his friend.

"Let me see him," Eryx said urgently. Leo hesitated only for a moment before stepping aside, his gaze locked on Finn.

As Eryx assessed Finn's condition, Leo couldn't help but ask, "How is he looking, Eryx?"

"I can try and help him, but we need to get him back in the house," Eryx responded, his eyes scanning their surroundings. He called out to Alex, a call filled with urgency, "Alex, help us, we need to hurry."

With a sense of shared determination, they all rallied. They carried Finn, who was barely holding on, out of the house. Time was slipping away.

They arrived at their estate sooner than Leo had expected, the urgency of the situation driving them to move with remarkable speed. Leo gently cradled Finn in his arms as they entered their bedroom and laid him down on the bed.

Eryx entered the room, his eyes reflecting a combination of determination and concern. He motioned for Leo to step back, and Leo complied, his only wish being for Finn's safety.

The room quickly filled with people who cared about Finn - Alex, Leo's team, Finn's parents, and his brothers. They all stood in silent support as Eryx prepared to work his magic.

Eryx's body began to emit a radiant, golden glow. The room was bathed in the ethereal light, and the sight left everyone in awe. Leo couldn't help but glance at Alex, who wore a rare expression of pride on his stoic face.

With unwavering focus, Eryx began the process of healing Finn. The golden glow transferred from Eryx to Finn's lifeless body. It was a mesmerizing and powerful sight.

As time passed, the glow on Finn's body gradually dimmed, until it eventually faded away. Eryx turned toward the group, a reassuring smile on his face, and explained the miraculous feat he had just performed.

Eryx described how he had used his magic to regenerate all of the blood that Finn had lost, sparing him from scarring, as his magic had taken care of that as well.

Leo couldn't contain his worry and asked the question that weighed on his mind, "How long until Finn wakes up?"

Eryx's answer was filled with gentle uncertainty, "It's up to Finn now, and the time it takes for his magic and body to heal."

Alex placed a reassuring hand on Leo's shoulder and spoke softly, "We'll give you and Finn some space. You both need it."

Once everyone had left the room, Leo moved closer to Finn's side. He took Finn's hand in his and pressed a loving kiss to it. His voice trembled with emotion as he whispered, "Please, be okay, Finn. I need you. I love you."

Tears welled up in Leo's eyes, and for a moment, it felt as if the world had come to a standstill.

24

Finn

Finn felt like his entire body was made of lead - heavy yet somehow aware. Slowly opening his eyes, he saw Leo's sleeping head nestled next to him. Finn smiled softly at the sight and reached to gently play with Leo's beautiful wavy hair.

Leo began to stir. Finn quickly withdrew his hand as Leo lifted his head, blinking awake. Doing a double-take at seeing Finn conscious, Leo bolted upright.

"Finn! You're awake!" Leo moved closer, face alight with relief and joy. "How are you feeling? Can I get you anything? Some water?" The questions tumbled out in an excited rush.

Finn chuckled weakly. "Water would be amazing," he rasped, throat dry as ash.

Leo nodded eagerly and grabbed the glass from the nightstand. "Here, just small sips," he said, helping Finn drink.

The cool water soothed Finn's parched throat. With a contented sigh, he rested his head back against the pillows. "What happened?" he asked. "My memory's fuzzy."

Tenderly brushing hair off Finn's face, Leo replied, "What's the last thing you remember?"

Finn turned his head to kiss Leo's palm nestled against his cheek. "Alicia draining my blood during some ritual. After that, it's blank."

Leo's expression darkened. "She took so much blood that I almost lost you. I can't go through that again." His eyes shimmered with tears.

Reaching up, Finn gently thumbed away a stray tear from Leo's cheek. "But you didn't lose me. I'm here now, and that's what matters."

Leo gave a small nod, seeming to take comfort from the words. He pressed a soft kiss into Finn's palm. "Eryx was the one who healed you," he explained. "Kid's more powerful than we realized."

"Well, he is a god's vessel after all," Finn replied knowingly. At Leo's look of confusion, he just chuckled. "You'll have to ask Eryx about that later."

Taking Leo's hand, Finn asked, "Any word on freeing Rory?"

"Bliss thinks he can finish the process now that you're awake again," Leo assured him. "You were unconscious for nearly a day, had us all so worried."

Finn gave Leo's hand a grateful squeeze. "Stay with me?" he requested through heavy eyelids.

Leo softly brushed Finn's hair back. "I'm not going anywhere. Get some more rest."

With a tired smile, Finn let his eyes drift closed again, comforted by Leo's nearby presence. The horrors were behind them now. As long as they were together, he knew everything would be okay

Finn was woken by the sound of voices arguing nearby. He recognized Leo and Alex seeming to be in a serious discussion.

"Leo, I know you want to join the team, but now isn't the right time," Alex said firmly.

"Give me one good reason why I can't," Leo challenged, frustration clear in his tone.

Alex explained patiently, "We need someone on the inside of the HIB to feed us information. I want you to be our mole, like a covert spy."

Finn opened his eyes and saw them standing by the door. "Alex is right, Leo," he spoke up. They both turned to look at him. Finn gave a tired smile. "As much as I'd love having you on the team, your role in the HIB is too important to lose."

Leo came over and gently cradled Finn's face in his hands. "Are you sure about this?"

Finn leaned into the touch. "I'm positive."

Alex cleared his throat awkwardly. "I'll give you two a moment. Leo, we'll need to do the ritual soon, hopefully today. I can have Eryx come check on you first, Finn."

Finn shook his head, already feeling stronger. "That's not necessary, I'm doing much better now. Thank you. Could you let the others know we'll be down shortly?"

After Alex departed, Leo asked with concern, "Are you really feeling up to this?"

Finn chuckled. "Honestly, I'm fine now." He met Leo's eyes earnestly. "Leo, I want you to move in with me. That way we can still be together when not working. I love you. Will you move in?"

Leo's face lit up joyfully. "Yes! Of course I'll move in. I love you so much." He leaned in for a fierce, passionate kiss.

When they finally broke for air, Leo said excitedly "You won't regret this, I promise."

Finn cupped his cheek tenderly. "No regrets when I'm with you." He slowly sat up, steadier than before. "Help me get ready? We could shower first if you want to join me…"

Leo readily agreed. Supporting Finn to the bathroom, they enjoyed a steamy shower before heading down to reunite with the others, ready to take the next step together

They stepped into the warm cascade of water. The sound of the water hitting the tiles created a rhythmic melody to accompany their desires. Finn's heart raced as Leo's eyes met his, filled with longing and passion. The air was heavy with the scent of desire.

"Leo," Finn whispered softly, his voice filled with adoration.

Leo pulled Finn closer, his touch sending shivers down Finn's spine. "I've been dreaming about this, about us," Leo murmured, his voice laced with desire. "I wanted to make every inch of you mine."

Finn's breath caught in his throat, his body trembling with anticipation. "Take me, Leo. Take all of me."

Their lips crashed together in a fierce kiss, their tongues dancing in a sensual tango. Finn wrapped his arms around Leo's neck, pulling him even closer. The water cascaded over their bodies, intensifying the heat between them.

Leo's hands roamed across Finn's back, leaving a fiery trail in their wake. Finn moaned against Leo's lips, the sound filled with raw need. He arched his back, pressing his body against Leo's, craving the touch that would ignite him completely.

Leo's fingers trailed down Finn's spine, sending electric jolts of pleasure through every nerve ending. Finn gasped, his eyes closing as Leo's touch became bolder, more possessive.

"You're so beautiful," Leo whispered, his voice husky with desire. "I couldn't resist you, Finn."

Finn's senses were overwhelmed by a mixture of desire and love. "I am yours, Leo. Completely and utterly yours."

Leo's hands moved lower, cupping Finn's ass and lifting him effortlessly. Finn wrapped his legs around Leo's waist, their bodies pressing together in a perfect fit. Their eyes locked, and Finn could see the hunger and love burning in Leo's gaze.

"I want you, Finn," Leo growled, his voice filled with primal need. "I want to taste every inch of your body, feel your warm skin under my lips."

Finn's breath hitched as Leo lowered him onto the tiled floor, the water still raining down on them. Leo's lips trailed a hot path down

Finn's neck, leaving a trail of wet kisses. Finn's back arched, his body writhing in pleasure.

"Oh, Leo," Finn moaned, his voice filled with ecstasy. "Don't stop. Give me everything you've got."

Leo's mouth found Finn's nipple, sucking and teasing with expert precision. Finn's fingers tangled in Leo's wet hair, urging him on. The sensation shot waves of pleasure straight to Finn's core.

Leo's lips continued their journey southward, leaving a trail of fire along Finn's abdomen. Finn's cock throbbed with anticipation, eager for Leo's touch. He watched as Leo wrapped his hand around it, squeezing gently.

Finn's breath hitched as Leo's tongue circled the sensitive head, his thumb brushing over the tip. The combination of the warm water, Leo's skilled mouth, and Finn's overwhelming desire sent him spiraling into bliss.

"Leo," Finn gasped, his voice filled with need. "I am so close... please..."

Leo's lips wrapped around Finn's cock, his mouth engulfing him in a wet heat. The sensations became almost too much to bear as Leo's tongue danced and teased, driving Finn to the edge of ecstasy.

Finn's body tensed, his release building to a crescendo. "Leo... I'm... I'm..."

Before Finn could finish his sentence, his body convulsed in pleasure, waves of ecstasy crashing over him. He gripped Leo's hair, his moans filling the bathroom as his orgasm took hold.

As Finn came down from his climax, Leo held him close, their bodies still entwined. The steam and water created an intimate cocoon around them.

"I love you, Finn," Leo whispered, his voice filled with tenderness. "You mean everything to me."

Finn smiled, his heart swelling with love. "I love you too, Leo. Always and forever."

After showering they immediately went to Rory's room. The room was heavy with anticipation as the group gathered in Rory's dimly lit bedroom. The somber mood was thick enough to be cut with a knife. Leo's parents sat on the edge of the bed, clutching each other's trembling hands, their faces etched with a mix of hope and fear.

"Leo, Finn, step forward. Stand right in front of Rory's bed." Bliss said.

Leo and Finn obeyed without a word. They stood before the motionless body of Rory.

Bliss continued, "Hold hands and tap into your own magic. Feel it coursing through you." The words were gentle, encouraging, meant to coax the power within.

The room seemed to hush as Leo and Finn closed their eyes in unison. Their faces tensed with concentration as they reached deep within themselves, searching for that inner wellspring of magic.

"Find the magic that connects you together," Bliss instructed. "Weave it, like threads of destiny binding your souls." The instructions were laden with a sense of urgency, the tension in the room mounting.

Finn, in his state of intense focus, began to sense Leo's magic, a unique and brilliant force that sang to him. It was like a melodic tune only he could hear, resonating deep within his being. He could almost feel it, like the warmth of the sun on his skin, its energy flowing between them.

Bliss's voice pierced through the silence, "Release it, together, towards Rory's body." Their words hung in the air, a command pulsating with purpose.

Leo and Finn opened their eyes simultaneously, their hands still firmly clasped. The room was awash in a breathtaking display of magic as they followed Bliss's instructions. The glow that emanated from their entwined hands was a breathtaking mixture of vibrant violet and pure, radiant white. It shimmered and danced like a celestial phenomenon, casting dazzling patterns on the walls and floor.

In unison, the two of them raised their free hands and placed them gently on Rory's still form, their eyes locked on his pale, lifeless face. With unwavering determination, they focused their combined power into the spell.

Rory's body began to respond to the surge of energy. The room quivered with an otherworldly presence, and the air became charged with a palpable tension. The bed seemed to vibrate beneath their touch as they poured their collective magic into their fallen comrade.

Bliss's voice offered a gentle but firm command, "Now, give it everything you've got."

Finn and Leo, their brows furrowed with effort, channeled every ounce of their willpower into the spell. The magical glow intensified, casting a blinding radiance that filled the room with its brilliance. The boundaries between the physical and the mystical blurred as the room seemed to exist in a realm of pure magic.

With beads of sweat on their foreheads and the echo of their shared resolve in their hearts, they held on until they had given their all. The room seemed to hold its breath.

And then the impossible happened. Rory's eyes, which had been sealed in an eternal slumber, began to flutter. The miraculous transformation was subtle at first, a mere glimmer of life in his vacant gaze.

The room erupted with an emotional chorus of gasps, sighs, and choked-back sobs. Leo's parents, unable to contain their elation, wept openly. "Rory, my dear boy," his mother sobbed, her voice quivering with emotion,

Rory reached out to embrace his parents, and tears of joy shimmered in his eyes. "I knew you'd find a way to bring me back," he said, his voice trembling with emotion. "I missed you all so much." He gripped

Leo's shoulder. "Thank you."

Leo swallowed the lump in his throat. "I'd go to the ends of the earth for you guys." Justin and Harry joined the familial embrace.

At last Rory turned to Finn and the others. "And thank all of you. I can never repay what you risked for me. But I intend to try." His smile was full of renewed life.

Alex stepped forward. "Having you back safe is reward enough. But more work remains. Will you stand with us?"

Rory met his gaze squarely. "Gladly."

A portal suddenly opened, depositing an unexpected visitor - King Demetrius. "Sorry to interrupt. I'm here to offer my assistance, Alex."

Alex nodded in thanks. "We'll take any help we can get. Lyandros still has allies lurking." The two shook hands, magical beings united.

Over the next days, Alex's people prepared to return to New York. But first, Alex pulled Finn aside. "Take a few more days to recover. But Manhattan still needs its protector soon."

Finn agreed, though reluctant to leave Leo's side. But their paths would reunite again someday. For now, he would savor the time given.

On Finn's final night in Salem, he and Leo escaped to the moonlit garden. They lay gazing at the blanket of stars overhead.

"Part of me wishes we could stay like this forever," Leo murmured, head resting on Finn's chest.

Finn pressed a kiss into his curls. "Me too. But we'll see each other again soon." He tilted Leo's chin up. "And you'll always have my heart."

"As you'll have mine," Leo replied tenderly. He pulled Finn into a lingering kiss under the starry sky.

Tomorrow would bring bittersweet partings. But though miles would separate them for a time, their souls remained linked by bonds of loyalty, camaraderie, and love - unbreakable no matter the distance.

They would carry the memory of this night together, a touchstone until joyful reunion. And one day, their paths would reunite once more.

But for now, they had each other, and that was enough.

# About the Author

Introducing Ken Sanchez, the visionary behind spellbinding M/M romance-fantasy worlds where love and magic entwine in a mesmerizing dance. With a heart devoted to the art of LGBTQ+ romance and an unbounded imagination, Ken is your guide to immersive realms he's painstakingly crafted. A dreamer who infuses passion into every stroke of his ink, he's conjured tales that not only enchant with fantasy but also stir the deepest emotions of love, taking readers on a spellbinding journey through his vivid narratives.

# Also by Ken Sanchez

242

**Echoes of Destiny (Shadowguards Book One)**
Eryx, a gifted musician, channels melodies that bridge the realms of the seen and unseen. Little does he know that his haunting tunes are echoes of his godly lineage, a connection he's yet to unearth. When a sinister encounter alters his reality, he finds solace in an enigmatic guardian named Alex, whose presence sparks a connection that defies explanation.

Unbeknownst to Eryx, Alex is Hades, the lord of the Underworld, and a sentinel between the mortal realm and the divine. Possessing an air of danger and allure, he battles malevolent forces threatening to tip the balance. As he guides Eryx through the labyrinth of their intertwined destinies, an undeniable attraction forms between them, challenging the very fabric of their worlds.

Amidst the backdrop of a contemporary New York City tinged with ancient mystique, Eryx and Alex's love story unfolds. With the looming resurgence of ancient prophecies and an encroaching darkness, their bond becomes a beacon of hope. As Eryx's godly ancestry awakens and their love deepens, the duo embarks on a quest that will test their resolve, unravel hidden truths, and determine the fate of humanity itself.

"Shadowguards" is a spellbinding gay urban fantasy that marries the ordinary with the extraordinary. In a world where shadows hold untold power and love defies all odds, this novel explores the complexities of destiny, self-discovery, and the unbreakable ties that bind us. Prepare to be captivated by a tale where music and shadows converge, and where the line between the mortal and divine blurs beyond recognition.

**No Matter What**

In the vibrant heart of London, amidst iconic landmarks and hidden gems, two lives collide in a tale of unbreakable bonds and unwavering love. When David's memories are stolen by a violent attack after a promising date, his best friend Ryan steps up to mend the shattered pieces. As they navigate the city's playful quirkiness and emotional depths, David and Ryan's friendship blossoms into something unexpected. Guided by a series of

heartfelt letters, signed with the promise 'No Matter What,' they embark on a journey of self-discovery, tracing their shared past and forging a future full of hope and passion. Amidst the backdrop of playful banter, stolen glances, and the rich tapestry of London, they unveil the truth about their connection and embrace a love that transcends memory.

'No Matter What' is a heartwarming and witty novel that captures the magic of friendship, the power of resilience, and the joy of finding love where you least expect it."

**Enchanted (Willowbrook Book One)**

In the mystical town of Willowbrook, secrets are written in the whispers of the wind, and magic hides in plain sight. A gifted young man named Benjamin, with the power to breathe life into stories, embarks on a journey of love and mystery. His path converges with a reclusive, cursed Beast named Adrian, and their destinies become enigmatically intertwined.

"Enchanted" unveils an enigmatic, gay retelling of a timeless legend, where every word holds hidden power. As their story unfolds, the heart of Willowbrook stands on the precipice of a chilling, unending winter. A fading enchantment, veiled truths, and a love as mysterious as the tale itself will rewrite the destiny of a town and its inhabitants.

Unlock the Magic Within, and Let Love Rewrite the Story. Journey into a world of mystery, where secrets and enchantments await your discovery.

**Light Redemeed (Shadowguards Book Two)**
Coming Soon…